SARA SARQUE
&
THE DEMON
EXECUTIONER

and Other Stories of Mystery,
Terror, Heartbreak, Hope and Humor

D C MALLERY

TESSELESSET BOOKS
VALENCIA, CA USA

SARA SARQUE & THE DEMON EXECUTIONER and Other Stories of Mystery, Terror, Heartbreak, Hope and Humor

Print ISBN: 978-1-7353386-6-8

eBook ISBN: 978-1-7353386-7-5

"The Trauma Eater" Copyright © 2015 by DC Mallery. First published by Sanitarium Press in Sanitarium Magazine, Issue #37, September 2015.

"The Woman and The Maze" Copyright © 2022 by DC Mallery. First published by Hobb's End Press in Dark Horses Magazine, Issue #9, October 2022.

"Temples of Fire" Copyright 2020 by © DC Mallery. First published in Hypnos Magazine, Fall 2020.

"The Frequency of Souls" Copyright © 2020 by DC Mallery. First published by GLAHW in Ghostlight Magazine, Fall 2020.

All other stories are first published herein with Copyright © 2023 by D C Mallery.

Front and back cover images/design provided by The Cover Collection.

Note that the book cover includes a distressed design with various white streaks and scuff marks. This is intentional and does not indicate the book is damaged.

TESSELESSET Books: http://www.TesselessetBooks.com

Published in the United States.

A BRIEF PREFACE

A dozen eerie and tantalizing tales with mystery, terror, heartbreak, hope, and, yes, sometimes even a bit of humor. Several of these stories were first published in various magazines. Others are presented here for the first time. Strap yourselves in tight and prepare for...

The Trauma Thief: A tormented man—who suffers vivid memories of families he never had, each day a different family, each memory tragic in its own way—meets a mysterious fellow who claims he can rid him of those false memories, for a price of course.

Tessa Thrope and the Unholy Venom: A rogue priest embarks on a bold experiment to build up a tolerance to demonic possession by injecting one drop of blood at a time from a possessed young woman into his veins, with quite unexpected results.

The Woman and The Maze: An aging woman—who loves to become lost in hedge mazes—finds herself somehow turned into one after she collapses in a strange glen in the woods and soon fears for the children of nearby towns who come to explore the maze.

Acts of Absolution in the Circus of the Night: In 19th century Paris, a boy with hemophilia learns his older brother and sister—who fled the city years ago under mysterious circumstances—have returned with an enigmatic Night Circus. Defying his stern father, the boy sneaks out one night to watch the circus, setting off a chain of events that will change all their lives.

The Night of Blood Perfume: Neighbors in the San Joaquin Valley of California find themselves in a desperate fight for survival as a strange fog descends on their town and, within the fog, comes an unusual "call of the wild" that only some can hear.

Temples of Fire: A woman traveling with other tourists in the Zagreb mountains of Iran fears something dangerous was unleashed from beneath an abandoned Fire Temple in a cave they visited but no one will believe her until it is far too late.

The Frequency of Souls: A desperate father takes desperate actions as midnight approaches on the midpoint between winter solstice and spring equinox in a frantic attempt to save his family.

The Last Canvas: In a secluded art studio, an arrogant artist picks the wrong muse to mess with.

The Society of the Never Coming Back: A bachelor in 1920s New York responds to an invitation to join an odd social club that changes its name with each new member until one day it becomes *The Society of the Never Coming Back.*

Arabella and the Stone of Tarrenton County: A sculptor in 18th century England believes he can conjure a finished sculpture from raw stone, but his young daughter knows the truth of what will happen if he tries.

Her Best Feature: A young girl is often told her long hair is her best feature but she understands that strength comes from within and to survive she must be willing to make painful sacrifices.

Sara Sarque & The Demon Executioner: A feisty young junkie reluctantly joins forces with a former seminary student to battle terrifying demons—but these are not the usual sorts of demons and these are definitely *not* the usual sorts of exorcists.

No tree, it is said, can grow to Heaven
unless its roots reach down to Hell.
Carl Jung

THE STORIES

THE TRAUMA EATER

M ONDAY:

My wife had her auburn hair pulled tight in a bun. Her name might have been Anne. I'm not sure. She was about thirty, a few years younger than me. Our son was twelve. Arthur, I think. He'd gotten his best grades ever in school, so we were driving downtown to celebrate at a favorite pizza parlor. It began to rain hard, *very* hard, another wicked Midwest thunderstorm, the wipers struggling now to keep up, fighting against the downpour, failing badly. My wife tried to say something that I couldn't hear.

But I never had a wife. I never had a son.

Tuesday:
She was a sun-drenched blonde this time, her hair tangled by the summer wind of our convertible. I think her name was Jocelyn. Our daughter was thirteen or so, tall for her age. I don't recall her name. We were heading home from a day at the lakeshore. The drunk was headed the other way, fast approaching stopped traffic, oblivious. Too late, he tried to swerve. He struck the rear end of a VW hard. His massive sedan went airborne, careening up—but

1

not quite over—our Olds Cutlass, shearing the windshield off, cutting my wife and daughter down like blades of grass.

Yet I had no wife. I had no daughter.

Wednesday:

She had short hair tucked under a knit cap, a few brown curls peeking out. Maybe her name was Amber. We had been arguing. The twins were in back, Terry and Teddy, eleven or so, rambunctious as always. This time the drunk ran a stop sign and sideswiped us on 3rd Street, sending our Olds into the nearby curb at just the wrong angle. We flipped over and were upside down as we plowed through the vacant storefront. The impact sheared the car roof off, clear down to the side doors, ripping the roof away like flimsy tin foil torn from a TV dinner.

But I *never* had a wife. There were *no* twins.

Thursday:

My wife was thin and nervous and she said something I didn't hear. The pale boy in the backseat was about ten or so, fidgeting. We were crossing the 10th Street Bridge and it was snowing now, wet snow, slushy snow. This time the drunk was driving a truck, overloaded with heavy machinery. He didn't hit us; he hit the bridge abutment. Then we struck him. Soon, we were sinking fast in icy water. Only I came out. But there was no truck. There was no bridge.

There was no wife. There was no family.

Friday:

The nightmares were *not* nightmares. They were memories, impossible memories. Nerves shot, I could no longer sleep. I could no longer dream. But those memories haunted me worse than any nightmare ever could. Here is a simple truth: voices that never were can never be silenced. On Friday, we weren't even in a car—my fake wife, my fake children, my *fake* family—we were in a seedy motel off the highway, on the second floor. Acrid smoke choked the room. Some vagrant set the fire. I was the only one to get out.

No! No fire. No motel. No wife. No kids. Yet none of that truth mattered. The pain of it was real. The anguish. The heartbreak. The deep and crippling despair.

Saturday:

I had now taken enough speed to keep a bull elephant awake for a month and a day. I paced the apartment, bare feet creaking across the scratched hardwood floor. Sagging sweatpants and a sour T-shirt, neither changed for as long as I could remember. I kept up my relentless search, looking for anything that wasn't mine. Yet the drawers, the dressers, the closets, held only my clothes. My shoes. My belongings. No one else's. Just two rooms. The bedroom and the cramped main room with my desk squeezed alongside the kitchenette. A used Selectric typewriter, reference books, dictionary, thesaurus. I wrote my freelance articles there.

I hadn't written anything in how long? I could not remember.

No one seemed to mind. The phone never rang. The mail was all junk. Into the trash it went. Earlier, I found a wad of cash in a desk drawer. The landlord would come by sometime. I would crack the door open and push enough sagging bills through to make him go away. That hadn't happened yet, had it? I kept searching, my body begging now for rest, my mind ever more frantic. I checked the closets yet again, the drawers, opening and closing them until the runners grew hot. No honeymoon mementos. No snapshots of kids. No holiday souvenirs. No nothing.

No family.

Now and then, I paused to stare at the man in the stained mirror above the toilet sink. Gaunt and pale, he looked a dozen years older than he should. I knew everything about that man. *Marshall Devon Adams*. Born in Chicago in 1940. Thirty-two years old now. I knew when he had his first smoke and his last, when he had his first drink, when he lost his virginity. When he got drafted. When he got sent home from boot camp. 4-F. Childhood asthma.

I knew everything about that man.

He had no goddamned wife. There were no goddamned kids.

What the hell was happening to me?

In the dim and flickering light of the bathroom, with the drip drip *drip* of the sink loud now in my ears, I spotted a glint of plastic in the dust and darkness behind the toilet. Hunkering down, my fingers found a yellow vial that must have rolled back there. A goddamned prescription vial. I hurried to the main room where the light was better to read the label.

Take one tablet as needed. Side effects include vertigo, nausea, excessive thirst, loss of appetite, loss of libido, confabulation, fraudulation, prevarication and various and sundry combinations thereof.

Below was the doctor's signature, hard to read. Ornate. I think it read: *The Trauma Eater.*

The Trauma Eater? I popped the vial open and peered inside. Empty. I smelled it. An odd lingering odor, medicinal. I stuck a finger in, licked it. Bitter. There was writing on the backside of the label. An address. 1717 1st Street. Just a half mile away. I checked the time and saw it was after midnight. If it was a proper medical office, I'd have to wait outside until morning. But if it were the sort of office found in the front room of an older residential house, maybe the doctor would be home. I'd pound the door. Wake him up. I'd find out what the hell was going on.

Before I left the apartment, while searching for keys to let myself back in, I found a clean knife in the kitchenette. A paring knife. Short and sharp. It could come in handy.

Outside, it felt colder than it was, but my bones were close to the skin now, no thick warming layer of fat, so I kept moving. The neighborhood deteriorated badly after a block or so, cheap apartments giving way to tenements, then to abandoned commercial properties. Vagrants. Addicts. Pimps and whores. No one gave me a second look. A first look maybe. Never a second look. For tonight I looked like the sort of guy you did not want to mess with. I looked like the kind of man who would slit your throat before you had a chance to ask the time of day.

It wasn't raining, not yet anyway, but it would soon, so I quickened my pace. Sweat trickled along my neck, damp against my collar, my hair slick now. The address was no doctor's office, though. It wasn't an office at all. It was a bar. It was a gawddamned bar. I must have been here before—I'd been to every joint in town—but I didn't remember this one. Maybe the name had changed. Now it was called *The Downtowner*. It had one of those script neon signs that buzzed and flickered. It didn't bother me that the doctor's "office" was a dive bar. Plenty of doctors didn't work out of offices. Yet they prescribed what was needed by folks like me who just weren't gonna sit still in some brightly lit waiting room, fat nurses padding in and out, soft Muzak piped in, goddamned National Geographics stacked on the end tables. In a dark bar, after midnight, you met the kind of doctor who had the shit you *needed*.

There was a surly bouncer at the door. As I pushed past him, he muttered that last call was in a half hour. I threw him a look. It was only 1:00 a.m. Last call should be at two, not a moment sooner. Inside, there were fake ferns and plenty of cheap mirrors and a row of dim and quiet booths. I slapped cash on the bar and called for a couple of whiskeys, straight. When the barman handed them to me, I told him to send "the doctor" on over, then slipped into one of the dark booths in the back to wait. I liked the privacy. Heavy partitions separated the booths. The upholstery was blood red, torn in places. Cigarette burns. Stains. Dried gum stuck under the table. I was just finishing my shot of whiskey when a man slid into the seat across from me.

I'm not sure what a doctor who called himself *The Trauma Eater* was supposed to look like, but this man probably fit. He was younger than me, his beard trimmed neatly, his dark hair plastered in place. Too much Brylcreem. His black suit might have been fashionable years ago, decades ago. Pale, he looked much like a mortician. And he had flint blue eyes. There was something un-settling about them. They were the sort of eyes you couldn't look straight at for long. There seemed to be something watching from behind those eyes.

Looking at him, I recalled a short article I'd written a couple years back about the inner eyelids some animals have, so-called nictitating membranes. We all still had them, small and vestigial, hidden down in the corner of our eyes. In cold-blooded animals, they were often translucent. Reptiles could close those inner lids and still see. They could sit on a rock with their goddamned eyes closed and still watch you. Maybe it was just the whiskey, or the fact I hadn't slept one *gawddamned* minute all week, but it occurred to me that maybe those flint blue eyes of his were just such a membrane, the real eyes hidden behind.

He didn't seem to recognize me at first. Then he looked closer, startled. "My goodness, Mr. Adams, you look awful."

"Of course I look awful. I haven't been sleeping. What the hell was in this?" I tossed the empty vial on the table.

He didn't bother to pick it up, nor even look at it. He grinned. "A sugar pill, Mr. Adams, with a dash of Angostura to give it a bitter taste, a medicinal taste. It helps with the metaphor."

"Metaphor?"

He palmed the vial like a magician, deftly slipping it into his suit pocket. "You didn't come here to talk about metaphors. I take it you've had some memory bleed. How bad?"

Memory bleed? "Well, if by that, you mean I remember things that goddamned never happened, never could have happened, and it's driving me batshit crazy, then yeah, I guess I've had some memory bleed." I took his whiskey now because he hadn't touched it and gulped it down, felt the burn strafe my throat.

"Well, Mr. Adams, I already explained this to you." He sighed heavily, then leaned in close. "When you remove a memory, *any* memory, it leaves a space, a void. The bigger the memory, the bigger the void. But it gets filled in. Imagine shoveling mud from wet and sloppy ground. The hole won't last long. It gets filled in soon. And the things that shift and wriggle in to fill that void are not always pleasant things. So, too, with our most traumatic of memories."

Anger surged within me. "Is that what you did? You took my memories? What the hell for?"

He gave a patronizing smile. "You paid me to, Mr. Adams."

"Bullshit! How come I can't . . . " I meant to ask why I couldn't remember any of that but I realized the question would be pointless and stupid.

"If you recalled our earlier meeting, Mr. Adams, you'd remember me taking your memories. That would defeat the purpose."

"Yeah, yeah, I get it." My mind was finding traction now, catching up. "It was an accident of some sort? A car wreck?"

He shrugged. "I couldn't tell you. Once I've consumed a trauma, once I've eaten it, it's gone. Like yesterday's dinner." He dabbed a handkerchief to his mouth for emphasis.

Memories of our earlier meeting were shifting now into focus, as if an inner eyelid were slowly opening deep within me. He had told me how the mind would "confabulate" false memories to replace those taken away, but those new memories would be less painful. If your wife had died of cancer, suffered horribly, you might instead remember that she had divorced you, moved far away. That was less painful, right? And the pill? It was just a way of giving the Trauma Eater permission to do what he did. Swallowing that pill gave him the right to consume your most painful and private memories. Because that's what it ate. That's what it found nourishing. It. Him. Whoever or whatever was sitting across the table from me now. Grinning. Those goddamned flint blue eyes. The eyes that never seemed to blink.

He had warned me to get rid of anything that might bring the memories back. I had to do that first, before I swallowed the pill, otherwise it wouldn't work. I recalled, vaguely, throwing stuff out. A box of photographs. Polaroids from a brief honeymoon. A lock of a child's fine hair in a keepsake book. I couldn't remember who was in those photographs. I couldn't remember whose hair that had been. Boy? Girl? Maybe my mind was just "confabulating" now, but I vaguely recalled being married for several years. She must have left me. She took the kids. That's why none of her clothes were left in the flat, none of their toys.

No. We had a house. A craftsman with a little front porch. Maple trees in the yard. She'd thrown *me* out, my belongings dumped in sagging cardboard boxes, left on the curb in the rain. My type-writer. My books. Clothes. Shoes. So my bachelor flat never had much of anything to throw out. But was that really what I had so badly wanted to forget? That some bitch had divorced me? Maybe for another man. Maybe because I drank too goddamned much.

That didn't seem right.

I leaned into the doctor now. "The memories you make up, the ones you invent, they're not as bad as the ones you want to forget, right?" I asked and he nodded. "So if I . . ."

Suddenly, I didn't want to tell him of the false memories my mind had concocted. Horrific memories. Grotesque memories. I didn't want him to know any of that. For if those tortured memories were truly less painful than what I'd chosen to forget . . .

He saw my anguish. "Bad, is it?"

"The worst part is that they keep shifting. The memories. They're never the same but each is godawful in its own way."

He looked worried. "That should have stopped by now. New memories settle in. They congeal. They become your own. They shouldn't keep shifting."

"Well they goddamned are!" I slapped the table.

Just then, the bartender came by. "Last call."

"Two more whiskeys. Doubles." I laid out a twenty, my last. The barman took the cash and retreated to fetch the drinks.

The Trauma Eater kept his voice low. "It's rare. But in some cases—when the invented memories are quite bad too—they leave their own void as they shift away. That, in turn, brings in still more false memories. They keep cycling through. It's quite rare. But it can happen."

"I don't care how goddamned rare it is. What are you gonna do to put an end to it?" I felt under my jacket for the paring knife, warm now against the sweat of my body.

He gave a nervous smile. "It's quite simple. You'll need to eat someone else's memories, Mr. Adams. Their real memories will fill the void so your mind will stop concocting fake ones."

Eat someone else's memories? I wanted to grab the collar of his black suit and throttle him until those damned blue eyes of his fell out, but the bartender returned with the drinks. I leaned back against the booth to cool down until he was gone.

Maybe it was not such a bad idea, I thought. If I could somehow stop my memories from changing every day, every hour, every minute, if they would just sit still, maybe I wouldn't go mad. "But how will we find someone who'd agree to that?"

"Mr. Adams, in this town, there's always someone looking to

forget. Desperate to forget. I don't find them. They find me."

I nodded. "Okay. Now we're getting somewhere. But then what do I do? When you bring him to me, what do I do?"

The man reached into his coat and withdrew the vial. It now held one pill. Small and brown. He handed it to me. "Give him this. Tell him all the things I told you when we first met. Tell him to swallow it. When he does, your mind will eat a part of his mind. You will consume his trauma. Your shifting void of remembrance will be filled with something stable."

I guzzled one of the last whiskeys, felt the burn again along my throat. The bar would be closing soon. They'd send me into the rainy night. "You'll call me when you've found someone?"

The Trauma Eater cocked his head as though listening to unheard voices, as though tuning his ear to some ethereal radio. He grinned. "I have the perfect man. Tortured by guilt. His trauma will fit nicely into your void."

"Who the hell is it?" I asked, worried now.

"The drunk from your nightmares, Mr. Adams. The one who killed your wife and children. The one who got away with it because the cops couldn't prove it was him."

His blue eyes now shifted. Those outer eyelids began sliding away, revealing dark and haunted eyes beneath. His skin seemed to tighten. He became gaunt. Pale. Older.

I should have seen this coming.

Of course, I should have seen this coming. But you don't see these things when they're happening to you. You blind yourself. No amount of hindsight will change that.

His patronizing grin faded, replaced now by a ragged and familiar leer. I didn't have to tell *that* man to take the pill. He grabbed the vial greedily, fumbled at it, popped the bitter tablet in his mouth, washed it down with the last of the whiskey.

When the bartender returned, I was still staring into my reflection on the far side of the booth. The barman said something about closing time. But I wasn't listening. I was remembering.

All of it now.

TESSA THROPE AND THE UNHOLY VENOM

*F*IRST *TRANSFUSION, AUGUST 28, 1870*

Andrew thought of snakes, venomous ones. He thought of deadly vipers and the brave snake handlers Father Ricardo had told him about, the ones who injected a little of the venom into themselves, lest someday they be bitten and die.

Mithridatism. Known since ancient times, it was named for a suspicious king who feared he'd be assassinated by poison. So he poisoned himself, bit by bit, building up a tolerance.

There were no snakes here, not the Earthly kind anyway. Lit by flickering oil lanterns hung from oaken rafters, the old barn was cavernous and oddly silent. Outside, the warm Pennsylvania summer evening was hushed. The Estate's horses were stabled closer to the manorhouse, the servants sent away for the night. The barn's massive wooden doors were locked. None could enter. None could leave. Andrew wished he were anywhere else.

Demonic Mithridatism, that was madness, wasn't it?

"What are you waiting for?" Father Ricardo demanded.

The harsh tone snapped Andrew from his reverie. Father Ricardo lay upon a canvas cot in the middle of the barn, his arms and legs bound, his priest collar set aside. Although sixty years old, he was stout as an ox. Stubborn too. Sleeves rolled up, muscular biceps exposed, the man waited for the transfusion to begin. Andrew searched his eyes for madness but saw only well-justified desperation. Yet desperation often hid its insanity beneath.

"Has your faith wavered?" the priest taunted.

His faith had indeed wavered, Andrew knew, but he would admit no weakness now. Father Ricardo nodded to the needles, long and sharp, then to the tender flesh of Tessa.

Andrew now looked reluctantly upon his beloved.

Twenty-five years old, Tessa wore a thin white nightgown, soaked in sweat, her mouth gagged, her elegant hands draped in white gloves. She was tied to a cot too, her wrists bound by thick twine to its top corners, her ankles to its bottom corners. She was Father Ricardo's devoted niece, and the woman Andrew intended to marry after this nightmare was over.

She was also—Andrew had no doubt—possessed.

Andrew had never bothered much with stories of devils and unholy possessions. He understood there was evil in the world. The War of Southern Rebellion proved that to him. He'd been a medic for the Army of the Potomac. He'd seen battlefield carnage, bodies torn asunder, viscera spilled to dusty ground, flies feasting. There surely was evil in the world. Now he understood, there were demons too. One was inside his precious Tessa.

Alongside a well-worn copy of the Bible, a jug of Holy water rested upon a nearby crate, the water blessed by Father Ricardo himself. Earlier, the priest had dripped a bit onto Tessa. It had sizzled upon her pallid flesh. She had winced and spat and swore until Andrew begged the man to stop. Gruesome lesions had formed on her pale skin and crawled across her flesh. Now, her skin was again unblemished. She gaped up at Andrew, pleading with frightened eyes to be set free. It was the demon conniving to trick him.

Andrew wondered if the Beast inside Tessa understood what Father Ricardo had planned. Ricardo was a catholic priest, a rogue one to be sure, but still ordained. He had told Andrew that, although the Church sometimes authorized the Rite of Exorcism, it always ended with the death of the victim. The Rite was never intended to save their human life, only their eternal soul.

There were just two ways to end a true possession. Death of the possessed, or transference by physical touch of the demon into another. Neither was acceptable. The first would send the demon back to Hell, yet Tessa would be dead. The second would just trade one unholy possession for another. The only way to save Tessa's life was to draw the demon into another, and the only way to prevent that other from himself becoming possessed was the way of the snake handler, the way of the snake charmer, to partake a little of the unholy venom. A mere drop at first, drawn from Tessa's body, fed into Father Ricardo's veins.

When Andrew had first entered the barn earlier that evening, the contraption had already been set up. Father Ricardo called it a blood transfuser. Recently invented, Ricardo had seen one demonstrated at the renowned Pennsylvania Hospital in Philadelphia. Hand-cranked, the machine had bellows and beakers and four catgut tubes with sharp needles fixed to their ends. Two of the needles were already secured into the priest's forearms. Andrew was to secure the other two into Tessa.

Then, a turn of the crank would feed a little blood from her into Father Ricardo and an equal amount of his blood into her. A drop at a time. They hoped that, as each drop of her blood passed into him, he'd build an immunity against demonic possession.

It might take days or longer, but once the priest gained resistance against the demon, once he could take it inside him without letting it possess him, he could save Tessa without dooming himself. Andrew feared the demon might fully possess Father Ricardo once the first drop of Tessa's tainted blood seeped into his vessels. Yet they must try. Tessa's life depended on it. It depended on Father Ricardo's unwavering spiritual strength, and Andrew's strength too, what little he could muster.

"What are you *waiting* for?" Father Ricardo repeated.

Andrew tugged on a pair of thick leather gloves. He understood he couldn't let his bare flesh touch Tessa's, not for a moment, not even a gentle caress. The demon was eager to find another vessel. Father Ricardo had explained a demon would often enter a woman first for they were the weaker sex, but it would then connive to possess a man.

Hands trembling, Andrew worked one of the needles into a vein in Tessa's right forearm, careful not to tangle the catgut tube that coupled the needle to the transfuser contraption. She squirmed and writhed, but the needle held. Next, he secured the last of the four needles into Tessa's other arm. She screamed through the gag that bound her mouth. If he chose too, he could free her from her horrific burden with the briefest of kisses. Yet he feared if he let the demon into his body, its first cruel task would be to use Andrew's own hands to strangle her.

No, he must adhere to the plan. Mercifully, Tessa passed out. Andrew took hold of the crank-wheel of the transfuser and looked again to the priest.

"Do it!" Father Ricardo demanded.

Andrew turned the crank. Blood filled the intervening beakers. The priest's blood seemed healthy and vigorous, Tessa's thick and sluggish. Turning the crank more, some of her blood was now pumped toward the priest's left arm. Tense, Andrew slowed the crank to ease just a drop or so of Tessa's blood—*the demon's blood!*—into Father Ricardo's veins. It seemed to have no effect.

"More!" Father Ricardo yelled.

Andrew turned the crank a bit farther, and a little more of Tessa's blood seeped into the priest, while some of his blood went into her. Still nothing.

More, Father Ricardo demanded, yet still nothing. Andrew was about to give up when the priest's eyes went wide. He howled.

It was not a human howl.

FURTHER TRANSFUSIONS, AUGUST 29, 1870

Andrew tended the two sick and suffering souls. After the initial bloodcurdling howl, Father Ricardo passed out. He and Tessa both remained unconscious throughout the long night. By morning the priest began to buck and strain against the thick twine that bound him to his sturdy cot. As he did so, Andrew was transfixed with astonishment, for lesions and scars seen first on Tessa rose now upon the priest's flesh. The man's eyes twitched violently beneath closed lids. Andrew feared that a furious war raged now between the priest and the demon within unholy battlefields. He feared the priest was losing that war.

As Father Ricardo bucked and strained against his bindings, Tessa writhed and twisted and tried to free herself too. As he watched with growing panic, the strange lesions and scars faded from Father Ricardo and returned with vengeance upon Tessa.

Wearing the thick leather gloves, Andrew struggled to secure the loosening twine that bound Tessa's wrists to her cot. She woke and begged through her gag for him to release her, pitifully at first, then seductively. He understood it was not her. It was the demon.

It broke his heart to see her this way. He considered Tessa to be his fiancée, though she had never answered his many proposals. She neither declined nor accepted. She always just smiled coyly. Yet he knew he was her favorite for whenever any other man asked for her hand she promptly rejected him, sometimes gently, often brusquely, especially arrogant men. She had seemingly endless suitors, her beauty well-known throughout the county.

After the War had ended, many a dashing and well-moneyed Officer had proposed. She rejected them all. Those men would never have truly loved her anyway. They would have found her too headstrong, too independent, too impulsive. She loved to ride for hours and would often mount a favorite filly and canter up alongside Andrew as he was riding into town. "Well, Andrew, are you joining me or not? I shall not ask twice."

If he hesitated, she would be gone.

Tessa was hard to fathom, one day reading the honored classics in Latin and Greek, the next day delving into the profane and the forbidden, books on ancient mystics, pagan magic, the occult. Her parents died when she was but a toddler. Her uncle, Father Ricardo, inherited their sprawling estate and raised Tessa in the manorhouse. Whenever he found her reading those forbidden books, he'd take them from her, but he would never scold her, nor strike her, nor burn the books, for he too was fascinated with that dark and mysterious side of the world.

Maybe both had been far too fascinated with the dark arts, Andrew considered. For how had Tessa become possessed to begin with? Probably a foolish occult ritual gone awry.

He feared Father Ricardo had indulged too many of her shifting passions. One year, he gave her a powerful telescope and tomes on astronomy and astrology and astromancy. Another year it was a collection of laboratory flasks, a pharmacy's worth of aromatic compounds, a dozen books on chemistry and alchemy. For her, it was never enough. She always craved more: more knowledge, more freedoms, more adventures. So perhaps it was no surprise that her fascinations turned eventually to the mystical and the forbidden.

She writhed and twisted yet again. He cranked the wheel of the transfuser to pump more of her blood into Father Ricardo and, more importantly now, to pump more of the priest's blood into her. She passed out.

As he worked again to secure the twine, Andrew recalled when he had first met her. She was twelve and had commandeered a room in the manorhouse to stage a theatrical production. She was playwright, director, and star. Andrew, the son of one of her many nannies, was recruited into her production, a silly play about a girl who craved to know all there was to know of the world. In its last scene, she threw off shackles that had bound not just her body but her mind. He'd been given a small part in the play with but one line. The line was long ago forgotten, but Miss Tessa Thrope could never be forgotten. That day, Andrew had fallen forever in love.

A sudden noise arose at the barn door, a rattling of the lock, a key turning. Andrew spun to see the wide doors swing open.

A man strode in. Probably forty years old. Tall, strapping, dressed in a military uniform, a well-oiled pistol slung at his side. The man didn't acknowledge Andrew. Instead, he hurried to Tessa's side and cupped her head gently in his leather-gloved hand.

"Tessa dearest, can you hear me? I am here," the man intoned.

Andrew struggled to recognize him. Perhaps a cousin of hers. He eyed his insignias. He was a Major, a very well-decorated one.

"You, fetch water," the man told Andrew. "Not Holy water. Fresh drinking water. There's a pump outside. Quick now!"

"You do not belong here!" Andrew cried out. "She is *possessed*."

"Of course she is! Who do you think carried her here, tied her down? It broke my heart to do so, but Father Ricardo solicited my help. I could not refuse him. Nor Tessa, of course." The man noticed the poorly tied twine about her wrists. "She is nearly loose! Why have you not kept her secured?"

The man quickly and expertly re-tied her bindings.

Andrew stared at him. "Who exactly *are* you?"

"You must be Andrew. I am Caspar Kerrington. Major Caspar

Kerrington." His stern bearing now softened. "Water, please. Tessa needs it. Can you not see that?"

Andrew left to fetch a jug of fresh water from the pump. When he returned, Kerrington carefully poured water past her gag and into her mouth. He then moved to Father Ricardo's side and peeled back the priest's eyelids to check his eyes. Satisfied by what he saw, Kerrington cranked the transfuser, drawing not just a little of Tessa's blood into the priest, but a lot of it. Andrew tried to stop him, but Kerrington shoved him aside.

"Can't you see Father Ricardo is ready for more?" Kerrington glared back at Andrew. "Did he not tell you to keep pumping the blood often? As much as he could take."

"Major, I must insist you tell me how you know Tessa," Andrew demanded.

"I am her fiancé, of course," Kerrington declared.

Fiancé? Andrew's knees buckled as though punched in the gut.

"How dare you!" Andrew sputtered. "How dare you claim *that* about my beloved Tessa?"

"*Your* beloved?" Kerrington mocked. "When did Miss Thrope—and I must insist you refer to her as such—ever agree to marry such as you? Did you ever even ask her?"

"Many times, I assure you," Andrew replied indignantly.

"Did she ever say yes?"

Andrew's bluster faded. "Not in so many words."

"Not in *any* words." Kerrington laughed. "I asked for her hand just *once*. She assented. We shall be married when this ordeal is over, when she is cured of this cursed demon, and—"

"Impossible! She would never marry such as you. It is the demon that tricks you!"

"We were engaged a week ago, before this all began, while you were away, and she was quite sound of mind and body. Quite. The priest was there. He assented to the engagement too."

Andrew shook his head in limp refusal.

"Did you not notice the ring on her finger?" Kerrington asked.

Andrew looked now at Tessa's gloved left hand. There was a slight bulge beneath the rumpled cloth he had missed before. It had the shape of an engagement ring.

Andrew staggered back and plopped onto a wooden chair.

"It can't be. She was to be my wife. Some day. Why didn't Father Ricardo tell me?"

"I was called away before the commencement of this unholy experiment. One is never truly free of one's military duties. In my absence, Father Ricardo needed your help. Would you have come, if you'd known Tessa was betrothed to another?"

"Of course! I would do anything for her. Anything."

Kerrington eyed him as if verifying his resolve. "Good, for your further assistance may be needed before this foul day is done."

Questions boiled in Andrew's mind. Before he could ask any, Father Ricardo awoke with a gasp. Andrew and Kerrington hurried to his side.

"I see you two have met," Father Ricardo said wearily. "How is my niece?"

"Still possessed!" Andrew dribbled some Holy water upon her to prove it. She howled in pain.

Kerrington yanked the water from him. "*Never* do that again! While the demon howls, Tessa suffers inside. It is torture."

"Worry not, Major," Father Ricardo interjected. "Our experiment is working. I am subduing the demon. I'm close to taking its powers."

"Powers?" Andrew asked, confused. "We're here to save Tessa. Nothing more."

"Of course, that is our most important task, Andrew. Not the only one. As I absorb the possessed blood, I'm able to fight the demon in a realm between Earth and Hell. In our battles, it appears

20

to me as a fallen angel with a crooked crown. This is not just any demon. It is Satan himself."

Father Ricardo paused to let that sink in.

"The crown is where his power lies, I know it!" he continued. "If I can weaken him further, I can take his crown and send him back to Hell, while I retain the crown's powers. Think, Andrew, what a just and righteous man might accomplish with such a gift."

Andrew glanced at Tessa, bound to the cot. "But, Father, if the demon has such fearsome powers, why does it not simply snap those twines? Why does it not—"

"In *our* world its powers are constrained by God. The Beast mostly uses its unholy crown to wield power in Hell. Here, it must rely on influence and persuasion for its devilry. If I can capture the crown, I have no doubt God will allow me to use its full force here on Earth for good and just deeds."

Andrew gasped. "That is far too much power for one man, no matter how devout."

"I shall wield the power for benevolence. You understand that. You trust me, don't you?"

Tessa moaned. The scars and markings seen before flared once again upon her skin, but not as bad as before, not as gruesome.

"The demon is weaker!" Father Ricardo exclaimed. "Pump more blood. Faster now!"

Kerrington cranked the transfuser and more blood surged within the tubes and beakers between Tessa and Father Ricardo. The priest howled again, deep and inhuman, and passed out.

Tessa howled too, then slumped back to pale silence on her cot.

Andrew spun to face Kerrington. "Has he gone mad? Trying to take Satan's powers is insane! How can you condone this?"

"Andrew, Tessa told me you were an army medic. You saw the slaughter of war. Imagine if one could use such powers to defeat enemies without carnage and without sacrificing lives?"

Andrew conceded the Major had a point. Perhaps such powers could indeed be used for good, if in the right hands.

Kerrington noticed that the barn doors were still open. As he strode to close and lock the doors, Andrew eyed the pistol that swung at his side. He wondered why the man had brought a hand-gun to an exorcism. The Major didn't strike Andrew as a fool. Father Ricardo was no fool either. They must have a plan if their experiment failed.

Andrew now feared if they couldn't get the demon out of Tessa, the Major would force Andrew's hand upon her flesh. She'd be freed of her possession as the demon took over Andrew instead. In that instant, a quick bullet to Andrew's head would send the demon back to Hell. He again eyed Kerrington's well-oiled pistol. No doubt it was loaded and ready.

FINAL TRANSFUSION, AUGUST 30, 1870

All afternoon and into the night, Andrew and Kerrington wait-ed in worried silence, often pacing nervously, sometimes sitting restlessly, rarely talking to one another. The Major would oc-casionally crank the transfuser to exchange more blood. They watched Father Ricardo's closed eyes as he fought the demon within unseen battlefields. They kept an eye too on Tessa, hoping her pallor would improve. It did not. She grew ever more pale.

As Tessa became worse, Andrew noticed Kerrington fussing more with his pistol. Andrew wondered how many lives that gun had taken during the long and accursed War. He recalled now when Tessa was eighteen she demanded Father Ricardo let her join the armies of the North to defeat the Southern Rebellion. She begged to travel south to serve as a battlefield nurse. When that was denied, she threatened to cut her hair short, disguise herself as a man to fight alongside others so she could make a difference in the world. Father Ricardo had thankfully talked her out of joining the war. He assured her she would indeed make a difference someday, when the time was right, when the Lord was ready.

The only time Andrew ever truly impressed Tessa, he figured, was when he announced he was joining the army as a medic. The day he left was the only day she ever kissed him. A quick peck. She tried to hide her tears that day. "You come back Andrew Vaines. You come back safe." He had indeed come back safely from the Hell of those battlefields. Now he needed for her to return from the Hell she was trapped in.

It was after midnight when Father Ricardo finally woke again. Andrew and Kerrington rushed to his side. The priest gasped when he saw how bad Tessa now looked. Deathly pale.

"She is dying," Father Ricardo declared with panic choking his voice. "We have no choice. She'll be dead in minutes if we don't draw the demon completely from her, and do it now. You must pump *all* of her blood into me. And mine into hers. All of it!"

"There's far too much of a risk!" Andrew protested.

"I have fought that Beast hour upon hour within battlefields you cannot imagine. I know I am stronger than it. God stands with me! Will you not stand with me too?"

"I stand with you," Kerrington replied and cranked the trans-fuser, pumping blood as fast as he could, as fast as the contraption would permit.

As a surge of Tessa's blood reached the priest's veins, he passed out again.

Andrew looked to Tessa and gasped. She was no longer breathing. "Tessa! Beloved!"

Kerrington saw Tessa's condition too. "Pray for her! She's in God's hands now."

"Not yet!" Andrew shoved Kerrington aside and grabbed hold of Tessa's right wrist.

Andrew's ungloved hand was now against her uncovered skin.

"Take me!" Andrew demanded. "Take me, you Unholy and Cursed Thing!"

In an instant, Andrew found himself in a terrifying realm. He could still see the barn around him and its occupants glowing in some ethereal light, but where the far wall should have been stood a gateway. Hell itself lay beyond that gateway with all its fiery and molten terrors. Nearby, the demon itself stood. Father Ricardo had been right. It appeared as an angel, but a fallen one. It indeed wore a crooked crown, which glowed with eerie and otherworldly power.

The demon turned to Andrew, a fresh body now to possess, a *willing* soul to take.

It stretched out its unholy arm and clutched at Andrew's heart. Despite the fires of Hell beyond, the grip felt as cold as arctic ice. As the demon worked to possess him, it lost sight of Tessa on the cot nearby, but Andrew kept his eyes locked on his beloved.

A spectral version of her suddenly leapt from her dying body and tore the crown from the demon's head. Stunned, the demon staggered back, letting go of Andrew's heart.

"Andrew, shove the demon through the gate!" Tessa yelled. "We have but moments!"

Peering through the gateway into Hell, Andrew could see the demon's minions coming now, racing to defend their Master. Andrew didn't think he could possibly shove the demon through that gateway, but he had strength here he lacked in the mortal world, a strength that came from the Heavens, no doubt. He put his shoulder into the demon and shoved it back. Without its crown, it was weak. It howled and kicked and spat, but Andrew drove it backward, step by step, toward the heat of the open gateway. One final push and Andrew shoved it through.

Tessa slammed the gateway door shut; the howls of Hell silenced.

Everything went black.

When Andrew came to, he found himself sprawled on the floor

of the barn. Major Kerrington was checking on Tessa. She was breathing again, taking in gulps of air, her pallor improving fast. Kerrington turned to Father Ricardo, removed the transfuser needles, and quickly untied him. The priest rose shakily from his cot, rubbing his sore forearms.

Father Ricardo looked confused and shaken. "What has happened? What went wrong?"

"Andrew *touched* her!" Kerrington exclaimed. "He took the beast into himself! He did so willingly! He ruined everything!"

Kerrington drew his pistol and leveled it at Andrew.

"Stay where you are, Demon!" Kerrington growled.

Father Ricardo and Kerrington were both so intent on Andrew they failed to notice that, behind them, the needles in Tessa's arms fell away. The twine that had bound her to her cot also fell away. She rose to her feet. Not long ago she had looked near death. Now, she was as healthy as Andrew had ever seen her. All scars and marks and wounds gone, her skin fresh. Her eyes bright again. She tossed her gag aside. Finally, Kerrington and the priest noticed her.

"Is it true, child? Is it gone from your flesh?" Father Ricardo asked Tessa while he kept a wary eye on Andrew. "Does it now possess poor Andrew?"

"I'm fine," Tessa replied patiently. "The demon is gone. Defeated. Returned to Hell. All is as it should be. All is as I had planned."

Kerrington backed away, tense, his pistol still aimed at Andrew.

"Put the gun down, Major," Tessa told him. "You'll find it no longer fires anyway."

Kerrington scoffed and aimed the gun at the rafters of the barn. He pulled the trigger. It clicked uselessly.

"What *plan* do you mean, Tessa?" Father Ricardo asked her.

"Uncle, have you forgotten where you first got the idea of demonic Mithridatism?"

Father Ricardo stared at her for a moment, then seemed to remember. "It was you."

Tessa nodded. "I told you of it months ago, after you first told me of the blood transfuser you'd seen demonstrated. I knew I could use it to take Satan's power. So I let the demon possess me using an incantation from one of my occult books, knowing you'd then construct a transfuser and gallantly try to save me. But for my plan to work I needed to trick both you *and* the demon. It needed to be convinced that you Uncle, an ordained Priest, was its true adversary here, not me. It needed to exhaust its strength battling you. You fought so bravely and for so many long hours. You weakened the demon, Uncle, left it vulnerable. I never could have done that."

"But . . . " Father Ricardo began, then trailed off, clearly struggling to understand.

"But once you weakened the demon, I couldn't let you take its power," Tessa continued. "Although you would surely plan to use it for good, for just and benevolent reasons, you'd soon invoke the power to wage war and vanquish enemies. I will use it to liberate those who have been unjustly vanquished, to free those who so desperately need to be freed."

Tessa turned to Kerrington, his former bluster all gone.

"And you, Major, I needed your help too. I could not take the demon's crown without assistance. I knew your presence here would inspire the unselfish sacrifice I needed to guarantee that crucial aid at just the right time. The presence of a romantic rival can encourage the most remarkable displays of bravery, isn't that right Andrew?"

Andrew was too dumbfounded to reply.

Tessa pulled her glove from her left hand, withdrew the engagement ring, and tossed it to Kerrington. "I'm sure you know we never would—and never could—get married."

"We are engaged. We are engaged before God!" Kerrington bellowed. "You assented!"

"Major, have you forgotten you are *already* married? You've been married for a dozen years. I'm sure Mrs. Major Caspar Kerrington misses you."

Kerrington's face went red with embarrassment. "She suffers consumption. She's quite frail. She'll be dead within the month. It will be a blessing. Then you and I shall marry."

"Major, when you return to your wife, and I will make sure you do, you will find she is suddenly quite healthy again. Consider it a miracle. Trust me, I will check upon you often to make sure you remain a dutiful and faithful husband. And that you cease pursuing other, younger women. Besides, I could never marry you. My heart belongs to another, one far more worthy of my affections than you ever could be."

Outside, a sudden thunder of hooves. She nodded toward the barn door and it burst open. Two steeds waited just outside. She strode confidently to the horses and the night beyond. As she did, the stained and flimsy nightgown she had worn throughout the ordeal ripped itself from her body, swirled briefly around her as a dust devil might swirl furiously about, then reformed upon her, now as a leather jacket, clean riding pants, and high black boots.

She mounted the nearest of the horses, then glanced back at Andrew with a coy grin.

"Well, Andrew, will you be joining me or not?"

Andrew didn't need to be asked twice. With haste, he mounted the second of the steeds.

Side by side, Andrew and Tessa galloped into the night, the stars winking bright in the heavens above.

THE WOMAN AND THE MAZE

T HE WOMAN WAS LOST, she knew that now. Not in the way she liked to be lost, not in the delicious manner of the maze, not as a child might thrill to running amid tall hedges, dizzy and out of breath, turning this way and that, finally finding its elusive heart, triumphant. Not that way. She was *lost*. Now, oddly weak.

She found herself in a marshy glen, the woods of late autumn close all around, dark woods. She could not recall ever seeing this glen before. She knew the route from the Convent by heart, over the thick wooded ridges, down to the farmland of the valley below. She took the path often for within that valley stood a hedge maze. She knew children would be there today. A penny to enter, hot apple cider awaiting them in the center of the maze, stronger cider for the weary mothers and fathers. It was Sunday afternoon. Kids would be running and thrilling there, as she had done so often as a child in such labyrinths, as she still did whenever she could.

Well, not running. Not anymore. It was 1935. Maybe 1936. She was not good with dates but knew she was in her sixties, her eyes less sharp than when younger. Perhaps that was why she'd gotten lost. No, she'd taken the path too many times to lose her way.

Something must have lured her here.

She realized she was in the center of the glen now, her feet sinking into its thick marshy bog. She lost her shoes in the mire. She meant to find them, to root them out of the mud, but then the pain came—fierce and fast—all along her back, her left arm, her chest.

And so the woman who so rarely spoke, and almost never to others, screamed.

The pain eventually eased a bit. She prayed it was over. Catching her breath, she recalled how the Sisters told her when she was but a child, that she was a Child of God, they all were, all the orphans, and there was a plan for every one, even those who could not or would not speak. She never doubted that. It was one of the few beliefs she and the Sisters agreed upon. But as the fierce pain now returned, as it surged, as it threatened to sever soul from flesh, she wondered if she and the Sisters had been thinking of the same God.

#

She sank, helpless, into the thick and sodden bog. As her back settled within a deep trough, she caught a final glimpse of the sky, a few clouds drifting past, then darkness. It was cold here, but the cold oddly comforting, the last warmth of her body a fading nuisance. She understood she would not be found. The glen was too far from the thin trail, the trail too far from the county road, the road too far from the Convent where she still lived, a ward of The Church. The Sisters would not search for her.

She had often left that sanctuary for days, sometimes months, even years, riding railway boxcars, crossing the forlorn country, wandering among its rural enclaves, far from the towering cities—those beasts of steel and stone—the wrong kind of mazes. On her travels, she had sought the charity of others amid small towns and farms and ranches and so often found it, rarely ever left hungry. She always felt protected in her travels, guided to shelter and meals and safety. She wondered now if she had been guided here for some reason. She wondered, too, how she could still wonder for surely she was dead.

Her body was decaying; rotting would be a better word.

The many crawling and slithering denizens of the Earth, the blind things, were consuming her, eating her. Her mind somehow survived, though, carried within thin tendrils that wound their way from her moldering flesh, creeping into the thick bog, worming through moist and fragrant soil, ever closer to the edges of the glen, ever closer to the dark woods.

#

The terrified boys *ran*. They were no more than six or seven years old. She watched them, somehow, though surely she had no eyes. She heard their screams though surely she had no ears. They ran through collapsing passageways of burning branches, across smoldering ground, their faces dark with soot, eyes wet with tears, hearts pounding. She understood, vaguely, this was her fault.

They were trying to escape from her.

She needed to save them. Yet none of this made sense. Was this now? Maybe it was a flickering memory. Or a future fate foretold. Time seemed irrelevant, as if part of her had no need for it anymore. She wondered if this was how it was for all who died.

The screams of the children faded and she could no longer see them. She feared they were dying and would soon join her. She craved their simple companionship, was desperate for it, but understood that was wrong; part of her understood at least. Part though wanted to devour, to absorb, to feast on decaying animal flesh. That part of her seemed so strong and was growing ever stronger. She feared she would forget who she was and then there would be no hope. She tried now to remember as much as she could for she too had been a child.

#

She had a mother and father once. They'd given her a name, one long ago forgotten. They had loved her, no doubt. At least until it became clear she was different, that she did not talk as other children would. That she did not laugh with glee at silly peekaboo games as others would. That her eyes rarely bothered to find the eyes of others. So they had left her at the doors of a convent orphanage, swaddled in linens within an old orchard basket.

The Sisters had taken her in, as they had taken in so many other orphans of that era. Back then, it had been a mere handful of years since the end of the first great war, the War Between the States, the war of brother against brother. The Sisters had given her a new name, Eleanor, and told her it meant Child of God. Later, she learned they told every orphan the same thing regardless of their name for they were *all* Children of God.

The Sisters, too, saw the distance in her eyes and were troubled by the silence of her lips. They assumed, as her own parents no doubt had, that she was a mute. That she could not speak. She chose not to. She understood words. She knew how they could be pulled apart, rearranged in her mind, and fitted back together, forming new and different sentences. Speech was a puzzle. But a simple one. She had grown bored with it. The puzzles she liked were those she could feel, those she could trace a finger across, those she could draw. She found her first maze in an old grammar school primer in the orphanage library. She was soon obsessed.

With pen and paper, she had drawn endless mazes. When paper was taken from her, she drew along the dormitory walls of the orphanage. When pens were taken, she traced mazes with her fingertips across the tile floor, along the thin sheets of her bed at night, along the tabletop beside her meals, and, sometimes, in the convent gardens, amid flowers and weeds and other growing things. She had dug deep into the loamy soil with dirty fingers, burrowing amid roots and worms, forming mazes there, finding mazes there, finding them everywhere. The Sisters would spank her when they saw her clothes dirtied, their flower gardens disheveled.

Yet the Sisters were never so furious as the day they took her to her first life-sized maze.

It was in October one year. The Sisters took her and the other children to a sprawling hedge maze. She loved it so much, she refused to leave. The poor Sisters thought she couldn't find her way out. They thought her stupid as well as mute. She was neither. She was home.

She had quickly learned the trick of that maze, a trick the Sisters, for all their wisdom, could not discern. It was an island labyrinth, its inner maze subtly and cleverly separated from its outer maze. So the simple right-hand-rule would not work. One could not just place one's right hand—the hand of God—along a hedgerow, then turn right, and right again, and then right and right and right, until reaching the center, then proceeding in the same manner to find the exit. The inner island prevented that for it was separate from the rest. The same but different.

It had grown dark and cold that day before the last of the Sisters had been found by the proprietor and led, shivering, from the maze. Shivering and livid. By then, she'd been waiting for hours outside the maze along with the other children, many of whom were crying. She was smiling, at least inwardly. The Sisters refused to take her or any of the orphans to that or any other hedge maze ever again. So she would go on her own, often leaving the Convent before dawn, returning after dark. Each time, she could feel the disappointment in the Sisters. Not that she had left for the day, but that she had returned.

The Sisters gave up trying to teach her grammar or arithmetic or even The Bible. They were content she busied herself. Though she couldn't express it, she was grateful to the Sisters for all they did, providing food and shelter, a place to sleep. In time, they reached an accommodation. Since she insisted on tracing endless mazes with her hands across every tile floor and along every wall, they gave her wet rags to hold as she did so. The Convent was never so clean, never so sparkling. The Sisters otherwise left her alone.

The other kids left her alone too. It was the distance in her eyes that pushed them away. It was that same distance that kept adults from her later in life, men especially, for she was not an unattractive woman. Yet, when she rode railcars by herself, or wandered rural byways, she was left alone. She never married. Never had children of her own. As an adult, she often sought their innocent company, in playgrounds, in parks, in mazes, not to play with them, nor even talk to them, but to be in their presence, to commune with their life, their exuberance, their simple joy.

#

Amid the cool darkness beneath the ground, it was hard for her to reckon time. Had weeks passed since she died, or months? Her tendrils wound ever wider across the boggy glen, North and South, East and West. She sensed the shape of herself and realized her tendrils were a wild profusion of underground growth, chaotic, meaningless. That must be the plant in her, she understood.

So she sought to shape herself, guide her growth. It was difficult for already much of her was plant, not person. Yet with effort she wrangled her tendrils into a shape of her pleasing. A maze. An underground one, for her tendrils had yet to turn upward. Soon, though, they became roots, the roots sprouted, the sprouts became shrubbery, the shrubs grew ever taller. It was spring, the long winter over. Her hedgerows grew fast. By summer she was tall—tall enough for children at least. The soggy bog dried and hardened into firm pathways. She was a fine maze but not a perfect one. With effort, with focus, she found she could wither the hedgerows she didn't want and grow new rows, form new pathways, make new dead ends. She turned herself into a maze children could truly lose themselves in, a vast island maze.

She puzzled over just how fast her new hedgerows grew. Days

and hours were for people, not plants. Still she was pleased with the maze, pleased with herself, pleased to know she now filled the wide and flat glen, surrounded by the woods. But where were the children? Judging from the heat of the sun, and the length of the days, it was well into summer.

Children should be free by now. Free of school. Free to play. Free to wander. She set about to call them. She cast her mind out, but no child heard her, perhaps she was too far away, too far from the nearest trail, the nearest road, the nearest town.

She feared she would remain alone, then she realized there were other minds she could call too, minds far more tuned to the magic of the woods than even children.

She called out again. This time something else heard her.

From a small town a few miles away, a hound dog heard.

It came. And it brought a few rambunctious boys.

#

They were ten or twelve years old, she figured. She was happy a hound had brought them, for the dog would know its way back to town. These children would not become lost, as she had. They dove into her now. They ran headlong and headstrong along her narrow pathways, under her archways, turning this way and that. It felt to her like blood flowing through veins. She felt truly alive again. It was thrilling.

When they went home after the sun set, she knew they'd be back. They would return with brothers and sisters and friends, maybe girl-friends, never any parents. That pleased her too. For this glen was a place of magic and few adults understood magic. Those that did, like her, were deemed broken. She thought again of the Sisters. She hated how they had seen her and others like her as just that—broken. She hated too that The Sisters, and indeed most people she had met in her travels, assumed those who were not normal were all the same. A silly notion. She understood that those who were different were different in different ways.

#

It was a glorious summer.

Almost every day, children came. One night a few of them, older boys, brought sleeping bags and slept within her grounds. As they lay beneath the stars, a part of her hoped they would put down roots, that they would stay. They left soon after the sun rose. She felt a pang of intense loneliness when they left. A week then passed with no children, and she worried they'd grown bored with the maze, that it was now too easy for them, even the younger ones. She tried to change herself. She tried to wither parts of her and grow new hedgerows. She couldn't. She wondered if that was something she could do only in the spring when she was young and vigorous. Or perhaps the other part of her, the plant of her, didn't want her to make changes now.

Her leaves grew brown and dry.

#

For over a month no child came. Her loneliness festered. It ached. It hurt. She called out with her mind again. She called to those older boys who had slept within her, but they couldn't hear her. She called to the older girls who sometimes played within her maze. No answer. She called again to the hound dog. If it heard, it refused the call, maybe now it feared her call. She called then to a few of the younger children, their minds still fresh, still tuned to the natural ways of the world, not yet stifled by school and chores. She had never even tried to call any so young, but she did so now for loneliness was too powerful a tide. It was late October when they came, three boys, six or seven years old, so young, so fresh.

Since she was now dry and ugly, they had to dare one another to enter, but enter they did. Again, she felt the thrill of blood in her veins as they ran within her. Soon, their little legs and hearts and lungs grew weary. They turned to leave. She could not let them go.

Parts of her withered and fell away. New parts grew, fast and vigorous. The fresh hedgerows closed off the only exit. It took a while for the boys to realize there was no way out. She hoped they would be happy. For they were in a perfect maze. For a perfect maze was one that a child could explore forever and never risk finding the exit. She cherished the feeling of warm blood in her veins as they ran, and screamed, and ran still more. They tried to cut and claw through her branches, but she was thick and she was tough. Eventually, she knew, they would calm down. They would lie on the ground. They would finally cease their incessant breathing. They would put down roots too. They would join her. They would join her perfection.

She realized these thoughts were not her thoughts.

She understood, dimly, at least the last of the human in her understood, that the plant in her craved the flesh of the children, the decaying nutrients plants always needed, that plants always sought to take from animals, to feast upon, and the woman in her craved companionship. It was an unholy combination of the two needs that doomed the boys. Try as she might, she couldn't free them. She could no longer force parts of herself to wither, while other parts grew.

She had lost that control.

#

Desperate, she called to the town. She screamed into the minds of the men and women there and the older children too. They heard nothing. The hound heard, and now it didn't ignore her. Later that day, led by the dog, the townsfolk arrived, mostly men. They brought guns and knives, even hatchets. They called to the three trapped boys. The boys called back through the dense hedgerows. The men tried to cut the thick branches with knives and hatchets but could not for she was too tough. One, then, came at her with fire, a burning branch, lit from a match.

The plant in her, and the woman too, trembled at the flames. Fire was a force both animals and plants could fear together. She understood the man's plan. The boys were told to hurry to the center of the maze. By the time the fire might reach those inner hedgerows, the outer rows would have burned. A path would be open for the children to escape. It was their best hope. She didn't want to burn, but she would do so to save the innocents.

As the man poked the burning branch toward her dry and brown leaves, fresh vines erupted from the hedgerow, darting out far faster than she thought possible. They took hold of the man's arm and twisted it back. He howled in pain as his bones snapped.

The flaming branch dropped harmlessly to the ground. The plant in her was in full control now. The man and the other townsfolk fell back in terror, scrambling away in abject fear at this unholiness. But the hound had no fear. She called to it. It understood. It understood all too well.

The dog grabbed one end of the burning branch, the flames now singeing its fur, no doubt burning its tender eyes. It ran bravely along the outer edge of the maze, along those dry hedgerows, her dry hedgerows, leaving a path of fire, a ring of fire.

The flames grew fast. The woman in her roared in agony, and the plant in her did too. The fire spread, burning in toward where the boys cowered, but she was still an island maze. So the flames of the outer half of the labyrinth didn't reach the inner half, not yet. When enough of the outer maze had burned, and the flames there had abated, a path was left open. The plant in her tried to hold onto the children, it tried to clutch their arms and legs with fresh vines, but it had lost too much strength from the fire. The boys pulled free of those tangles.

They ran now through collapsing passageways of burning branches, across the smoldering ground, faces darkened with soot, eyes wetted with tears, hearts pounding.

This now was *now*, she felt. Maybe it would be the last now that ever mattered to her.

Soon the boys were free. The townsfolk grabbed them and hugged them, then they turned, all of them, and scrambled up the hillside, hurrying into the woods, toward home, none looking back, none but the hound. It gazed back once. It watched as flames caught the inner maze. That part of her burned now too. She couldn't read the look in the dog's eyes. Was it fear? Or maybe sympathy. Or was it just an animal thing acknowledging the magic of a plant thing.

Admiring it. Fearing it. Turning, finally, and running from it.

#

Below ground, she was content. For she was still a maze. Not a maze of hedges and leaves and branches, not a maze that reached toward the heavens. She was a maze of roots and tubers, a remnant of—and a reflection of—the hedgerows that had perished above, with the same pathways, the same in's and the same out's. Here, she could no longer endanger children. She missed them dearly but, should any ever return to the glen, they would be safe from her, from the dangerous blending of the needs of a plant and the wishes of a lonely woman.

Things soon began to crawl in and around and through her, worms and other blind creatures. Although they moved very slowly, she was no longer on the rushed time of men and women and children, nor was she on the time of hedges and flowers and trees. Here, even seasons barely registered. Time itself found little or no traction here, so she could slip forward or back in it if she wanted, but why bother, for she was content. Here, the slow meander of a worm, the lazy slither of a slug, felt *quicksilver* fast in her dark passageways. And so once again—and now forever—she felt the thrill of blood in her veins.

ACTS OF ABSOLUTION IN THE CIRCUS OF THE NIGHT

1.

Monsieur Dubois Presents... An evening of High Acrobatics and Low Comedy, Lust and Limberness, Sweat and Fire. Featuring the most skilled and daring performers from all of Europe, the Far Orient, and All the Corners of the Globe. Three Nights Only. The 23rd-25th of November, 1893. 123 Rue de Chatel. Paris. Midnight. Attendance by invitation only.

T HE BOY CLUTCHED THE embossed invitation in trembling hands, careful to keep his pale skin from its sharp edges. In his excitement, he might cut himself. He would bleed.

He might never stop.

The envelope had his name—Stelian Cojacarú—in floral script. His sister's handwriting. Yet, oddly, different. It *had* been ten years. Ana would be twenty-five now. He could smell the perfumed scent where her hands had brushed the paper. He recalled her tucking him into bed each night when he was a child. Ten years older than he, she was the only mother he'd ever known. He had despaired he would never see her again. Now, she was here. In Paris!

He read the invitation again in the candlelight of his bedroom. Why midnight? His papa had taken him to a circus one afternoon in the *Jardin du Luxembourg*. Jugglers and mimes. Elephants and other tamed beasts. This circus must be quite different. Steli was now almost fifteen. Nearly a man, despite his small bearing and frail physique. This circus must be for grown men, he thought, and ladies of ill repute. *Other women*, he scolded himself, not Ana. Maybe she sold oranges and other sweet *argumes* during act breaks. Maybe she just mended costumes.

It wouldn't surprise him, though, if his older brother Anton was a performer. Strong and athletic, Anton had been lucky to escape the condition that haunted Steli and so many others in the Cojacarú family. Haemophilia. It was why their father had brought them from Bucharest to live here. He had hoped that here in Paris they might somehow avoid that blood curse. Ana and Anton had avoided it, at least.

Steli eased the invitation back into the envelope. He'd found it on the floor of his bedroom earlier that day after returning home from market with the housekeeper. Ana must have climbed the rusted iron ladder in the alley, then made her way across the sloped roof to slip the invitation through the dormer window. No doubt, she had hoped to avoid their father. He was an unforgiving man. After she and Anton had run away, he forbade Steli to even mention them. He had also forbidden Steli to ever leave home alone, even by day, and especially at night.

Steli did not disobey the man often, but he would do so now.

With his father's deep snores rumbling from the main bedroom, Steli tugged on a long coat. He stuffed the invitation in a deep pocket along with a map of the Arrondissements of central Paris. Testing his bedroom door, he found it locked from the outside. Had Papa somehow *known*? Steli eyed the dormer window. Gathering his courage, he climbed onto the roof. He'd never been on the rooftop before, never dared. If he cut himself on the sharp drainpipes or the splintered roofing tiles, he would bleed. There were other ways to die too. A loss of balance. A sudden slip. A fast drop to the cobblestones below.

A thin iron railing stood outside his window, mounted along the slippery roof tiles. He clutched the rail and eased his way along the steep roof to the rusted ladder that led down to the alley. It wobbled as he climbed on. Its cold rungs were wet with the misty night. Each handhold, each foothold, each step terrified him. Yet he was exhilarated too. The night was chilly, but he was *sweating* and he felt alive for the first time in years. Before long, he reached the alley below.

He drew his coat close around him and headed into the dark city.

2.

As Steli worked his way through winding streets, he looked about, fearful. This was a different Paris than the one his father sometimes showed him by day. Dark shapes hunkered in dim corners and loitered in narrow passageways. Thieves and murderers, he feared. Cutthroats. And the poor, the destitute. He followed his map and was relieved no one bothered him. He checked to make sure he still had the invitation from Ana.

It had broken his heart when she'd run away years ago with Anton. The two had left with a traveling carnival, one Papa called cheap and vulgar. Were they even still together? So different from one another, Ana and Anton, always squabbling. It had been a shock to Steli when they'd suddenly left together, but their father was a strict and unpleasant man, so perhaps it should not have been a surprise. Steli had hoped Ana would quickly tire of Anton's antics, his arrogance and his endless bullying, and she would grow weary of the dangers and discomforts of the road. Yet she had not returned. Neither had Anton. *Ten years.*

Steli reached a side alley. According to the invitation, the circus must be at the far end of that narrow *venelle*. Yet there could be no circus tent there. He might have turned back, but a carriage pulled to a stop behind him. Well-dressed gentlemen climbed out. Ladies too, their evening dresses coal black or blood red. They showed curves that made Steli blush. Quietly, he followed them. At the end of the alley, he found no circus tent, just an old theater. The place looked abandoned for years but a stout doorman emerged from shadows. The gentlemen handed him their invitations and escorted the ladies inside. Steli fumbled with his own invite, dropping it in the grime of the alley. He tried now to brush the dirt off but the doorman ripped it from him.

"Where'd you find this, boy?" He squinted down at Steli. "This is no place for a guttersnipe," the man growled, towering over him. "Run along home."

"It's *mine*. My sister left it for me."

"I said run along!" The man ripped up the invitation.

Other gentlemen now arrived and the doorman stepped away to greet them. Steli heard muffled voices down a side passageway and hurried in that direction. He hoped it was the chatter of circus hands. Maybe Anton would be among them. He could fetch Ana. The voices seemed to come from beyond a heavy wooden door, left ajar. Steli was thin, so he slid through easily and found himself in a dim and musty room, bustling with activity. Circus performers, roustabouts, seamstresses. He must be backstage somewhere. He searched for his brother. He knew his sister was not here for he would have noticed her perfumed scent if she were.

Suddenly, a big paw grabbed his coat and hoisted him high.

"What have we here?" a gruff voice demanded. A gas lamp was thrust beside Steli's face. "A wisp of a boy. You are a *boy*, ain't you?" Harsh laughter barked from others in the room.

A shape strode forward, smiling. "Stelian?"

"You know this waif?" the rough man asked.

"From a past life. From a memory," Anton replied. "Put him down. Let me hug him."

Anton's strong arms closed around Steli, crushing him to his broad chest, and Steli thought maybe there was a tear in his brother's eyes. He'd never seen that before. Not even when they were younger and Anton hurt himself badly at play, not even then.

"Stelian, you haven't changed a bit!" Anton exclaimed, and Steli supposed it was meant as a compliment. Anton, though, had changed. Bigger. Stronger. A man now. In the flickering light, Steli peered at his face. He saw some of his father there, in the sturdy chin, in the strong brow. But in the eyes, he saw a haunted look, not quite hidden.

"Is Ana here?" Steli blurted. "Can I see her?"

Anton laughed. "Of course. I'll put you up front."

Before Steli could protest, Anton carried him through another room, a bustling area just backstage where performers readied themselves. Mimes. Contortionists. Acrobats. Steli looked for his sister. She was not here. Anton then took him into the old theater itself, packed with well-dressed gentlemen and ladies, laughing and drinking. Thankfully, Anton didn't put him in the front row but to one side. He hoisted Steli up and set him high upon a wide brick ledge with a good view of the stage over the heads of the audience. Anton waved to an usher.

"This is my honored guest," he told the man. "My brother. Let him watch from here."

Anton ruffled Steli's hair, squeezed his cheek and grinned.

43

"It's so good to see you again Stelian. Ana will be thrilled to meet you after the show. I won't get a chance. I've things to do. But Ana will talk to you. There's much to tell. So much."

The lights went out, Anton went backstage, and the show began.

3.

Steli gawked at a series of lewd performances from mimes and comédiens. The jokes were bawdy and Steli didn't understand them, didn't *want* to understand, but the audience howled. There were also skilled acrobats and contortionists from around the world. *Chinois. Brésilien. Indonésien.* Some spat fire into the smoky air, nearly scorching the rafters above. Between acts, young ladies took to the stage, dressed scantily, and danced provocatively. Steli was embarrassed for them. He was relieved, each time, that Ana was not among them.

As the show went on, he sensed the crowd grow restless, waiting for something different. Finally, the last act of the evening was announced by Monsieur Dubois himself, a portly man who winced from gout. As he left the stage, the crowd leaned forward. Two figures appeared, backlit behind a white curtain. The way the light cast their shadows, they looked huge. *Olympian.* Distorted though they were, Steli recognized them, both of them.

As the thin curtain was raised, Anton and Ana were revealed on stage to much eager applause. Anton wore tight shorts. His physique was like that of a Roman statue, a body taut and powerful. Steli's heart broke to know he'd never look like that. He would become a man, soon maybe, but never like Anton. He'd remain slight. Frail. And there was Ana. She was just as he imagined. Poised and perfect. Bold and beautiful. She was dressed scantily as well, her breasts and loins wrapped in swathes of tight cloth, the rest of her was but oiled skin.

He knew he should be embarrassed for her as he'd been for those other young women who had bared too much of their skin, but he was not for her body was flawless. Somehow it was *right* that she presented it as she did, as it was right that the stone sculptures of the *Jardin des Tuileries* displayed the unclothed perfection of classical Grecian women. Perfection should be heralded, not hidden.

Juggling implements were tossed to them from backstage. For Anton, sharp knives, maybe from the Orient, curved and deadly. The blades shimmered in the hot lights of the stage. For Ana, torches, as yet unlit. Anton began juggling. It was like nothing Steli had seen before. What Anton did with those flashing knives was unique, dangerous, highly skilled.

Though Steli was no expert on such matters, he could tell from the audience that they too were dazzled. As Anton's performance ended, Ana touched a half dozen of the torches to nearby footlight flames to set soaked wraps afire. She began an act that soon became even more dazzling than Anton's. It was as different, though, as night from day. As she juggled, still more torches were tossed to her until the stage was a blur of twisting fire. Steli understood that for an act as intricate as this, it must have taken endless practice, all day, every day. No wonder Ana had no time to write or visit. For Anton, it must have been the same.

Ana's performance ended with a roar of applause but the audience soon quieted and leaned forward still further. Steli realized the show wasn't over, maybe just beginning. Anton and Ana approached one another, their bodies sweaty. The thin white curtain lowered again, encircling them and the brightest of the stage lights. Silhouettes of their backlit bodies were cast on the curtain to the size of Olympian Gods. Stagehands waved large fans that billowed the curtain. Rhythmic drumming came now from backstage.

Anton and Ana began a slow and undulating dance, not touching one another, but moving around each other. Steli had seen many dances: simple folk dances and elegant waltzes. This was nothing like that. This was primal. Animalistic.

The dance grew ever faster and more frantic and the drumming ever louder. Anton now threw his head back and something began to wriggle from his mouth. A snake? At least, it looked to Steli as though a large snake—or maybe an eel—was slithering from Anton's open mouth. Thick and strong, the creature lunged at Ana. As if transfixed, she didn't flinch. While its tail was still inside Anton, its head wormed its way around Ana's lithe body, around her waist, her breasts. Then, Ana reared her head back and it plunged into her mouth, quickly working its way down her throat. There were gasps from the crowd and some retches.

Appalled, Steli prayed this macabre act would not grow worse, but it did. While the tail of that writhing creature remained within Anton, its head emerged from Ana's belly as if wriggling from her flesh. *No!* This must be an illusion. Trickery. Steli peered more intently, trying to make out what was happening behind the billowing curtain. The snake—or whatever it was—now seemed to plunge into Anton's stomach, writhing its way into him as its tail finally emerged from his open mouth.

The stagehands waved the fans even faster and the curtain gusted even more, so it became even harder to see, but the tail of the creature seemed to disappear into Ana's mouth, then emerge from her belly, before slithering into Anton's stomach and vanishing within him.

Abruptly, the drums stopped, the billowing curtain fell.

No sounds now from the audience. No cheers. No applause. Clearly, the act was not over. Ana and Anton grabbed their juggling implements and began to juggle once more.

Now, it was Ana who juggled the sharp and deadly blades. Anton tossed the flaming torches. Steli was amazed that Ana could juggle the blades as well as Anton had. Anton could likewise juggle the torches just as Ana had. Both showed uncanny skill. Yet it seemed to Steli that they mimicked one another's acts with too much precision, too much perfection.

Steli feared something truly unholy had occurred behind that curtain and now wanted to run home, but Anton had set him upon too high a ledge. With his frail bones, if he jumped down, he might hurt himself. He wondered if Anton had put him there on purpose so he'd be forced to watch. Soon, Ana and Anton reached a crescendo. They flung their blades and torches high into the rafters of the theater, then caught them with a final triumphant flourish. The audience burst into rapturous applause. The main curtain thumped down, and the crowd surged to the exit, fanning themselves. Steli sat, alone, trapped atop the ledge.

As the last of the patrons left, and with the smell of stage smoke and stale sweat still thick in the air, Steli noticed a perfumed scent, then Ana was striding toward him, smiling brightly, wearing a flowing cloak. His perfect sister fetched him down from his perch, then crushed him to her bosom. Steli nearly passed out from the exhilaration and confusion of it all.

4.

A thousand questions boiled in Steli as Ana led him backstage, past other performers, then to a quiet dressing room. She plopped onto a chair, kicked her feet up on a divan. Nearby, there was a box with juggling knives and spent torches. A sturdy crate held a thick snake. So it was a snake, after all, Steli thought. Yet it didn't look nearly as large or as long as the one on stage. Ana eyed Steli now, a slow smirk growing on her face.

"Oh, Stelian! It was just an *act*. A bit of bawdy theater. A macabre burlesque. But the juggling was quite good, don't you agree?" Ana took one of the curved knives and drew a bead of blood from her fingertip with its blade, proving its sharpness, its deadliness.

Steli nodded, not knowing what to say. He doubted the audience would even remember the juggling. They'd recall what he recalled, the sickening snake, how it had writhed its way into her, then *through* her.

Ana laughed. "Smoke and mirrors. Puppetry and illusion, I assure you." She nodded to the crate. "You can hold it, pet it."

Steli found himself growing sweaty, though the room was chilly. A large window was open high above to the cold night air. His sister noticed his distress and gave him a coy look.

"Did you enjoy watching me, Stelian?" Ana asked. "Precisely which part did you enjoy the most? Was it when my mouth opened wide and the snake thrust its way down my throat?"

Steli was swooning now, almost passing out. Then, sudden motion behind him. A man grabbed him and carried him away. It was Anton! His brother looked furious. Not at Steli, but at Ana. He glared at her. "You will not *see* him again! You will not *talk* to him!"

Anton hustled him along a dark passage to a side street. He whistled for one of the roustabouts Steli had seen earlier, the man who'd called him a mere wisp of a boy.

"Gregor! Take my brother home." Anton rattled off the address, and Steli was impressed his brother still knew it. "Do not knock there. Do not wake my father." As Steli was passed to the other man, Anton caught Steli's eye and lowered his voice. "Say nothing of this. Papa will be furious if he knows you came tonight. He will come for us. He will kill us."

Steli was then carried off through the streets of Paris by Gregor, relieved he wasn't on his own now. The night had grown darker, the moon gone. Fog had settled in. He knew cutthroats and night thieves were watching them, maybe following them. He closed his eyes in fright. Before long, though, Gregor set him down on the cobblestones not far from his home.

"I will take you no closer. Quick now!" Gregor told him, then disappeared into the night.

Steli eyed the ladder he had climbed down earlier. To climb up, he would need to tug on those rusted rungs. They'd dig into his tender skin. He might bleed. Then he'd have to cross the sloped roof, slippery now from the fog. As he stood in the cold night, staring at the tall ladder, with the sounds of the dark city all around, closing in, the front door burst open.

His father stomped toward him, enraged.

5.

Inside, the evening fire still burned. Steli was shoved into a chair. His father was so angry it took him time to speak. When words came, they were little more than rough whispers.

"I forbade you to see her again. *Them*. Either of them. I *forbade* you. I knew they must be back in Paris. With that vile circus of theirs. That *perversion*."

Tears filled Steli's eyes now too. "I'm sorry, Papa."

"Promise me you'll not see them again." He glared at Steli, eyes fierce in the firelight.

"I promise." Steli nodded. "I saw something tonight, Papa. Something *unholy*. I saw—"

"Do not speak of it." His father glared at him, then his expression softened. "Because you are still so small, so frail, I forget you are now almost a young man. It is time for us to talk."

His father stirred the fire and embers fluttered to the wood floor. Papa would always stomp out such cinders right away. Now he just kept stirring the fire, staring into it. Steli understood that whatever his father would say now, it had to be spoken to himself, a soliloquy, a confession.

"Do you know the true reason we are here? In Paris. Not Bucharest." His father didn't wait for an answer. "It's *shame* that drove us. One of our forefathers did something unspeakable, though we no longer even know what it was. There was an old crone in his village. They called her a *vrăjitoare*, a witch. Who knows what she truly was? Long dead now, she's mere dust in a grave. But she cast a curse upon him and his descendants. When they come of age, those sons and daughters, they are drawn to one another to perform a profane ritual, passing a vile serpent back and forth, mouth to mouth, stomach to stomach, letting it wind its way *through* their bodies, letting it *defile* their flesh, defile all who witness it."

"Did the snake really come out of Ana's belly?" Steli was stunned. "How could that be?"

"Satan has many powers. We must fight his machinations."

Steli puzzled over the curse. *Sons and daughters drawn to one another.*

"Papa," Steli began, choosing his words carefully. "Can that snake cause the brother's sister to . . . well . . . to then bear a child?"

His father winced, then nodded tersely. "Eventually. Of course. That is how the curse is passed from generation to generation. Seed from the brother may be carried by the snake into the womb of the sister. It is *Unholy!*"

Steli gasped. "*Not Mama?* Not you and Mama?"

His father threw down the fire poker. He hoisted Steli in his strong hands and shook him hard, harder than ever before. "Never speak of her! *Never* speak of your mother!"

Shaking, he threw Steli back down. Now he understood *that* truth too. He understood why an old daguerreotype of his mother, the only memory he had of her, showed a haunted woman who looked more like a sister to his father than a wife. He understood too why Ana and Anton had run off. Father would have murdered them, or maybe just Ana.

Steli sobbed. "Did you try to kill Ana? Is that why she ran away?"

"I had hoped the curse was over. I had hoped mine was the last generation and she would be spared. A foolish wish, I know. I should have spared her all that misery long ago. By the time I knew the curse still festered, she and Anton had run off. I hoped, never to return."

"Do you mean to hurt her now?"

His father refused the question. "Speak of her no more. You will not see her again." He pushed Steli toward the stairs. "Go to bed. Ask no more questions."

His father turned away to tend the fire, leaning heavily against the hearth. Below where his papa stood, Steli spotted a glistening on the wooden floor, a puddle of tears. He sensed there was more his father was not telling him, maybe more to that shameful *vrăji-toare* curse, something his papa could not bear to speak, something Steli hoped never to hear.

Steli hustled upstairs to bed, praying to forget all he had seen and heard. When he woke the next morning, Steli found the bedroom door locked, a bowl of cold porridge on the washbasin, a bucket on the floor for urine and night soil. He understood he would not be leaving the room until the circus left town. Hearing noises outside, he hurried to the window. His father was removing the roof railing, tossing its metalwork to the cobblestones below. Once done, his father climbed down the iron ladder, out of sight. Then came loud prying noises. He must be pulling the ladder from the alley wall, Steli realized. There'd be no way to climb down now, even if Steli wanted to, even if he needed to.

He wondered why his father had not simply nailed the window shut. That would have been easier than removing the roof railing and the iron ladder. Maybe, *probably*, it was done to prevent Ana from climbing in. For she could have brought a hammer with a sturdy claw and pried out the nails to slip into his room at night. Or maybe, Steli realized, his heart sinking, there was another reason his father left the dormer window alone but removed the safety of the roof railing. Maybe he *wanted* Steli to climb onto that slippery tile roof. Maybe he wanted him to fall.

As Steli's frail body hit the cobblestone below, he'd be freed of the cruel blood disease, and that other curse too, the one brought upon their family by that old *vrăjitoare*.

6.

Growing up, Steli had been content to spend entire days in his bedroom, not even venturing downstairs, let alone outside. Now, with the door locked, with meals brought in by the housekeeper, he felt like a prisoner. He spent long hours that day by his window, watching Parisians on the street below, hurrying about. Some carried luggage, perhaps heading to *Gare du Nord* for passage to distant lands. He took out his maps, a small collection given to him over the years by his father. They showed all of Europe and The World itself, at least those parts charted.

With a pale finger, Steli traced railway routes leading away from Paris, some east to Romania. He knew little of that homeland but felt its tug anyway. There were other exotic cities too. *Istanbul. Jérusalem. Caire.* If not for his deadly blood affliction, he too might travel far from Paris, to the deserts of the Middle East, to the wilds of Africa, maybe across the Indian Ocean to the Far Orient. *Malaisie. Vietnam. Singapour.*

He set the maps aside when he saw his tears were staining them.

There was a small fireplace in the room. The housekeeper had left fresh wood. He started a fire to warm himself that night. The next day was spent much like the day before, peering out the window, reading his books and maps, waiting. He checked the time often, begging for morning to turn to afternoon, afternoon to evening, and then for evening to pass through the night to the safety of another day, for this would be the last night of the circus.

Then it would be gone; *she* would be gone.

He didn't bother to set a fire that final evening and went to bed early, hoping to sleep through the night, hoping to wake in the morning with the circus gone, Ana gone, this nightmare behind him. The brief time he spent in her dressing room had been *unsettling*. She had changed. She was not the sweet Ana he cherished from years before. Performing that unholy snake ritual each night had changed her. It had warped his beloved Ana. He fell asleep and dreamt of her sitting beside him, her hand lovingly caressing his brow, as she had done many years before.

He dreamt of her in his room.

He jerked awake. She was *there*.

7.

Steli gasped, but Ana placed a finger to his lips. "Shhh."

He sat up quickly, drawing the covers close to him. "*Ana?* How did you get in?"

"I climbed the brickwork. It was hard, but I *needed* to see you. I can't stay long. It'll be midnight in an hour or so. I had to see you, though. I had to see my precious little Steli."

He peered at her in the dim light of his room. He tried to reconcile the caring girl beside him now with the debauched woman he'd talked to in the circus dressing room two nights before, the one who had taunted and teased him.

"Steli, there is so much I want to say. So much to apologize for. I should have come back to Paris long ago to see you, but we were so far away for so long. Asia. Shanghai and Peking. It was Anton's idea to make an *act* of it. To pretend as though it was a stage trick

53

with a trained snake. It allowed us to be actors. It was easier that way, he told me."

"Did Mama truly die giving me birth? Or did she kill herself?"

Ana shook her head. "No, Steli, our mother didn't kill herself, but I do think she gave up living. That is something different. You see, we can't kill ourselves. The curse is too strong. Otherwise, that would've been done years ago by our forefathers. The curse would have died out. We can't kill our brothers or sisters either. We can't even separate from one another for long, we are driven relentlessly back to consummate the snake ritual at least once each night."

"But *Papa* can kill you? A father can kill a daughter?"

"He can and he will if he gets a chance." There were heavy footsteps on the wooden stairs beyond the door. "Steli, there's so much I need to tell you about the curse but there's no time now." She hurried to the open window. "You must promise me something. It's *important*."

Steli nodded. "I know, I must stay here. I must not follow you."

She gave him a sad look. "No, Steli. You must come tonight. You *must* come to the circus. But after the show. We'll be packing for our next city, but there'll be time."

Steli was stunned. Time for *what*?

A key rattled in the door lock. Father must have heard them. The door swung open but was jammed for a moment by the nearby chamber pot. That gave Ana time to save herself. She dove out the window. A gun went off. In the small bedroom, its roar sounded to Steli like all the thunder in the world. The shot missed. Steli darted to the window and saw Ana leap from the rooftop to the building across the alley. She then half-climbed, half-slid along a drain pipe to the ground. His father pushed his way into the bedroom and thrust the barrel out the window but must not have had a good shot for he didn't fire. Instead, he stormed into the hall and soon returned with a hammer and nails. With a few quick pounds, he sealed the window shut. He left and slammed the door behind him and locked it again from the outside.

Steli returned to the window, fearing he would soon see his father charge into the night with his rifle. But his father didn't. Perhaps his threat of killing Ana was all bluster.

The curse was not her fault.

8.

As Steli tried to start a fire to warm the bedroom, he despaired that he wouldn't be able to keep his promise. Ana needed his help, yet he could do nothing trapped here. He couldn't break the window for his father would hear. Steli lit another match and tried again, futilely, to set the stubborn fireplace wood alight. He felt a waft of cold air from the open flue and realized he'd almost made a foolish mistake. He tossed the matches aside.

If he had been bigger, if he'd been of normal size for his age, he would have had no hope. But with his slender body, he might make it. He dressed quickly and grabbed his long coat. He cranked the flue as wide as it would open and climbed in, coughing at the stench of soot. The chimney was narrow and if he weighed but a few pounds more, he would have been too big.

Squirming and wriggling up the shaft, the cold and crisp night air above slowly drew closer. Eventually, he got his head, then his shoulders, and finally his whole body out of the chute. Gasping, he perched atop the chimney. Shivering, he tugged his coat on.

Legs still wobbly from the hard climb up the chimney, Steli worked his way across the slick tile to the edge of the roof. He peered down to where the ladder had been bolted. His father had indeed removed it. Steli looked across the alley to the neighboring rooftop Ana had jumped down to. It seemed too far. She was bigger. Stronger. He feared he couldn't reach it, or even if he did, his thin ankles would break when he landed. But there was no time for cowardice.

He took a few steps back, gathered speed as quickly as he could, and leapt from the edge of the roof. Sometimes it was good to be thin and light. He landed on the roof on the far side of the alley, one floor beneath the rooftop he'd jumped from, the cobblestone street still a couple of stories below. His ankles hurt from the impact but they didn't break.

He looked now at the rusted drainpipe Ana had climbed down earlier. It appeared flimsy but if her weight had not tugged the pipe from the brickwork, neither would his. He now worked his way down the drainpipe. He didn't know how long it took him—maybe just a minute, maybe more—but his feet were then on solid ground. He wiped sooty sweat from his eyes and headed into the dark streets, past beggars and thieves.

He made his way once again to The Circus of the Night.

9.

When Steli arrived, the audience was just leaving the theater following the midnight performance. No doubt, the circus had ended this night—as it had the first night—with Anton and Ana on stage. That *unholy* snake act. With the show over and the roustabouts packing their gear, no one cared about the soot-covered boy who worked his way to the dressing room.

He eased the door open and peered in. Ana was slumped on the divan, her loose blouse unbuttoned. She looked possessed of laudanum or maybe some stronger form of opium. Steli's father had once shown him an opium den, derelict souls wasting away. Ana had the same dull look. To one side lay the sharp knives of her juggling act. The crate with the snake was not here.

Suddenly, someone pulled him into the room and locked the door behind them.

It was Anton! He must have drugged Ana. Steli feared Anton would drug him too, or strike him hard, maybe kill him. Instead, Anton got down on a knee, tears in his eyes. Anton took his shoulders and turned him gently so he wouldn't have to look at Ana.

"Steli," he began. "I know you won't understand. But it's me. It is *me*. It's *Ana*."

Steli didn't want to believe it, but he did. He saw the Ana in Anton's eyes. It *was* her.

He understood now what he should have figured out before, but he was still a child and there were things no child should ever have to understand. This was part of the curse, a part his father hadn't told him about. The unholy snake didn't merely writhe from brother to sister and back, forming a demonic loop, it must somehow carry their souls from body to body. That was how Ana could juggle the deadly blades as well as Anton and how he could juggle the flaming torches in the same fashion Ana had. It had been Anton that first night, here in the dressing room, not Ana. And it was Anton on the divan now, eyes droopy, barely awake, not Ana.

Using Anton's strong muscles, Ana shoved a dresser against the door, blocking it.

"There are things you need to do, Steli, while Anton is still drugged within my body." She nodded to the divan. "But the laudanum I gave him won't last. We must hurry."

Steli shook his head, started to sob. "I can't. I won't. It is *unholy*."

"No, Steli. There is nothing satanic or demonic about it. The Curse is indeed a *curse* but for a far different reason. Listen carefully. I have not much time to explain."

She turned him again from the divan so he would not be distracted.

"Long before the Birth of Christ," she began, "there was a ritual.

The Passing of the Snake. Some lucky wives and husbands could swap bodies with their spouses, allowing them to experience the feminine *and* the masculine, to gain wisdom from that. They say it was a gift from the Pagan Gods. That witch, that *vrăjitoare*, somehow learned the ancient incantation but perverted it, forcing it upon brothers and sisters, then upon their children, and theirs, and on and on."

Steli shook his head in horror.

"Occasionally, the passing of the snake causes the woman to conceive a child. It's not a problem with husbands and wives, of course. It's a blessing. But it is a *perversion* with brothers and sisters. It causes the inbreeding. It's why you have haemophilia."

Steli gagged at the thought of a sister bearing a brother's child.

"Understand this, Steli: it's *not* incest—for the ritual is not sexual and the brother and sister take no pleasure in the act—but its consequences can be the same. That is why papa will kill me when he gets a chance. We need to put an end to all of this tonight."

She nodded to the divan.

"I'm sorry for Anton. I truly am. But the three of us cannot all live on, and Anton . . . Well, you remember what a bully he was. He has become far worse now that he is full-grown. God may choose to save him. I will not. Steli, you know what needs to be done."

Steli felt he understood what she had in mind, some of it at least. He would try to forgive himself. This was what Ana wanted. This was what she needed. He pulled his coat and shirt off.

He approached Anton on the divan, who looked up at him with listless despair.

Steli turned back to where his true sister stood. "What do I do?"

"Take his hand," she replied. "The curse will do the rest."

On the divan, the woman who held Anton's soul muttered "no" but Steli could see a change come over her once he took hold of her hand. Her head tilted back, her mouth opened, and a snake's tongue soon appeared from within, licking the air.

The head of the snake worked its way from her mouth. Steli would have retched at the sight but now his own head was tilting back. His own mouth was opening wide and he could do nothing to stop the snake as it writhed its way down his throat to his gullet.

Steli could feel the head of the snake wriggle deep within his stomach, then somehow his belly was splitting open near the navel, painlessly at least, and the snake head poked out, its tongue again licking the air. Transfixed, Steli watched as the creature thrust toward Anton on the divan. It wriggled its way through the un-buttoned blouse and into her belly.

Moments later, Steli felt as though he were fainting *inside* himself. When his eyes fluttered open, he found he was looking up from the divan at himself, just in time to see the tail of the snake disappear into the mouth of the boy who stood before him. That pale and weak boy now looked down on him with fury and frustration. Steli recognized *that* look. It was the look of Anton. Steli's frail body now had the arrogant eyes of his brother.

Anton was blubbering. "No, no, *no*. This cannot be!"

Anton was now in that weak body, that haemophilic flesh. Ana was still in Anton's body. Strong and lean and powerful, she grabbed the frail boy and flung him hard against a wall. His head struck stout woodwork. He slumped to the floor, limp.

Lying on the divan, Steli could barely move. The laudanum was thick in him now. From where he lay, he could see his former body sprawled on the floor, a nasty gash across its forehead, bleeding badly. He knew there was no hope of returning to that body.

And why would he *want* to?

Loud voices suddenly barked in the alleyways outside. Shouts of gendarmes. Men running, women running. Panic and chaos as the Night Circus was raided.

Steli heard a familiar voice rise above the others. "Find them!"

It was his father. He would find him like *this*. Papa would find him in Ana's body. He would know *why*. He would kill them all. Or they'd be hauled away by the gendarmes, excommunicated from the church, hung for their blasphemies.

Ana shook him, trying to get his attention. She looked at him through Anton's eyes.

"We're almost done, Steli," she said. "We must be quick now."

Harsh shouts came from just beyond the door. Someone rattled the doorknob.

"Open up here!" Men pounded on the door. They kicked at it.

Ana tossed the shirt she wore aside and grabbed hold of Steli's hand as he lay on the divan. The snake now emerged from Steli's mouth. It quickly worked its way into Ana's throat as she waited within Anton's strong body. It soon looped around, emerging from his stomach and plunging into Steli's belly where he lay, listless, on the divan.

Now, Steli was fainting once again, fainting inside himself. Then he was looking down on Ana. There were tears in her eyes. He staggered away from the divan, flexed his new and powerful muscles, then hastily pulled the shirt on. He peered at the frail and sickly body he'd been imprisoned in since birth, slumped beside the wall, starting to stir, blood seeping from the forehead. The men outside were pounding harder on the door, trying to break in.

Ana looked up at Steli from the divan, her eyes heavy from the laudanum. "You *must* leave, Steli. Never return. Go with the circus. They will give you work. Simple labor at first. But you will learn skills. Become one of them. Go, never come back."

Steli didn't want to leave her but knew he must. He spotted the window high along the wall. In his own sad body, he could never reach it. With Anton's physique, it was easy. He climbed quickly, effortlessly, to the open window. He ducked through and perched on an outdoor ledge. He would need to jump down to the alley below, but his new body was sturdy.

With a sharp crack, the door to the dressing room broke open. Looking down from his perch, he watched as gendarmes shoved the dresser aside and forced their way into the room, his father close behind. The police hurried to the frail boy slumped by the wall, blood oozing from the gash on his head. His father instead approached Ana who lay on the divan, listless.

"Let this be the *end* of it." His father grabbed one of the curved knives from nearby.

Through drugged eyes, Ana looked up. In those eyes, Steli could see relief, acceptance of her fate, a final hope for atonement. Before the gendarmes could stop him, their father brought the knife down hard, drove it deep into Ana's chest, impaling her heart, killing her instantly. Her eyes remained open, but her soul was gone now, the curse along with it.

Shocked by the brutal murder, the gendarmes muscled his father to the floor. In the commotion, no one spotted Steli peering down through the high window. His father was pinned to the floor beside the frail body of his youngest son. He sobbed at the sight of the blood that seeped from the deep gash in the forehead. The frail boy looked at him. *"Father?"*

The pale boy passed out and Steli knew he wouldn't survive, the wound too deep. The bleeding wouldn't stop. He took a last look through the window at that dying boy, then let himself drop from the ledge, falling fast to the cobblestone alley below. He hit the ground hard, rolled easily, and came up running. He heard the shouts of circus roustabouts ahead. He saw Gregor waving now for him to hurry, waving for him to join the others, scattering now into the thrilling night. He ran with them.

Stelian Cojacarú ran and he never looked back.

THE NIGHT OF BLOOD PERFUME

1956

A WAFT OF RED mist drifted from the hazy evening sky. Cindy had been watching an old Clarke Gable movie from the 30's on the Philco but had lost interest and gone to the porch for a smoke. Andy and the kids were at the Bowling Center for league night, so she had the house to herself. She wanted to enjoy the still of the evening.

The evening was indeed still, except for that waft of mist that caught her eye.

Without quite knowing why, she strode out onto their quiet suburban lane and stuck her tongue out, as a child might in hopes of catching a snowflake. Cindy let the mist settle on her tongue, on her whole face. The mist tasted of red meat. It tasted of blood. She didn't mind. It tasted *right*. She was suddenly hungry again. The pot roast she had served for supper seemed so long ago. She ran a finger along her splattered brow and dabbed the fingertip to her tongue to taste the blood again. Fresh. She figured that high above a hawk must have caught a smaller bird, killed it, eaten it, and the gentle waft of red mist was all that was left of that evening meal.

Cindy noticed her neighbors were now coming out of their homes too, looking skyward as more gentle sprays of red mist appeared. Perhaps an entire flock of birds had been taken by the hawk, one after the other. Maybe a whole kettle of hawks had swooped in, silent in the dusk.

Someone, probably her next-door neighbor Evelyne, must have gotten on the party line and told the other neighbors. Folks all along the lane were gazing skyward. A few tasted the mist too, enjoying it as she had. Others seemed appalled. Cindy wondered why she was *not* disgusted by that mist, why the taste of warm fresh blood in her mouth seemed so right.

When Cindy looked up again, the high haze thickened into fog and quickly descended.

Like a massive gray elevator, it lowered toward the ground, as far as she could see in all directions. It now hung close over the neighborhood, probably the whole town, maybe the entire Central Valley of California. It looked to her like a Tule fog but an odd one. Tule fog often clung to the ground, thick along highways, making driving dangerous, making it deadly. This fog instead looked like a blanket of dull gray snow held aloft, upside down. The moon and evening stars were now lost from view. The street should be dark, she realized. It wasn't. The fog seemed to glow. She tried to judge its height. It rested about ten feet above the street.

Rested. That seemed to be the right word. The fog was resting, as if gathering strength, as if readying itself. The neighborhood dogs grew eerily quiet. Not even whimpering, they hunkered close to their masters. Children too came out of the houses to look up, even a few of the younger kids who'd been put to bed early. All marveled at the odd sight. No one seemed much troubled by the fog until one of the Caruther boys tossed his football into it. The ball didn't come back. Now, the neighbors grew worried. Some of the houses had attics. A few had second stories. The fog sat at just that level.

Next door, Sam Henderson announced he'd check his attic. Evelyne, his wife, told him not to, but Sam was stubborn. Their attic had a window. He would call down once he got up there. So Cindy and Evelyne and a dozen others waited in their front yard.

Soon, a creaking sound could be heard above them in the fog. The attic window opening, no doubt. At about the time Sam should have called down to them, a fresh mist of red drifted out of the fog. Like a spritz of heavy crimson perfume. All understood; the mist was not mist.

Evelyne screamed and ran into her house calling for Sam. Cindy almost got to her, almost stopped her, but Evelyne was too quick to catch. There was a pulldown ladder in the hallway her husband had climbed to reach the attic. Evelyne was halfway up when Cindy finally got hold of her and pulled her back. All that came back were legs and half a torso that fell heavily to the floor. Other neighbors were entering the house now to try to help.

Cindy shoved them back. She yelled at them. *Get the hell out!*

Then it didn't matter whether they were inside or out.

Lightning quick, shapes speared out of the fog. Far too fast to see clearly. Maybe claws. Maybe fangs. Maybe things for which there was no name. Whatever they were, they were wickedly quick. Many were snatched into the fog. Not everyone. Not yet, at least, and not in any apparent order. Cindy saw that some who ran were taken. Others who stood still, terrified, were killed too. Some who had embraced the taste of the red mist, whose faces were still wet with it, were slaughtered. Others, who'd been appalled by those who savored the blood from the sky, perished now too. As each was snatched into the fog, a moment later, a mist of savory red.

Cindy fought the powerful urge to taste the mist again. She wandered in a daze down the street, panic all around. Two men from down the block pried open a manhole cover and climbed into the sewer. The *things* somehow reached through the ground, through the pavement, and snatched them up. Other neighbors raced to a backyard fallout shelter one had built last year. What was the point? The ground offered no safety. Survival wouldn't be that simple.

Suddenly, a screech of brakes. A crazed driver nearly struck her.

He lurched his car to a stop just beside her, yelled at her, screamed at her. She was still staring at the chaos when she realized it was Andy. It was their own goddamned Packard. The kids must be in the big back seat, Jill and Joey, no doubt terrified, no doubt hunkered low on the floor, out of sight. There were splatters of blood on the car's side doors, dripping off the gleaming chrome door handles. Cindy's hand slipped and slid as she tried to get the front passenger door open. Finally, she yanked it open and scrambled in beside Andy.

The powerful engine roared as they tore down the street, neighbors leaping out of their way, others snatched by the fog as they approached, replaced with a waft of red from above. The wiper blades whacked back and forth, valiantly trying to wipe away all that crimson. Andy had trouble keeping his eyes on the road. He kept looking over at the shiny little power door lock button to his left. It was the first year that Packard offered the feature, and they were the first in the neighborhood to own a 1956 Four Door Patrician, the envy of all.

Andy was sobbing, trying to say something, choking on his words: "I thought I was unlocking the doors. I *swear*. I thought I was unlocking them."

Then, only then, Cindy understood her kids were not in the back seat, not hunkered on the floor.

"I swear, I thought I was *opening* the doors," Andy mumbled in a daze.

In a flash, Cindy understood. Her own blood went cold.

Andy and the kids must have made a run from the Bowling Center for the car. Andy got in and tried to open the passenger doors. He had pushed that damned little button. The power door lock. He must have locked the doors by mistake, the kids still outside tugging at the handles, probably crying, probably screaming, probably—

"I thought I *unlocked* the doors."

Cindy was shocked and sickened and heartbroken her kids were gone, taken by the fog, but she was relieved they were spared the terrors she and Andy now saw, the horror of *living*, the horror of surviving to watch others perish. She was certain they were in a better place now. She was not particularly religious, never had been, but there was a place souls went.

There *must* be.

Cindy looked around to gather her bearings and saw they were now on Telegraph Street, racing along a gentle downhill stretch of road that led to the main town square. In the summer, they held the Soap Box Derby along this street. Yet it looked like they were somehow headed uphill. It took a moment for her to figure out why. The fog was descending yet again. Andy didn't slow as they approached the town square and soon barreled through it, the Bijou to the right, the Woolworth's to the left. The square was full of terrified folks. Many had just come out of the cinema. Panicked, they ran about, some straight into the car's path. None struck the front bumper. None crashed off the windshield. All were turned to blood mist before they could be hit.

With the town square behind them now, Andy found a street that led out of town through a deserted commercial district. Soon they were on a long straight stretch of rural road, vast orchards to the left and right, the flat ceiling of gray ever-present above. Here the fog was still twenty or thirty feet above the land, but slowly and relentlessly descending.

"To the river?" she asked Andy. "Is that where we're headed?"

He nodded and Cindy understood. If they had any hope, it was there, the lowest land around. Maybe the fog would not drop that low, maybe it would eat its fill before then, maybe it would spare the last of them, the ones who made it to the river. There was a small marina there. The river fed into the estuaries of the San Joaquin delta, and the delta led to the San Francisco Bay, maybe to safety. With a boat, they might survive after all.

Her thoughts then turned to other matters that nagged and pestered her mind.

She was heartbroken by the loss of Jill and Joey but oddly not as devastated as she figured she ought to be. It was as if she were instead mourning the loss of nieces and nephews or maybe the children of a cousin. Blood relatives—but *relatives*—not close family, not part of her.

"Did you taste it too?" she finally asked.

Andy glared at her like she was insane.

"When the blood mist began dropping from the sky, did you *taste* it?"

"Of course not," he hissed.

"And the kids, did they?"

"No!" Andy's face went pale as if the very thought sickened him.

"But others did, right?" she prodded.

"Sure. Some of the folks. They stuck their tongues out and . . . "

He didn't have to finish. She understood. They had thrust their tongues out to taste that blood, as she had, as some of her neighbors had, while others just stared at them, appalled.

Andy sobbed. "They didn't know what they were doing."

Cindy was not so sure of that. Instinctively, those folks had answered the call, as she had.

She thought of the old movie on the TV console she'd been

watching. Clarke Gable. Loretta Young. *Call of the Wild*. Cindy had devoured the book as a teenager. She loved how the domesticated dog had embraced the primal call of its ancient cousins, the wolves, and joined them in the end. The movie version had annoyed her since it was more of a frontier romance.

Cindy wondered now whether humans had ancient cousins too. Not apes, not monkeys. Those were certainly cousins, but biological ones. She meant cousins of a wholly different order. Ancient cousins who long ago left this realm but returned occasionally to feed, to replenish their numbers, to call upon some of their human cousins to join them.

"Did you?" Andy asked.

Cindy looked at him, his fists tight on the wheel, his eyes tearstained with anguish.

"Did *you* taste the blood from the sky?" he persisted.

She didn't answer, but her silence was enough.

"How *could* you?" he wept.

She chose not to reply. He wouldn't understand. He was a good man, a good husband, a good father, but he was not the sort of person to hear the call she had heard, nor answer it.

His eyes grew worried at the road ahead. An overpass. It would take them over a wide stretch of railroad tracks. Atop the overpass, the fog was much closer to the road. They would have to risk it. There was no other route to the river beyond.

Andy floored the gas pedal and the Packard barreled uphill. Soon, the fog was level with the roof of the car. Then, loud scraping sounds. Cindy saw flashes of bones striking the top of the windshield, cracking the glass. Clean white bones. Sucked free of flesh.

The bones were somehow held aloft by the fog, suspended just where the deadly mist ended and clear air still reigned. Cindy figured that when the fog finally left, when it had eaten its fill, it would drop the bones, thousands of them, all at once, all across the valley.

The Packard crested the overpass. They were finally descending again but were not yet out of the fog. The roof was still plowing through the floating ossuary, the noise deafening.

An especially large bone struck the driver side of the windshield, shattering it. The safety glass buckled. Air rushed in.

Cindy turned to Andy and screamed, but he was already gone.

A spray of red mist was left on the seat where he'd been. She thought of grabbing the wheel. What was the point? As the Packard descended the far side of the overpass, the fog descended too. The car was coasting on its own now, picking up downhill speed.

Cindy understood that although the car might reach the river ahead, she would not. The killing things would take her before that. She eyed the stain of blood on the driver's seat and once again embraced the hunger that beckoned her. She ran a finger across the wet upholstery, slipped her fingertip along her tongue, tasted a time when primitive humans ate their kill raw.

The Packard drifted into a guardrail, sideswiped it. A flash of bright sparks lit up the fog, and for a moment she could see eyes peering at her from within that fog, hundreds of pairs of hungry eyes. Now the car was out of control. It spun lazily along the slick road, tires squealing.

She was ready. The fog grew even thicker around the car, the *things* so close now, and—

#

It was quick, and the pain, though fierce, did not linger.

Cindy found herself in the fog, her body gone but her hunger still raging. Andy was not here, nor the kids. No doubt they were in a far better place. Safe. Some of her neighbors were here, though, warm and close, those who had embraced the call, their spirits at least. Many others were here too, some freshly taken, others dead

69

for centuries. Some were truly ancient, truly primal. They jostled with one another, all the spirits pushing in close, eager still to feed.

She figured there would be time to understand later. To learn why some answered the call while others didn't. Time to learn whether this was punishment for sins. Or instead a liberation of their true primal selves. Time to learn whether they were reapers, or those who had been reaped. Time, too, to learn where all these spirits went when they were not feeding.

For now, the hunger remained.

Down by the river, a handful of folks hunkered close to the water line, no doubt hoping the fog was done. It was not. Cindy reached down through the floating clog of bones, and with her new lightning-fast claws she snatched up one of the last men. She shared the feast with her neighbors and the others, her hunger finally sated, for a while at least.

Memories of her past life were fading now, but a few remained strong. She had first met Andy years ago when she worked a perfume counter at Hale's Department Store in Sacramento. He said he needed to buy perfume for his girlfriend and wanted her advice. Cindy could tell he had no girlfriend and just wanted to meet her. She didn't mind the innocent deception. That afternoon she had showed him how a proper lady embraces her perfume. Spritz it in the air, then walk through the mist, letting it settle upon her face. They were married within a year. Then kids and soap box cars and summer vacations and lemonade and barbeques and all that life.

She would miss them dearly, but not always, and never while feeding.

TEMPLES OF FIRE

A LISON WAS THE FIRST to notice. Seated in the front row of the parked tour bus, she saw the driver staring at his right arm, staring in puzzlement, in growing disbelief. His name was Sami, a likeable young guy from Shiraz who spoke little English but smiled a lot. He saw something on his arm, maybe something moving. Alison had a clear view. There was nothing there.

Sami scratched at his arm, then clawed at it, ever more frantic. Soon he was raving. No doubt, some on the bus thought he was shouting in Arabic. It was Persian. Sami was Zoroastrian, not Muslim. Their tour guide, Zahra, had explained that the first day. Where *was* she? They'd just arrived in Amira, a town in the Zagros Mountains of Iran, and were parked along a dusty street in front of their hotel. Zahra must have gone to the lobby to fetch room keys for the night.

Alison tried to calm Sami, but he shoved her away and staggered down the steep steps of the bus to the street. The road was mostly deserted. Mostly, not completely. It was just dumb luck a truck was coming. Dumb dead luck. When the truck struck, the sound of it was like a heavy bag of lumpy cement striking concrete. Alison had never seen a man die before. She charged down the steps to the street. Sami's eyes were still open, locked now in lifeless shock.

Alison knelt beside him and now saw what Sami must have seen. Something shifted under the skin of his right arm. It was hard to see amid the long shadows of the late afternoon, but something was swirling beneath the skin. It was churning and billowing like heavy cream stirred up from the bottom of a cup of coffee. That is, if cream could be as dark as thick blood. Yet his heart no longer beat. It made no sense. It could *not* be blood.

Alison noticed that the rest of the small tour group was gathering now, yet not wanting to get too close to the body, maybe out of respect but probably in fear the young man would explode, that he was a suicide bomber. Even the truck driver, an older guy with a grizzled beard, kept well back. But it was just Sami, their driver, the young fellow from Shiraz who smiled a lot.

The strange churning under his skin faded and was soon gone.

No, not gone. With growing horror Alison saw—or thought she saw—something shifting and swirling beneath the skin of her own arm. It was fleeting, and it too faded. She glanced toward the sun. It wavered behind thick smoke that billowed from a rooftop chimney across the street. That must have been it. A trick of light and shadow. A trick of the mind. The others still stood well back, and the truck driver was now on his cellphone, and no one was doing anything. Alison kept a couple of extra scarves with her for use as a *hijab* when in public. She pulled a clean white one from her hip pack and placed it over Sami's slack face, may he rest in peace.

As the tinny wail of a siren rose in the distance, locals from the neighborhood gathered, dozens, including children. One caught her eye, a scruffy little boy, face caked in dust, eyes transfixed, eyes haunted. Maybe he'd never seen death either.

Zahra, the tour guide, finally returned from the hotel lobby with a handful of keys. She stared at the body and began calling for Sami, not realizing it was his face beneath the scarf or maybe just not wanting to believe it. Alison rose and gave her a hug.

"He was my cousin," Zahra whispered to her, weeping now.

The room keys spilled from Zahra's hand and clattered to the grimy road.

#

Alison waited anxiously in the hotel lobby. Zahra had told the others in the tour group they could go to their rooms, but the police would want to talk to Alison. She perched on a leather couch beside a smoked glass window looking out on the street. She kept a nervous eye on the tour bus and the police and the milling crowd, and the ambulance that took away the body.

As she waited, she fussed with her outfit. She fussed with her luggage piled at her feet. Mostly, she fussed with her arm, trying to spot the shifting patterns she thought she'd seen before. She finally stopped fidgeting and looked about the lobby. A young man patiently staffed a reception desk, though there seemed little for him to do. Beyond the lobby, flickering gas lamps illuminated an inner courtyard. Guest rooms were set above the courtyard with balconies overlooking the enclosed space. All around: tile floors, tile walls, tile everything. And fine dust.

This hotel, like others they had stayed at on the tour, was just a few decades old but looked older. The dust that invaded all things in this corner of the world seemed to make even the new look dated. Dust was everywhere in Iran. It forever tried to reclaim cities and towns. No wonder, Alison thought, that so many who lived here felt a strong connection to the past, to the ancient world, to religions from before the Birth of Christ. The people were forever connected to history, to the long march of time. The dust helped keep them connected. She liked that.

The other reason the hotels often looked older than they were was more mundane. No matter how modern the building was, no matter how much marble tile was used in the construction—and marble was plentiful here—there were always thin cracks, in the floor, in the walls, in the ceilings. Alison wondered if it was from the many quakes and temblors. She knew what her ex-husband Karl would say. He'd tell her the buildings were built too fast. You have to let a foundation settle, he'd say, otherwise the tile will crack and fissure.

Marriages could be like that too, she mused. Hers had been. Karl was a good man, but they had gotten married in haste, and the cracks and fissures of their relationship had grown ever wider over the years. So, divorce finalized, and with their son James safely packed away to college, she had come here. Paris and London and Rome could wait. She would visit them when she got older, when she no longer had the energy for the more exotic and remote locales of the world. She was only forty. Well, forty-five, but she could still pass for thirty-five.

She fussed again with her arm, then stopped, forcing herself not to look at her skin, trying not to worry about those shifting patterns. Yet they nagged at her with a sense of familiarity.

"Alison?" Zahra called, startling her.

Alison hadn't been paying attention. Zahra had led two police officers into the lobby, along with the truck driver. The men eyed her with suspicion, as if the accident must have been the fault of a foreign tourist. Worse, she realized she'd been absentmindedly scratching at her right arm. There were red marks there now.

"Sorry," Zahra began, "but since you saw it all, they have questions."

The older of the two officers asked something in Persian, and Zahra quickly translated.

"The truck driver says Sami ran out in front of him. No time to stop. Is this true?"

Alison answered yes, and the driver looked relieved. Then, more Persian from the police.

"What possessed Sami to do that?" Zahra asked.

Alison paused at the question. It was an odd choice of words. Possessed. What *had* possessed the young man? She mulled over how best to answer. It was clear that not just the police wanted to know. Zahra wanted to know, she needed to know.

"I think he was stung," Alison replied. "On his arm, maybe by a wasp."

Zahra translated for the officers, who looked closely now at Alison's arm. There were no wasp-wounds there, no bites. Just long, lazy scratch marks. The policemen had another question and Zahra translated once more.

"They want to know if you saw a snake. I told them we were at the mountain cavern. There are vipers in those hills. You see a snake? Sometimes they wriggle into parked vehicles."

Alison shook her head. No snakes, but there was something about the cavern and the minor quake they'd felt there that was odd, something she now could not quite recall.

"You must have seen *something*," Zahra hissed, her voice now an accusation.

Alison shook her head but thought again of the strange swirling on Sami's skin, beneath it, beneath hers too. She would say nothing of that. They'd think she was on drugs. The police here probably thought all Americans were on drugs. She'd be detained. Before taking the trip she'd been warned by friends and family that the U.S. had no diplomatic relations with Iran. No consular services. If she got in trouble, the Swiss Consulate might help. Mostly, though, she'd be on her own. So she would say nothing to the authorities of what she'd really seen.

The police spoke again to the truck driver and, greatly relieved, the man left. The lead officer jotted a few notes on a little pad, eyed her scratched-up arm again, then left too.

"Are we done? Can I go?" Alison asked Zahra and she nodded.

Alison grabbed her luggage and headed for the stairs to find her room.

Zahra called to her. "We will talk more later. Please."

#

As Alison unpacked her luggage in her room, she thought again of the cavern they'd visited that day. They arrived mid-afternoon, a bumpy ride along a rutted dirt road that had the tour group wondering if the bus could even make it, but Sami got them there safely. When they reached the dusty parking lot, locals were waiting, not to visit the cavern, but word must have gotten out a tour group was arriving. Merchants hawked souvenirs and warm sodas in the March afternoon sun. They seemed disappointed the group was so small.

From the parking lot, Alison had taken in the impressive view of the town of Amira nestled in the valley below. Amid the old town stood mosques and minarets and a thousand years of vibrant history. The rugged Zagros Mountains towered all around. A rough trail led up from the valley. Alison felt sorry for the locals who had trudged up that steep trail in hopes of finding a bigger tour group with more sales for the merchants, more handouts for the poor.

Zahra and Sami had then led the tour group along a wide trail to the cave entrance, with a throng of locals following. Many were children, scruffy clothes, dusty faces, big bright eyes. Alison had dollars and *rials*, and made sure she gave to the poorest of the kids.

The cave itself was unimpressive from the outside but authentic and primeval on the inside. It had separate grottos lit by wall candles. There were no stalactites, but the stone walls were lined with heavily folded rock strata, a testament to the powerful geologic forces at work in these ancient mountains. Zahra had to roust the locals from the inner sanctum so the tour group could have enough room. A couple of small kids teased Zahra, darting to and fro, defying her orders, until she and Sami gave up trying to drive the last boy out who was especially feisty and defiant. Zahra then told the group the history of the cave. During the last ice age, cavemen had warmed themselves over a geothermal vent in the cavern. Later, pagans worshipped there, then early Zoroastrians. Geologists believed the vent was dormant by then. At some point around the fourth century, a fire-altar was mounted above it. The original was probably forged of fine copper, with a fire always kept burning in its mouth. An imitation now sat in its place, cheap and dented and scratched with graffiti. Alison had peered at the floor beneath the altar. The geothermal vent was sealed with concrete that seemed no more than a few decades old.

Zahra had gone on to explain that to the Zoroastrians fire was an agent of purity. She spoke of *Atar*: Holy Fire, Burning and Unburning, Visible and Invisible. Only priests could enter the inner sanctum itself where they tended the flame. This particular Fire Temple was abandoned in the sixth century for reasons unknown and was no longer considered holy. The tour group had been ready to leave when a temblor struck, strong enough to rattle the candles along the walls.

In the flickering flames, Alison had seen something, vapors she thought, swirling up from beneath the altar. Faint fumes mingled with fine dust that sifted down from above. Light from the trembling flames played across the cave walls, creating swirling shadows, oddly mesmerizing ones, she recalled. They looked similar to the swirling patterns seen later on Sami's arm, then on her own. That was why the patterns had seemed so familiar, she now realized. She had also smelled something in the cave. Not foul, not sulfur. Something else, an odor for which she had no word. Just as abruptly, the shaking had stopped, and they all returned to the bus.

Alison wondered now, as she sorted her belongings in her room, whether those vapors came from old chemical or biological weapons buried in the cavern decades ago during the Iran/Iraq war. Such compounds might cause hallucinations. Maybe some canisters had been stored in the cave and then, to dispose of them, the canisters were dumped in the vent and sealed over with concrete. Problem solved. As Alison mulled this over, she again tried not to scratch at her arm. The feeling was hard to describe. Although her arm didn't itch, somehow *she* itched.

There was a quiet knock at the door. She knew it would be Zahra. The woman would have awkward questions. Alison would have awkward answers. And she had questions of her own. She feared what had been released in the cave. Zahra wouldn't want to hear any of that.

Alison let her in. Zahra's eyes were red from crying. She was dressed in simple Western clothes. No *hijab*, no flowing robes. Though even with modern slacks and a blouse, Zahra still wore the requisite *Sudre* and *Kusti*, thin articles of Zoroastrian clothing that were symbols of purity and faith. She was attractive, quite striking really, probably thirty, maybe thirty-five. Alison realized she had kept her beauty hidden behind modest clothes and bland makeup.

Most of the women Alison had seen in the small towns and provinces they visited on the tour wore plain and shapeless clothes, especially young women, and girls. No doubt, for many it was a mandate of their religion. For others, a way of hiding a fetching body beneath a formless outfit, to keep certain men away, certain predators.

"They will send Sami's body to Shiraz tomorrow," Zahra told her, dabbing her eyes.

"You want to know what I saw when Sami died," Alison replied, getting to the point.

"You saw something you didn't tell the police about, right?" Zahra asked.

"Hard to describe. After he died, I saw strange patterns shifting and swirling on his arm. It looked like it was *beneath* the skin of his arm. Something I can't explain."

"Afternoon shadows, no doubt, but is there something else you're not telling me?"

Alison would say nothing of the same patterns she'd seen roiling beneath her own skin. Her arms were covered now by the long-sleeves of a blouse, her own scratch marks hidden. She thought again of the cavern. "In the cave, after that quake, you saw it too. Those vapors. Those fumes. They came from beneath the fire pit. You smelled it too. You must have."

"A dead animal," Zahra answered curtly. "Something crawled in there long ago and died beneath the pit. The quake released the foul stench. That is all."

Yet the odor was not foul, Alison recalled. It was almost sweet. "What if someone stored chemical weapons in that cave? Or biological ones. What if it was something like that?"

Zahra gave her an incredulous look. "Biological weapons? Chemicals?"

"Yes, left over from the war. The one with Iraq."

Zahra sighed heavily. "Good grief, Alison. That was ages ago, and we used no such weapons. That was Saddam. Why would any be here? We are far from the front."

Alison nodded. "Of course." She let it drop but wasn't convinced.

"Say nothing of that nonsense to anyone," Zahra told her. "Not even others in our group. They cannot hold their tongues. If the authorities hear such rumors, they will detain us. They will think the silliness of biological weapons in the cave might be true. They will quarantine us."

Alison blanched. "Of course. As you say, the notion there were any weapons in the cave is silly. I see that now." Yet something drove Sami mad. Something caused the strange churning beneath the skin of his arm. Something caused her to see the same roiling within her own flesh.

Alison sought to politely change the subject. "So what will the funeral be like?"

Zahra gave her a sharp look. "Normal. Dignified."

"Of course, I didn't mean to suggest otherwise."

"I know," Zahra softened. "In the past, the Zoroastrians did not bury their dead but left them in the wilderness to be consumed by vultures. Buzzards. The Ritual of Excarnation." Zahra could not hide her disdain. "I don't subscribe to that nonsense. Nor any nonsense." She glanced at a bedside clock and hurried to the door. "Dinner soon. Tell no one of what was spoken here."

Alison nodded. She would tell the others nothing, but she'd find out what they had seen, what they had smelled, what they remembered from the cave.

#

Three of the four couples on the tour were already seated at a long table in the hotel's dining room when Alison arrived. Zahra was not there yet. The table offered a nice view of the courtyard of the hotel, the sputtering gas lamps, the many Persian rugs. Only a few other tables in the dining area were occupied. Some businessmen, a couple of families. Judging from the dining room and the quiet lobby, there seemed to be few guests staying in the hotel. Every town they'd visited on the tour had good-sized tourist hotels, built back when it looked as though tourism might surge following the end of the Gulf War. The first Gulf War, that is. That surge never came and most of the hotels, and the restaurants they dined in, were sadly rather deserted. Oh well. Alison had come to this part of Iran to get off the beaten track.

The town of Amira was definitely off-track.

When the tour group had first met in Shiraz, the group was smaller than she had expected. The company brochure bragged of small group travel. Alison had thought that was a marketing ploy.

Yet it was just her and the four couples. All retired and in their late fifties or sixties. All living in Great Britain. The tour company was British, after all. Over the first few days of their tour, Alison had gotten to know each of the couples fairly well.

"So what do you think, Alison?" One of the husbands, Aarón Delgado, asked as she joined them at the table. He and his wife Èlia were originally from Spain but lived now near Oxford. "Are we stranded? With the driver dead, how will we leave tomorrow?"

"I'll drive the coach if it comes to that," Terry Thorpe offered. "I drove a lorry for thirty years. I can handle a tour bus." Thorpe was a tall and thin man with fine features. Alison had been surprised to learn he'd been a truck driver for he surely didn't look like one.

His wife Amy, a former pension administrator with bright and unruly red hair, rolled her eyes. "I'm sure Zahra will arrange something."

Alison glanced about to make sure Zahra was not approaching, then leaned into the others. "Forget the coach, let's talk about the cave. Have you been itching and scratching since then? What did you see there? What did you *smell*?"

The others looked at one another, puzzled.

Alison pressed them. "Have you seen anything odd, anything—"

"We'll have a new driver," Zahra declared loudly as she approached from behind. "He arrives tomorrow afternoon. We won't be able to leave until then. That will alter our schedule. I'm sorry for that. There's still so much to see."

"We were just going to visit another cave tomorrow, right?" It was Terry Thorpe again. "The big one yesterday, *Shapur*, that was impressive. Today's cave, not so much." He turned to Alison and said with a big grin: "You asked if there was a smell there. Sure. It smelled like piss."

Zahra threw a disappointed look at Alison, and she cringed.

"I for one found today's cave well worth the visit," Alethia

Boothe offered, and her husband Marques nodded in agreement. Both were of Jamaican descent with rich skin tones, but they had grown up in the Midlands of England and had barely a hint of island accent in their refined English diction.

Two smiling waiters emerged from the kitchen to serve dinner. Steaming plates of kebabs and rice and hearty stews, served with generous sides of *ghormeh sabzi* and *fesenjoon* and *doogh*. The aromas of saffron, turmeric, and pomegranate filled the dining room.

The remaining couple, the Hesters from London, was missing.

"Any idea where our colleagues are?" Alison asked, nodding to the empty chairs.

"A little pre-dinner tipple, I think," Èlia Delgado replied. "They brought liquor with them. Did you know that? If you're a tourist, you can bring some alcohol into the country. Wish I'd known that. I think they have a couple drinks each night before dinner. Good for them."

"We cannot wait," Zahra told the group. "Dinner will go cold."

With that, the group began to eat, digging into the feast.

With the waiters back in the kitchen, a scruffy boy snuck into the dining room. Alison recognized him. He'd been on the street after the accident, face dusty, clothes ragged. He now approached Alison with small scrolls, wishing to sell one. Zahra tried to shoo him away.

"No, that's okay. I have *rials*." Alison pulled money from her purse to buy one of the scrolls. With a bright and impish smile, the boy took the bills, a couple dollars' worth, and darted away. Zahra gave him a good-natured swat on his rump as he left.

Alison unrolled the thin parchment and found words written in calligraphic script. She had learned that, although most Iranians spoke Persian, often called Farsi, the written language was similar to Arabic. Zahra took the scroll and gave it a quick glance in the dim light.

"*Let your ruddiness be mine, my paleness be yours,*" Zahra read, her voice almost musical. "That is the literal translation and it is—"

"The song of *Chaharshanbe Suri,*" Terry Thorpe interjected with a beaming smile.

"Very good!" Zahra exclaimed.

"See, you thought I never pay attention. I do," Terry replied.

Zahra had told them of the festival on the first day of the tour. A combination of Halloween, Fourth of July and England's Bonfire Night all wrapped into one. Kids in disguise banged spoons in pots or bowls at doors to get treats, and there would be plenty of fireworks, but what interested Alison more was the tradition of leaping over bonfires.

"*Let your ruddiness be mine, my paleness be yours,*" Zahra repeated. "It's what's sung as we leap over rows of bonfires. A ritual of purification. We ask the flames to take away paleness and give us warmth and energy, to redden pale skin. That is the 'ruddiness' of the line. It is a prayer that we might be protected in the year ahead from all sickness, from all misfortune."

"It's a Zoroastrian festival?" Èlia Delgado asked Zahra.

"Originally, yes. It changed much over the years as it became more of a secular holiday. Devout Zoroastrians treasure and respect fire far too much to let it burn on dirty ground and jump over it. But many of us who do not hold close to the old traditions join in the fun."

"So you will lead us?" Amy Thorpe asked.

"I cannot. I have more calls to make. Difficult ones," Zahra replied, her voice catching. "And I am in no mood for fun. My heart is broken for Sami."

"I didn't mean to offend," Amy Thorpe told her.

"Worry not. And you won't need me. Downtown is not far. That is where most of the festivities will be. Ladies, remember not to walk alone and always wear your head covering. The town is safe, but many here will not tolerate a woman unescorted by a man. So it is best—"

Zahra was interrupted by that awful sound, the sound that reminded Alison of a bag of lumpy cement striking hard concrete. It echoed from the nearby courtyard.

Then a second thump, even louder, even more sickening.

#

The sight was gruesome. The missing husband and wife, Claire and Samuel Hester, were sprawled on the cracked tile of the courtyard. Both now dead, they smelled of liquor and blood.

"Stay back!" Zahra told the others as she hurried to the bodies.

Alison joined her anyway. In the dim light of the flickering gas lamps, Alison could see churning patterns along their arms. It appeared on both of them, husband and wife. Before, Alison had thought it looked like heavy cream swirling up in hot coffee. That was not quite right. It looked more like thick smoke boiling up from inside their flesh, seeking a way out.

As with Sami, the odd patterns soon faded, only to be reborn under Alison's skin. Hers *and* Zahra's. Both now had the strange swirling patterns. Alison peered back at the others in the tour group, and the hotel manager who now approached, and the other hotel guests who gathered. Some squinted at the dead bodies, eyeing the blood pooling around them. Others looked up at the balcony the couple had fallen from, but none seemed to see what she and Zahra saw.

As Alison stepped aside for the hotel manager, the scroll she'd bought fell from a pocket of her skirt. One end became soaked in the Hester's blood. She looked for a nearby wastebasket but saw none. She had wanted the scroll as a souvenir, but not now. She would throw it out once she found a garbage bin. Perhaps she could find another scroll to buy before leaving town.

"Poor drunk bastards," the lorry driver, Thorpe, grumbled.

Maybe that was true, Alison thought. Maybe the Hesters had slugged down too much liquor in their room, then tumbled off the balcony. Maybe Claire fell first and her husband Sam tried to catch her, or vice versa, and both went over the railing. Or maybe they'd been driven mad, like Sami, by whatever had been released in that cave, something chemical, something nasty, something that caused delusions.

#

Alison and the others waited in the lobby as the bodies were taken away. The same two policemen came to investigate, and now their boss too. A search of the Hester's room revealed they'd brought more liquor into the country than allowed. So maybe both were intoxicated when they went over the balcony. Yet that didn't explain what Alison had seen, the churning.

Zahra and the police then argued over something, with the officers looking over at Alison and the others and with Zahra finally nodding in reluctant agreement.

"What was that last bit about," Alison asked once the officers left.

"Nothing to worry about," Zahra replied, unconvincingly. "Well, they said we might not be allowed to leave town tomorrow, even once our new driver arrives."

"*What?*" Terry Thorpe asked.

"They say there is much paperwork to process. The British Embassy in Tehran must be contacted. With the festival there might be delays. Don't let it worry you. They are just annoyed they must now deal with the deaths of foreign tourists. They'll surely decide tomorrow it is better for us to leave town sooner rather than later, before they must do even more paperwork."

The explanation seemed to satisfy the others, though Alison feared what would happen if an autopsy of Sami and The Hesters found traces of chemical or biological agents from the cave.

"And now *Chaharshanbe Suri* awaits!" Zahra proclaimed, her face brightening. She urged the group toward the lobby doors and the night beyond. "Stay together! And take great care if you leap over those bonfires. Let's have no more accidents this night."

The Boothes balked. "You are all kidding, I hope," Alethia Boothe said, indignant. "The Hesters have *died*. Surely this is not an evening for fun and frivolity."

Terry Thorpe snorted. "I'm sorry for the Hesters. I truly am, but Amy and I have been planning this trip for a year. We'll not miss a moment of it." He glared at the Boothes.

"Now, now," Zahra cut in. "I'm sure the Hesters would want you to carry on without missing the festival. Keep Calm and Carry On. That's the English motto, isn't it?"

"We shall be in our room for the rest of the evening," Alethia Boothe declared and strode toward the stairs, with her husband Marques throwing a look of apology as he followed her.

In the distance, like gunshots in the night, a rattle of fireworks began.

#

Alison and the two couples—the Delgados and the Thorpes—merged with a stream of exuberant locals walking along the road toward downtown. No doubt, many folks had come in from surrounding towns and villages too. Some, especially children with faces disguised beneath colorful *chadors*, banged spoons inside metal pots. Occasionally, they'd dart down a side alley. Alison paused to watch as they banged their pots by household doors until handed treats. Farther along the main road, she could see smoke rising. More fireworks crackled, louder now. The night was alive with energy, and she felt her pulse quicken as she tried to catch up with her group.

The closer to downtown, the more crowded and chaotic the streets became. When she reached the main square, Alison found many bonfires burning there, some large, some small, most arranged in long rows. They reminded her of the rows of burning coals that firewalkers walked through, ones she'd seen on TV, except those were just coals and embers. These were wood fires with flames rising a foot or two or even higher in the air. Around each, adults and kids were running and leaping over the fires, while singing and chanting the same prayer Zahra had sung earlier. Now and then, others would toss dry branches into the fires to keep them burning. Alison took videos and photos with her smartphone. She then peered around the square but could no longer spot her group amid the crowds and thick smoke and clattering fireworks.

Abruptly, she felt she was being watched. Looking around she saw the same scruffy boy who sold her the scroll. He had the same impish smile as before. She put her phone away and pushed her way through the crowds, yet when she reached him, it was some other child, this one's face scrubbed clean.

Now, she saw the boy heading down a side alley and felt oddly drawn to follow him. As she hurried after him she dug a dollar from her skirt pocket to buy another scroll, or to just give it to him. He darted along alleyways that seemed to become ever narrower until she spotted him ahead in a small courtyard. There was a line of hot embers left there from a bonfire that must have been abandoned by others. He trotted and skipped along the embers, and Alison was surprised they didn't burn his feet, clad only in sandals. He beckoned for her to follow. Time seemed to slow, or just no longer matter, and she couldn't tell how long she'd been watching the boy. In a daze, she began walking along the same embers. It was exhilarating.

Those firewalkers she'd seen on TV were *real*. She too could walk along fiery embers!

Suddenly, a looming shape charged out from the shadows. She

was tackled and thrown to the dusty ground. She panicked and thought she was being mugged, then realized the man was beating the hem of her long skirt. Fires burned there. Horrified and confused, she looked back at the line of embers. It was a line of *fire*. In her daze, she had walked right into the flames.

The man finally snuffed out the last of the fires that had burned the hem of her skirt. Fortunately, her feet and legs were not burned. He pulled her to her feet and stared at her as though she were insane. He was in his twenties and looked familiar.

"You jump *over* the fires. Not walk, jump!" He spotted her scarf on the ground, dusted it off, and handed it back to her. "You should have stayed together with your group."

As she wrapped the scarf back around her head and neck, she looked more closely at him.

"I work at the Continental Hotel," he told her. "I'm one of the receptionists. Javon."

Alison realized that was indeed where she'd seen him. His shift over, he must have come downtown for the festivities. She now looked around the courtyard. "Where did the boy go?"

He shrugged. "I saw no boy here."

I wanted to give him this. "She waved the dollar."

A half dozen older men entered the courtyard. It looked like they were just passing through until one spotted something on a side wall. There was a burst of angry shouting among them. One shined a bright flashlight along the wall, and Alison could make out graffiti. Bold red, probably in Arabic script. Javon squinted over at the words and cringed at what he read.

He pointed to one word, then another. "Wolf. Death. Offensive words, this holy night."

The older men began gesturing angrily at Alison. Javon intervened. After some words were exchanged, he seemed to calm the men. He then turned to Alison. "They say it is written in red lipstick. They think it was you. I told them it could not be. You do not know our words."

He looked more closely at her, and his eyes said maybe he was not so sure she didn't write the graffiti. Those words could be easily translated from English using a smartphone or guidebook. A crazy tourist who walked through fire might do anything.

"It is not wise for a woman to be alone," he told her. "Nor to wave your foreign money around."

She hastily stuffed the dollar back in the pocket of her skirt. As she did, she felt her lipstick there. That made no sense. It should still be in her purse back in the hotel room.

"There you are!" It was the Delgados and the Thorpes. "Alison!" The two couples ran into the courtyard. "We've been looking all over for you!"

"What's going on?" Èlia Delgado asked, eyeing the crowd of men, then spotting Alison's dirty clothes and the burned hem of her skirt.

"I see your friends have found you," Javon said to Alison. "I think it best if you return to the hotel. All of you."

The Delgados and the Thorpes eyed the still menacing group of older men and nodded. Javon ushered Alison and the two couples back toward the main square, while staying between them and the still restless crowd of men.

"*As-salaam 'alaykum,*" Javon said as Alison and the others left. "Peace be with you."

"What was *that* all about?" Amy Thorpe asked Alison once the courtyard was well behind them. She eyed the burned hem. "What the devil did you do to your skirt?"

"I can explain later," Alison replied but knew she had no explanation to offer.

As they headed back to the hotel, Alison discretely pulled her lipstick from her pocket to examine it. The red lipstick was streaked in grime, as though scraped along a wall. She tossed it in a garbage can and quickened her step, eager to return to the safety and sanity of the hotel.

#

When Alison returned to her hotel room, she pulled off her long skirt with its burnt hem and tossed it in the trash. As she did, the paper scroll fell from one of its pockets, its end still red with the Hester's blood, dry now. She was shocked to see the scroll.

She was sure she'd thrown it out earlier. At least, she had meant to. She picked the scroll up. The inscription looked different from before. Maybe more words, or fewer, or just different ones. She could have sworn the lettering had been white. Now it seemed darker, more reddish. She quickly dressed and went to find Zahra. Downstairs, she found the night manager and asked where Zahra was. He didn't speak much English, but he led her to the stairs and pointed up. When she didn't understand, he uttered one heavily accented word: "rooftop."

Alison followed the stairs up several flights to a door that opened onto the roof of the hotel. Zahra was smoking a cigarette and staring pensively out over the town, watching as smoke from the bonfires and fireworks drifted under a moonlit sky past mosques and minarets. Alison took in the view in silence for a minute or so before handing Zahra the scroll. She pointed out the written words. Zahra shook her head as she read it, then looked up at Alison, confused.

"Is this the same scroll from earlier?" Zahra asked.

Alison nodded. It was definitely the same. It had the same bloodstain.

"I don't understand. It now says *Tonight the Wolf will Come and the Chosen will Perish.*"

Alison gasped and recalled the lipstick graffiti. *Wolf. Death.* Her own lipstick.

"I swear that's not what it said before. It was the prayer of *Chaharshanbe Suri*. I swear. The words are different now and . . . "

"What is it? There is more, isn't there?" Alison prodded.

"The words remind me of a parable I had all but forgotten, one told to me as a child. I haven't thought of it for years. Now I can remember every word as though I'm still sitting on my grandfather's bony knees. The parable was well known in my home province, though not much known elsewhere. You have your story of the wolf dressed in sheep's clothing. We have ours."

Zahra cleared her voice, then spoke from memory.

"A powerful wolf took too many sheep, devouring not only their flesh but their souls, so the Gods banished him to the underworld, never to return. But the wolf was a patient and clever trickster, and it feared no pain, so it burned itself in the fires of the deep until it was but smoke. As smoke, it seeped slowly back into our world and found a herd of sheep."

Zahra paused to eye the smoke that drifted across the sky as though it were a dark omen.

"Innocent and unknowing, each sheep breathed in a little of that wolf. Just a part of him. And that drove each, in turn, to kill themselves. As each died, the smoke of the wolf—and the soul that was consumed—were breathed into the remaining sheep, driving them mad too, until there was but one of the herd left. That last sheep was no longer a sheep. It *was* the wolf."

She handed the scroll back to Alison.

"My grandfather said the wolf went on to rule the whole of the world. For, you see, the wolf was no wolf. It was a demon in wolf's clothing. That was how it became incarnate."

Zahra paused as if remembering more of that childhood story.

"My grandmother once pulled me aside. She told me the wolf was really a she-wolf. Only men thought it was a demon. Women understood it was part of the Divine Feminine. It was no Angel, but no Devil either, for women are never that simple. According to her, the last of those sheep, the one who would become the wolf, and rule the world, must be female too. The souls she consumed would join her in that dominion."

"Is it from Zoroastrian folklore?" Alison asked.

"Not really. The *Avesta* does tell a story of Zoroaster and a she-wolf, but it's a different story. No mention of a wolf being burned and then returning to the world. Nothing like that. Who knows, though? Stories change from generation to generation as they are told and retold."

Zahra snuffed out her cigarette and eyed the scroll. "Give it to me," she said brusquely.

Alison did as told. Zahra drew a lighter from her pocket and lit the scroll on fire. She whispered what might have been a prayer and then, in silence, the two watched the scroll burn.

"Let us say nothing of this to the others," Zahra finally said before heading back to the stairwell. "And pray we have no more misfortunes."

#

At four-thirty in the morning, the Islamic call-to-prayer began, the *Adhan*, broadcast from a nearby minaret. Alison loved the musical sound of it, so exotic, but could they not wait at least until dawn? As she rose from bed to peer out at the town, with her legs illuminated by dim light from the crescent moon, she spotted patterns shifting on her skin. This time, her legs, both her legs. To see better, she flipped on a bedside light, but the bulb didn't work. She tried another lamp. No good. She found a flashlight and played the beam along her legs. The patterns soon faded. She then heard quick footsteps in the hallway outside her door. The power must have gone out. It was probably the night manager, maybe headed for the fuse box.

Alison then smelled the tang of burnt meat. She grabbed a robe and hurried into the hall.

Flashlight in hand, the night manager pounded on the door of the adjacent room. The Boothes, Alison recalled. No answer, so he worked to unlock the door. In the darkness, he fumbled with a set of keys until he found the right one. The door creaked loudly as he pushed it open. Alison followed him as he eased his way into the dark room, the smell worse here. He turned his flashlight on and pointed the beam around the room. The bed had been slept in but was now unoccupied. The manager turned his attention to the bathroom. He gasped at what he saw. Alison pushed ahead and saw it too. Two bodies. Alethia Boothe, probably awakened by the loud *Adhan*, had begun a bath. Her husband Marques must have dropped a hairdryer. He had tried to pull his wife from the water. Both had been electrocuted, burned badly.

Zahra arrived and was horrified by the charred bodies. Shaken, she led Alison into the hallway to talk. Zahra kept her voice low. "Did you see anything on your skin, like what we saw last night? Your room is next to their room. Your bed is close to their bath."

"It was on my legs this time," Alison whispered. "Can a chemical weapon cause delusions? Can it drive people to do crazy things? Can it drive them to kill themselves?"

"I don't know, but I know we must leave. We must get far from this place. Maybe far from one another." Zahra tried to push past her down the hallway.

Alison grabbed her sleeve. "What do you mean? Why far from each other?"

"What if it's true?" Zahra asked. "What if the wolf has come at last?"

Alison was too bewildered to reply. Zahra had been quite sensible earlier. Now, she seemed to believe an old parable, a myth, a wolf-demon who wanted to rule the whole of the world. No doubt, Alison and the others had seen and done bizarre things, dangerous things, *deadly* things, but surely those were from delusions caused by a chemical agent of some sort.

The night manager spotted them talking in the hallway and confronted Zahra. They argued. The manager then stomped off. Zahra told Alison the man was throwing them out. Not later that morning, not after breakfast. Now. The other two couples, the Delgados and the Thorpes, emerged from their rooms, no doubt awakened by the commotion.

"Collect your belongings," Zahra told them. "We leave. We return to Shiraz. I will drive."

When Terry Thorpe looked ready to declare, once again, that he could drive the motor coach, Zahra cut him off. "You have no license here. But I will appreciate whatever help you can give. And someone please fetch food for the trip back to Shiraz. It will take hours."

The Delgados offered to head downstairs to the kitchen to collect provisions for the journey. The Thorpes hurried back to their rooms to get their suitcases.

Alison needed to get dressed, so she hustled back to her room. Several minutes later, when she arrived downstairs in the courtyard, bags in hand, she smelled propane.

#

The power was still out, so the courtyard and the kitchen beyond were only dimly lit in the pre-dawn light. On her way to the courtyard, Alison had passed the night manager who was in a hallway alcove fussing with circuit breakers, swearing under his breath, trying to get the power back on. Now, as Alison set her bags down and peered through the dim light of the courtyard into the kitchen, she saw a tank of propane on the floor, leaking fumes.

The Delgados were gathering food and bottled water for the trip, seemingly oblivious to the tank at their feet. As Alison approached, the odor of propane grew worse, like rotten eggs. She called to the

Delgados and waved them away from the tank, but they just stared back at her with blank expressions. The tank must be another delusion, Alison figured, like the boy walking through the flames, beckoning her. Yet the odor seemed so real.

With a gasp, she realized she couldn't let the manager turn the power back on.

She spun and raced back toward the electrical alcove, or tried to, her legs oddly slow, as if moving through mud. Through the corner of her eye, she saw a shape darting through the darkness of the lobby. She had no time to find out who it was. When she finally reached the night manager, she waved frantically for him to stop what he was doing and follow her. He looked annoyed, but he saw the panic in her eyes and followed. When they reached the courtyard, his eyes went wide. The propane tank was no illusion. It was real, and it was leaking. Worse, now Aarón Delgado was trying to strike a match. He wasn't trying to light a stove, he was just staring back at them, his wife beside him, both seemingly oblivious to their insanity.

When the match lit, Alison and the manager dove for cover. The explosion sounded more like a roaring *whoosh* than a bomb. The blast of heat at Alison's back was fierce. When the surge of heat died down, she got shakily to her feet and tried to see into the now burning kitchen. The bright light of the fire hurt her eyes, and she had to look away. Yet she didn't need to see inside the kitchen to know the Delgados were gone, cinders now. She hoped they had felt no pain. She turned to the night manager to help him back up. He wasn't moving.

Alison rolled the man on his back and saw a nasty piece of metal—maybe part of the propane tank—pierced deep into his skull. He was quite dead. She also saw the swirling and churning pattern again on her hands and arms. It was faster now, more frantic. She saw no such swirling on the dead manager. Before she could puzzle over why, the Thorpes arrived from upstairs, running, frantic, dropping their luggage, stunned at the sight of the burning kitchen, the fires spreading. Zahra arrived too with a look of sheer terror. She waved for them all to run.

It was too late. Fire erupted all around.

The hotel must have been heated with gas, Alison realized. Pipes ran through the walls, beneath the floors. With the way the building had settled over the years, the pipes must have bent and buckled, cracks had appeared, then bigger ones. Flames from the kitchen had caught the gas. The hotel was now an inferno. The part of the courtyard in which they stood, terrified, was blocked by a wall of flame. Beyond those flames, she saw other hotel guests fleeing the building. Some saw Alison and the others who were trapped and tried to help but were driven back by the flames, driven outside.

Alison frantically looked for another way out and spotted a door to one side. She threw it open hoping for an exit. Her heart sank. It was a storage room. Boxes of dried food. Cleaning supplies. More propane tanks. She spun back to the others. "There must be some other way out!"

Through far windows, Alison spotted locals from the neighborhood who were trying to get into the hotel to save them, trying to fight through the thick smoke and flames with handheld extinguishers. She recognized some: the waiters from last night and the lobby receptionist, Javon. Maybe they lived close by, maybe they had just arrived for their morning shift. All fought valiantly to fight through the flames. It was hopeless, though, their extinguishers far too small. Fresh bursts of fire drove them back, drove them outside, back into the chaotic night.

Terry Thorpe now grabbed his wife Amy and pointed to a large rug hung along a nearby wall. If they could lay the rug down, it might clear a path. They tore the rug from the wall and dragged it across the floor. Alison and Zahra moved into help them, but Terry shoved them back. Then, rather than hauling the rug toward an exit to clear a path to safety, he and his wife veered deeper into the flames. Another act of sheer madness. Another act of self-immolation.

Alison and Zahra tried to wade into the fierce heat in hopes of pulling the Thorpes back. Before they could reach them, more gas pipes ruptured. Flames exploded around the couple, turning them into human torches. In that horrific fire, Alison could see churning within churning. The flames were frantic, eager, *hungry*. She and Zahra were forced to retreat to the center of the courtyard.

Alison gasped when she looked at Zahra, her face swirling with chaotic patterns. From the way the woman stared back at her, her own face must have looked the same. If there was a she-wolf here, Alison understood, it was nearly done consuming the sheep. It would become incarnate in the last of them who survived. The last woman standing.

Incarnate, it would be invulnerable. It was born of fire. It would not burn in it. It would walk through the flames and out into the world. Impossible, Alison scolded herself. Surely her frantic mind now read too much into that old parable.

Zahra approached Alison warily. They stood in the middle of the courtyard, as far as they could from the fierce heat of the surrounding fires, the flames closing in slowly.

"Alison, you understand now," Zahra spoke to her over the roar of the fire. "You understand the truth of it. I didn't truly believe until now either. But *it* has come. You were right, something was unleashed in the cave from beneath the ancient fire pit. Not a chemical. Not biological. It is seeking a way back into the world. I fear my grandfather was right, a demon."

What Zahra said was true, Alison figured, or they were both crazy. Either way, there was no way out of the hotel. The flames burned ever closer, ever hotter. And the itch that was not really an itch wriggled now along Alison's arms and legs. Not an itch, but an *urge*. An urge to hurl herself into the flames, to purify herself there. She fought the urge.

Outside, sirens wailed. Fire trucks would soon arrive, but too late to save the two of them. If Zahra was right, by the time firemen doused the flames, there'd be only one woman left standing. She would no longer be human. Alison hated that her life would end here, now. Never to see her son again. Never to see anything. Not The Coliseum. The Eiffel Tower. The Great Wall of China. A thousand other places she had meant to visit. With this journey to Iran, she had felt her life was just beginning. It was sure to end soon. She vowed to end it on her own terms.

"Zahra," Alison began, speaking slowly, assembling the plan in her mind. "We have no hope to survive. If what you say is true, we must die together. We must die at the exact same instant so it cannot possess the last of us. We can stop it. And if that old story is just myth and nonsense, well, we might as well die together anyway, and die painlessly."

Alison remembered the extra propane in the side storage room. She ran to fetch the tank. As she did, she had a grim thought. The demon was said to drive victims to kill themselves, and that was just what she was preparing to do. The itch seemed to be leading her to it, driving her to it. Maybe this was all delusion. The hotel. The fire. Maybe they were all still in that cave.

No, the flames were real. She could feel the heat. Caves do not burn. This was *real*.

Returning to Zahra, Alison opened the tank, allowing propane vapors to drift out.

"We don't have much time," she told Zahra. "When the fumes spread far enough, the propane will explode. A bomb. A small one, but big enough. We won't feel anything. Our minds will be gone before the pain reaches our brains. We will be gone before the fire consumes us."

Zahra nodded, tears streaming down her face. In the glow of the fire, she was radiant. Alison wished to kiss her now. That was an itch too, one she didn't fight, and Zahra didn't object, her lips soft. As Alison then drew away from her, something caught her eye beyond the flames.

Movement there, the same shape she had spotted earlier out of the corner of her eye.

The scruffy boy who had sold her the scroll was peering at them. Far enough away from the propane that he would not die from the blast, but the poor kid would surely be consumed by the fast growing fire. As the flames swirled, Alison got a better glimpse of his face. She recalled now why that boy had seemed so familiar. It was not just that he'd been on the street after Sami died, and downtown during the festival. He'd been at the cave too. He'd been *in* the cave. He was the feisty boy Zahra couldn't shoo away. He'd been the only one still in the cave besides the tour group during the quake, the only other person to breathe those unholy vapors.

That boy would be the last one standing. The poor kid was sweating now from the heat of the fire, shrinking away from it. Sweltering, he pulled away his cap and some of the ragged clothes he wore. In the bright light of the surging flames, Alison could see his face more clearly.

The boy was a *girl*. A girl who hid herself in the clothes of a boy, a feisty girl, a defiant one.

The last Alison heard was the whoosh of the propane as it ignited. The last Alison thought was that a feisty little she-wolf might soon rule the whole of the world. Good for her. Good for *them*.

THE FREQUENCY OF SOULS

*T*EN MILES.

The night races, the scattered woods a dark blur. I'm pushing the sedan hard, its engine straining up the steep grade leading out of town, racing now along the narrow road heading to the hillside enclaves where my home awaits amid cold thick pines. I brood again, obsess again, over what had been found in those videos, the ones I'd seen, that we'd all seen, everyone at the company at least. The horrific head-on crash videos.

Those *fatal* crash videos. There was always something missing.

Each time, each crash, each ghastly impact, each lethal impact, in that last moment as metal struck metal, as glass shattered, bones snapped, as lives ended, the moment was missing.

I come around a turn and a driver flashes his high beams at me, slow at first, then ever more frantic until I finally realize I've crossed the center line. I swerve back to my lane, slow down, a little, just a little. I check the time and speed up again. It's nearing midnight. Not clock midnight. True midnight, the exact moment between sunset and sunrise. Timing will be crucial. I hope that driver doesn't think I'm a drunk and alert highway patrol.

Crazy? Sure. *Drunk?* Not a drop for weeks, not since I figured it out. No, it's not just my imagination. Although, when I'd made the mistake of confiding in that prick, that asshole, that *shrink* in the back seat, he told me it must be a delusion. It is real. He'll understand soon. I will make him understand.

Nine miles.

I glance at him through the rearview. His eyes: desperate, panicked, locked on mine.

My eyes: calm, collected, in control now.

He's tied up, bound and gagged.

He's panting, hyperventilating, pretending he's suffocating, pretending the sturdy gag has cut off his air, that he's dying. He won't suffocate. That will not be his fate tonight, nor mine.

No doubt, he thinks I've gone insane. After all, I have coils wrapped tight around my head, so tight they cut into my flesh. Blood seeps from my wounds, now and then spilling into my eyes, dripping into my mouth, the taste of the blood metallic.

My personal crown of thorns, I suppose.

That's not what truly horrifies him, though. It's how I've worked the ends of the coils through the crude holes in my skull and deep into my brain. For the brain holds the mind, right?

And the mind holds the soul.

Eight miles.

I'm not the one who saw it first. The glitch. The test engineers found it. None could figure out why it was there. So they asked others of us who worked at the company for help. I was the only one to understand. Of course, I told none of them. They would have mocked me.

I eye the shrink again in the back seat, bound there, gagged, silenced. I wonder if he can read my thoughts, if the quicksilver

101

antenna looped around my head can do that too.

No matter, let him read my mind. Let him understand.

Here's how it began. Our newest front-mounted vids—installed within whole fleets of new vehicles—worked perfectly, recording high-res video at extreme frame rates, capturing whatever the vid-cam saw, whatever the driver saw, or perhaps didn't see until too late. The images were streamed to the net, automatically routed to our company's servers, stored there, the last ten seconds at least, enough time to see what happened and who was at fault.

The key part of the system was the ultra-high speed live stream. Most front-mounted vids were destroyed on impact. The wire-less transceiver in this new cam was hardened to withstand even the highest of high-speed collisions. Corporate had admitted the extreme frame rates were not really needed, that the use of super hi-res video was complete engineering overkill, but they wanted it all to be state-of-the-art. The best and fastest technology.

Complete overkill. I choke back a laugh.

Seven miles.

That's what all high-speed head-on collisions are. Complete overkill. You don't need nearly that much force, that much mo-mentum, that much *lethality*, to kill all occupants, despite seat-belts, despite airbags, for the human body was never meant to slam to a stop that fast, or worse, rebound in the opposite direction that quick, so every bone that could be broken would be broken, so every organ that could be ruptured would be ruptured.

That asswipe, that shrink, that *prick* in the back seat thinks I'm just obsessing over Helen and the kids. Well of course I'm *obsessing* over them. What else should I do? If I stopped obsessing, it would mean they were truly and forever gone.

How does the old adage go? *A person never truly dies so long as there's someone left to remember them.* Close, but not quite right.

It's not memory that counts, it's *obsession*.

Anything less is nowhere near enough.

Anything less is a betrayal of those who are gone. Anything less is a crime, anything less is a murder of their memory. Anything less is a desecration of the life they lived. So I sure as hell am obsessed, and will remain obsessed, right up to that last unseen moment. And beyond. Let the stupid shrink choke on that.

Six miles.

A truck now rumbles by in the opposite direction, its headlights set too high, and suddenly I can't see a damned thing. The sedan's tires catch in the gravel alongside the road. We almost plow into a ditch, the shrink wailing now through his gag, crying, pissing himself. I muscle the car back on the road and gain speed again, the engine whining now too.

I try to focus.

So this is the weird problem the engineers found, and here's what only I figured out. At the moment of impact, the moment the drunk who drifted across the road struck the housewife looking down at her phone, or the moment the drowsy driver who fell asleep, cruise control still on, rammed full speed into a massive concrete abutment, *that* moment, the system glitched.

That's the word the engineers used. *Glitched*. They couldn't figure it out. There was no sane reason why the system should skip that moment. I wonder now if it was more than just morbid curiosity that drove the engineers to even want to look into that final moment. Maybe they knew. Maybe they knew weird shit would happen, something that could not be explained, something—holy or unholy—something beyond the physics of this sad realm. Yet they didn't know the reason why that last moment of a moment, that last instant of an instant, was always missing from the video sent back from those crashes.

It's really quite simple.

There's a frequency to the human soul, one that radiates when soul is freed from flesh. When the spirit flees a dying body in a fatal crash, the frequency interferes with the video transmission, it resonates with the wavelengths of the transceiver, and *that* causes the so-called glitch. You never find that in anything but a fatal crash. Slam a vehicle with test dummies against a wall at a hundred miles per hour, no glitch. It only happens with death.

It is *proof*.

It's proof souls are real. It's proof they leave the body at death. Since souls exist, they must go somewhere. People never truly die. Sure, that that pisshead punk who squirms now in the backseat, bound there, gagged there, says I'm just rationalizing what I want to believe. He says if there are souls, they can't be something so crude as to have a frequency.

Radios have frequencies. Mobile phones have frequencies.

Souls, if they exist, must be ethereal.

Well, they are ethereal, just not the way he means.

Aethereal. Not ethereal. Aethereal with an A. It's not a radio frequency. Not anything science understands. At least, not modern science. Nineteenth century scientists understood, though. The Greeks understood. *Aether*. It's real. Those aetheric frequencies can bleed into radio frequencies, sort of like one broadcast station bleeding into another. Using the right antenna, formed of the right material, infused with quicksilver, one can sense it, detect it, control it.

As that other old saying goes: "Sometimes, the only way is *through*."

Five miles.

I take a curve too fast and the shrink is slammed back and forth as I try to get the car under control. Just now another driver comes round a turn in the opposite direction and, sure, I'm on the wrong side of the road again. I get us back just in time.

We barely even scrape metal with that other car, a shower of sparks in the dark night.

The shrink kicks and fights in the backseat, harder even than before. I glance back and he's red-faced now, veins bulging, eyes wild. Maybe the gag has shifted. Maybe he is suffocating. I reach back and yank the sash off. He takes deep gasping gulps of air.

Once he catches his breath, he hisses at me. "You don't have to do this! Let's go back to my office. Or anywhere you want! Let's talk about this. Or not talk. *Anything* you want. But you don't have to do this!" He's in tears now. The tears of a man who figures he soon will die.

"What exactly do you think I plan to do?" I ask, keeping my voice level.

"You're going to run us into something. Into someone. You'll *kill* us. It will not bring your family back!"

"They are *somewhere*. Beyond. I know that. There's proof now. I'll find them. Wherever they are, good or bad, Heaven or Hell, I *will* find them and bring them back, their souls at least."

"Okay. Sure. *Fine.* Best of luck. You don't need *me* for that, right? I've done all I can do for you. I've reasoned with you. I've been reasoning with you for two years now!"

"You think this was ever about your kind of logic?" I bark back at him. "*Your* reasoning won't take you there when *there* is not a place in this world. When there is *beyond*."

"You have gone insane. You understand that?" He sputtered. "We're never supposed to actually say that to our patients, no matter how bloody obvious it is, and in your case it's pretty damn obvious. You have gone insane. End yourself if you want but take no innocents with you."

By *innocents*, no doubt, he means himself first, and then maybe the occupants of some other car. Yet I have no intention of plowing headlong into an oncoming vehicle, snuffing out the lives of others, as the lives of my family had been taken. I have a different plan. A better plan.

Four miles.

Yesterday, I bought a wall-sized mirror, had it delivered to the house this afternoon, had the men leave it outside, leaning up against a towering pine in the front yard. I told my neighbors the delivery guys had left it outside, propped there against that sturdy trunk, that immovable trunk, because they couldn't get it through the front door of the house, and they'd be back tomorrow with more men. By tomorrow, there'll be nothing left of it for them to come back to.

You see, I coated the mirror with quicksilver too, rubbed the mercury in deep. The mirror will resonate with the coils around my head, the coils wound into my brain. I know this because the dreams told me, night after night, they laid it all out for me.

So it won't be some innocent family I'll see during my head-on collision. I'll see *myself*. The house is at the end of a cul-de-sac. Helen always worried that a drunk, lost and confused, would come roaring down the road late one night and plow straight into our bedroom. That never happened. The drunk found her out on a highway, plowed into her there. Killed her and the kids in an instant. There was no car-cam to record the last moment of horror. So I was spared *seeing* that. At least not for real, only in nightmares, only in fever dreams.

"So this is you still obsessing over that *glitch*?" the shrink demanded.

"It's no glitch. It is a moment that, once you're *in* it, it lasts for ages. Hundreds of years, maybe thousands, maybe eons. When your soul leaves its body, in that precious moment, that's when time slows to a crawl. For you. For your spirit. Time slows and slows and—"

"Really? That's your idea of Heaven? Trapped in that horrifying moment as you die?"

"No! Time slows to a crawl. In that moment, your soul can go anywhere. Another place. Another world. Another *something*. That's where they are now. I *will* find them."

"You know all of this *how*?" he scoffs.

I refuse his question. He would not believe me anyway.

Three miles.

After I first came to understand the so-called glitch, that it was the frequency of the soul that caused it, the dreams came. Some might call them nightmares. But nightmares, no matter how horrifying, no matter how grisly, never gave one hope. These were messages of hope.

The dreams told me facts about my family that even I didn't know. The dreams told me the password to Blake's schoolwork computer. He was twelve when he died. The computer is still in his bedroom, gathering dust on his desk—I never threw anything out—and the password *worked*. How could ordinary dreams tell me that? It was not anything on the computer that mattered. No, it was the password that mattered. It was given to me as proof.

Proof that it was my family calling in those dreams from beyond. Proof it was them.

The dreams gave me instructions. They told me how to convert a tungsten wire into a quicksilver antenna. Simple really. Plunge the wire into a tub of hot liquid mercury, scalding hot. Hold it there, let the wire absorb the quicksilver, let it become infused with it.

I gaze now at my hands on the steering wheel, at the nasty burns there. The pain was worth it. It *will* be worth it.

The dreams told me how to wrap the coils around my head,

forming just the right pattern, a crisscrossing pattern, around certain meridians, and then work the ends into my brain, into precise locations in the frontal lobes. Cutting the openings in my skull? That part I had to figure out myself. The high speed drill from my garage worked just fine. The pain was fierce, but the drill didn't plunge *too* deep. Not much gray matter came out, not much *ooze*.

The dreams also told me just when to ram into that quicksilvered mirror. *True* midnight.

This night. For tonight is the midpoint between solstice and equinox. My dreams called it a *cross-quarter* night. It all means something. It all must be timed just right.

I check the time again and speed up once more.

Two Miles.
"You need help," the shrink pleads. "It's not too late. No one has to die."

Behind, on a straight stretch of the road, I spot the flicker of blue lights. Highway patrol. Someone must have called me in. The officer is too far back, though. He won't catch me. More blood trickles now into my eyes, blurring my vision, turning the occasional oncoming headlights into flickering blood-red images, ghosts of sorts. I will be one soon enough.

"A ghost?" the shrink asks, begging disbelief.

I must have said that last bit out loud. Maybe I said all of it aloud. Or maybe the coil is projecting my thoughts into his thoughts. It's a psychic antenna after all.

"Projecting *what*, exactly?" he asks, patronizing me, yet no doubt intrigued now too.

"Aetheric signals," I reply, the spoken words rough in my throat.

"Signals in aether," he nods. Not a question, a statement meant to calm me.

"Listen! If souls fleeing dead bodies emit aethereal frequencies, then surely the soul ensheathed in the body can emit those frequencies too. You just need direct contact." I tap the coils wrapped around my head that entwine my brain, my mind, my immortal soul.

"And the point?" he asks, and I see him struggle against the sashes that bind him.

One mile.

"The *point* . . . "

I keep an eye on the rearview. The patrol car is gaining. I fight for calm against the rage that grows in me over the shrink and his patronizing questions, but I need him, the world needs him, so I will indulge him.

"The *point* is this. The frequency of the dying soul can be *modulated*," I stretch the word out, patronizing him now. "It can be set to resonate with that little glitch, with the gateway between here and *there*. It can be used to hold that doorway to the other side open so it's not just one way. It won't be open for long. Only a moment of a moment, but long enough."

"To bring your family back."

Now, he's getting it.

One half mile.

"They're dead and have been for two years," the shrink scoffs. "You'll be dead too if you do what I fear you're planning to do. Don't be stupid."

"My flesh will be gone, sure. Incinerated. I made sure the car has a full tank. Premium unleaded. But if you're understanding anything I'm telling you, flesh is not needed."

"So you'll return as what? Ghosts? *Spirits*?"

"I doubt there's any word in any Earthly language that truly captures what we'll be, since no soul has ever returned. The doorway has forever been just one way. No one ever had the technology to detect that glitch, or the means to exploit it, the necessary understanding of mirror resonance. I don't know what we'll be when we come back, but we *will* return, together."

"And if it doesn't work, if you're just bat-shit *insane*?"

"Either way, they won't be alone anymore. I'll be with them."

One quarter mile.

"Listen carefully," I tell the shrink. "I will let you out, but only if you promise me something. Something *important*. I set the transceiver in this vehicle so its electronics won't be interfered with when my soul departs my body. There will be no glitch. The video from that final moment will be transmitted. The aetheric frequencies will bleed through into optical ones, visible ones, the camera will pick them up. You'll be able to look into that final moment. You'll see proof. You'll see me—my spirit—free of its body, smiling. Grinning ear to ear. And so the promise you make now is a simple one. You'll give that proof to the world. That proof of a world beyond will bring a change to humanity greater than any ever before. Do you *promise*?"

The shrink nods. I look close into his eyes. I can see he's telling the truth. I slam the brakes. The sedan screams to a stop. We're now only a few blocks from my house.

"The video will be uploaded into a file labeled *Hope* and automatically sent to your email account," I tell the shrink. "Just those four simple letters. Just that one word. *Hope*."

The highway patrol is approaching fast, so I work fast. I free the shrink by yanking hard on the release tie of the sashes that had kept him bound. He clambers out the door. I expect him to turn and run like mad. But once outside, he leans in the side window to ask me something, no doubt another patronizing question. I floor it. Whatever question he still has, when he gazes into that final moment with his own eyes, recorded in vivid living color, he'll get his answer.

As I roar away, the police car is now just behind me, siren shrieking, lights flashing.

I ignore it and *focus*.

One Hundred Yards.

At high speed I steer hard around the corner leading to my cul-de-sac, tires screeching. The towering pine is dead ahead. I aim my headlights at their reflection in the mirror, waiting there against that immovable trunk. The speedometer shows ninety when I hit the curb and go airborne. Moments later, the car plows into the wide mirror and the sturdy trunk that holds it.

But, of course, I am already gone.

I'm *in* that moment. Time slows to a crawl.

For me, the sedan is frozen in air, the front bumper not far from the mirror. The camera tucked inside the front grill is furiously sending out its last high-speed signals, the proof of it.

I step out of the suspended car and glance back to confirm I've also stepped out of my body. It still sits in the front seat, safety belt off, airbag disconnected.

That body, that flesh, that *burden*, is not mine anymore.

I am relieved to know my soul was freed of its body before the actual impact. I am spared that final bone-crushing trauma, perhaps an act of grace by a benevolence that knows I have suffered enough. In real-time, my body will go through the window on impact and into the mirror, then into the sturdy pine trunk, leaving a mangled lump of splintered flesh. But I am free.

I pause to smirk back at the cop car that was just screeching to a stop on the street as I had gone airborne. For me, the patrol car is frozen in time too. I see that the officer is a young woman. Good for her. She will bear witness to this miracle. Once word gets out, once the proof gets out, it'll change her life. I make my way now around my car to peer at the space between its bumper and the wide mirror, two pairs of head lights glaring into one another, dazzlingly bright.

I peer into the vidcam's lens, nestled there just above the bumper. I'm grinning. I can't help it. Ear to goddamned ear.

I turn to look at the reflection of my car in the mirror, the quicksilvered mirror. I expect to see a reflection of me—my body, at least—in the driver's seat.

Something is wrong. *Very wrong.* There are four people in the car in the mirror reflection. That is impossible.

I don't need to look close to know who they are.

Helen is in the driver seat. Blake in the front right seat. Andrew and Amy in the backseat. I cannot look away. Why am I being shown *this*? Who or what is forcing me to see this? The look of horror on their faces, the look they had the night the drunk plowed into them head-on, it's the most horrifying image I've ever seen in my wretched life, far worse than any nightmare.

No, wrong. The *things* that surge now behind them, leering, grinning, those are far worse.

#

The psychiatrist watches the fireball rise above the woods, deep red, roiling skyward. He hopes it is just the car's fuel tank that is burning, and only that. He hopes the highway patrol officer stopped well back, well clear of the flames.

The fire grows, boiling ever higher into the night sky, and the psychiatrist now hopes it's just the woods that are burning, or maybe the whole neighborhood, but nothing more. He hopes what he sees is *not* the answer to his last question.

Yet the fireball rises still higher into the night sky. Now, lightning arcs from it and thunder cracks and rolls, and the sky itself is burning, writhing, seething, tearing itself open.

As fierce shapes now scream out of that nightmare fireball, the psychiatrist knows his final question has indeed been answered: *What if it wasn't the souls of the man's dead family who told him how to hold the gateway open but something else?*

The demons—and *multitudes* of them pour now from the torn and burning sky—rip flesh from bones in an instant, and rip soul from flesh in an instant of an instant. They swarm across and around and throughout the world.

The whole of the world, consumed now and forever, in a moment of a moment.

THE LAST CANVAS

G ROWING FRUSTRATED NOW, THE artist struggled to understand why the canvas kept absorbing the black paint, swallowing all of it, leaving no base layer upon which he could add colored paints later.

True, he had not sealed the canvas. He hated sealed canvases. He craved the texture of unprimed linen, its rough and flaxen weave, its humble charm. An unsealed canvas had character, depth, honesty. The oils in the paint would someday cause the fibers to decay and unravel. He liked that too for his works were never meant for dusty museums. Nothing should last forever. So he would let the bare fibers absorb his broad, dripping brushstrokes. Only when the thirsty threads could swallow no more would he paint atop that rough base, adding layer upon layer of color.

Texture. Character. Depth. His art had all of that.

Yet as he worked in the dwindling afternoon light in his mountain studio to slather more and more of the thick oil paint upon the canvas, the fibers just kept absorbing all of it, seemingly without end. Today, he had chosen ivory black—what some called *bone black*—for he was in a foul mood. His latest muse had left him. Usually, he was relieved to see them go.

114

Although the location of his studio was meant to be secret, now and then women would find him. They would make their way up the long dirt trail through the dense chaparral from the coast below. Some of the women, willowy and weak, would be in rough shape by the time they found his front door. It was a test, he supposed. Any fetching waif who could make the journey was worthy. Of course, there were many strong and fit women who could easily climb the trail, far more easily than he could. He had no interest in them. They could not inspire him. They would be sent away.

But the waifs, the pale ones, the humble ones, the alluring ones, they could stay.

Each wanted to learn from him, master what he had mastered, emulate his techniques. That would never happen. They could paint on their own if they wanted—acrylics, pastels, watercolors—but he forbade them oils. Some instead chose to write. Or snap pictures. Practice their music. Some were talented. Others not. He didn't judge. Let each have her own art.

He was arrogant, he knew. But it was a well-earned arrogance, honed over decades of adulation from the worldwide art community, from dozens of solo shows, hundreds of awards.

He would paint those waifs and in those works they would become famous; they would become immortal. It was his gift to them. If they chose to, they posed in the nude. It mattered not to him. It was the soul he captured in his art, in those layers and textures and tones. Then he'd make love to them. Paint some more. Make love again. He would cherish them—truly, madly—with a passion only a true artist could ever summon. For a while anyway.

Love, like wet canvas, dries in time. It hardens. It cracks. There would come a time, a decisive moment, when they'd realize they were no longer his muse. Once they understood they could no longer inspire him, that he had drained them, emptied them, that he was *done* with them, they'd feel profound emptiness and leave with swollen tears. Some would write to him later. Occasionally, he would read their missives. It was always the same. They told him how they had reached a point where the emptiness of their dying relationship would force them out the door. It would chase them down the dusty trail, back to the narrow road leading to the village below, then back to their cities and towns, back to their jobs, their careers. Often back to their dull husbands, their dull lives. But this one, this latest one, who had brought her old-fashioned film camera with its wide-eyed lens, he had wanted her to stay longer. There was still some muse left in her. It frustrated him that she had wanted to leave before he was done with her.

Now, he looked again at his thirsty canvas, at the flaxen weave that absorbed all the paint he offered. He slathered more on, more than ever before. Still, the weave was not yet sated. He worried he had not tightened the canvas correctly. Proper tension was crucial. To get the ideal texture to the canvas, the threads must be stretched quite taut. So maybe that was the problem. Maybe that was why it kept absorbing all the paint. Those thirsty little threads.

He scampered around the canvas on his hands and knees and cranked each of its corners tight using tensioners, tighter than he'd ever drawn any canvas before. He feared it might tear. The threads would rip. Yet they did not.He slathered more of the black paint onto the weave. Still, the thirsty threads drank all he gave them. He threw the brush aside and searched about until he found a can of leftover house paint in his storage room. He tore it open. The paint was thick and black with a hint of carnelian crimson. He poured it into the gaping mouth of the canvas. His wrists hurt as he held the heavy can. He feared he might have cut his forearms on the jagged edges of the canister. It was hard to tell for he had spilt so much paint on himself too.

Still, the canvas absorbed it all. Drank it all. The glutton. The insatiable bitch.

Of course, he understood this was not a canvas. He had known that for a while now.

This was her. Her arms and legs were pulled taut by the ropes he had bound her with. He had knocked her out when she threatened to leave. He had dragged her to his four-poster bed. He had tied her wrists and ankles to its four corners. He had meant—he had *honestly* meant—to just paint her face. To turn her pale and perfect and beatific face into a living canvas. A dab here. A dab there. Yet she was a glutton. Insatiable and demanding.

With growing fury, he now stuffed the wet paintbrush in her open mouth. He poured the last of the can of house paint into that mouth too. Still, she drank it all. She absorbed it all. She had depth, bottomless depth. So he found more house paint and poured it down her gullet too: bone black paint with still more of the carnelian crimson, a dusky hue some called blood red.

He tightened the canvas of her body even more.

Ear-splitting cracks tore through the room.

Were those the heartbreaking sounds of her bones finally snapping? Or maybe it was the bedposts splintering. Not his mind. He understood *that* had snapped already.

No.

He realized the splintering noises were coming from somewhere *behind* him. He became dimly aware there were men in the house: a sheriff and deputies with sledgehammers and axes. Medics too. They had broken open the front door. They had found him. And her. He wondered how they could have known. Who had called them? The nearest neighbor was miles away.

As the medics hurried to him, he was stunned to see that she somehow stood now at the end of the bed. She snapped photo after photo of him with her camera as he gaped up at her, confused, his raw soul exposed. He turned from her unflinching lens and stared down at the bed.

There was no body there. Just a mattress. All else had been mad delusion. He had pulled the sheets so tight they had torn and ripped apart. The mattress itself was soaked with gallons of black paint, soaked too with his blood, deep crimson, spilt from his crudely slashed wrists. He felt the deep emptiness of all those other muses now, an emptiness he knew would never go away.

She took one final photo of him, slung her camera over her shoulder and turned to leave. He called to her, begged to her, prayed to her. She ignored his pleas as she left.

He understood now she had drained him. Emptied him. Taken all she needed.

She was done with him.

THE SOCIETY OF THE NEVER COMING BACK

Luck can be so unforgiving.

Another of our venerable social club ended himself today in New York. No one cared. No surprise there. He would not be missed. None of us would ever be missed. It was not because we are bad people. That was never the problem.

Quite simply: each of us should have died years ago but didn't. When I first came to appreciate that melancholy fact, I worried Heaven or Hell would discover something amiss. Death or Fate or The Reaper, or whatever one chose to call him, would return to correct the error to balance the books. It wasn't like that. Not for me. Not for any of us. Definitely not for Abie—the one true and tempestuous love of my unlived life—wherever she is now.

For me, it all began on January 16, 1920. It was a Friday. My lucky day, I told myself.

Father had encouraged me to send my matriculation letter to

Columbia by post and to do so well in advance of the winter deadline. My fiancé Frances encouraged me too. Yet I had no desire to begin my collegiate career by post. I would hand-deliver the letter. I would meet the Provost, look him in the eye, shake his hand firmly. That is how one got ahead in the world.

I wore a clean-pressed suit and waistcoat that day, a freshly starched shirt, a neatly tied ascot. I would make it clear, discreetly of course, that although our family was not as wealthy as other legacies of the University, we were not without means. I would make an impression. I was an outgoing young man back then. That is hard for me to fathom now, after these many years, after all that happened, or *not* happened, or happened without happening.

There are no words to describe it adequately. Even language does not acknowledge us.

That day, I made my way with brisk enthusiasm along Broadway near 120th, a warmish day for winter, the smells of the city pungent and invigorating. How different it was from our estate in Connecticut where the dull odor of farmland wafted past our home, not the vitalizing aroma of city life. The express train I took into the city that morning had been delayed, so I was running late. The acceptance letter from the Provost made it clear all *Letters of Intent to Matriculate* must be received in his office by noon that day. January 16. My lucky day.

Approaching the campus, I quickened my pace. I darted across the busy street, my heels slipping on black ice made slick by the warming sun. There was a streetcar coming. Of course, I didn't see it until too late. Well, too late for one not as spry as myself.

Not as young. Not as agile. Not as lucky.

I darted out of its way, missing it by inches, and it rattled by noisily amid a swirl of wind, the driver cursing at me, I cursing back. Realizing I'd dropped the letter, I searched the grime and muck of the street. Not there. Perhaps I'd put it back in my coat. I double-checked each pocket.

No, the letter must have slipped from my hand as I dodged the streetcar, then stuck to the front chassis of that machine, dewy in the warming sun. I sprinted after the trolley, my arms waving, the driver ignoring me. No doubt, he thought I'd raise a complaint against his driving. He continued to his next stop and I continued after him, laughing at the absurdity of the scene. The trolley finally stopped and I rushed to the front of the streetcar. My letter was indeed plastered there. Stuck where, had I not been quite so nimble, I'd have been plastered too, momentarily, before being drawn beneath all that tonnage, under the grinding metal wheels, mangled. But I had been lucky.

I retrieved the letter and checked my timepiece. I was now truly late. I ran. Futilely. The bells of noon chimed before I reached the Provost's office. After some urgent words with the man's secretary, I was led into the main office. The Provost barely looked at me. That was understandable. I was now a mess, sweaty and disheveled. I barely looked at him either. Yet I was never one, not then anyway, to shy from eye contact. I puzzled over this as he explained that no exceptions could be made. The deadline had passed.

Rules were rules. How could the world function otherwise? It did not cease spinning for one tardy man. I would not be allowed to matriculate. However, given my father's modest, but appreciated, donations to the University, the Provost would not object if I chose to sit in on classes from time to time. Take notes. Learn what I found valuable. So on, so forth. I would not be admitted. I would not stand for tests. No credits would be accrued. No degree given.

And that was *fine*. That was the oddest thing. For me, the arrangement was acceptable, perhaps ideal. I reasoned there was some other Applicant, maybe from a lower standing in society, yet still worthy, who would take my place. I didn't *need* a degree. I would step aside graciously. I shook the Provost's hand, and again, no eye contact. The man's secretary barely looked at me as I left the office, nor I at him. I closed the door behind me and headed back into the world, a world that no longer had a place for me, a world that had already set me aside.

2.

Looking back, I suppose I should have discovered my affliction sooner. But when one is in the moment, when one is just trying to live life, it's hard to tell that life is not cooperating. I understand now that I should have been hit by the trolley. My head striking its front chassis might have killed me, or perhaps I would have survived until drawn beneath the churning metal wheels, crushed there, or maybe I could have lasted still longer, to expire later in the hospital. I should have died. I didn't. By the time I fully understood that, years had passed.

To be fair, my condition was subtle. I was new to New York. I was new to the University. I was outside my usual cluster of friends and family. I assumed that people, New Yorkers at least, were just standoff-ish. Maybe my clothes, my provincial accent, my bearing, or something else about me put them off. No one was ever impolite, *per se*. Or rude. I was simply left out. I tried to make friends but they could never seem to remember my name. Nor I theirs. I would invite myself along with others on evenings out after class when they descended *en masse* to the local speakeasies, but I found myself left out. If there was a group grabbing chairs at a table, no chair would be left for me, so I found myself standing at the bar, or vice versa.

At times, I would assert myself. I would insist on conversation. The response would be polite but with an odd disconnect. The conversation would soon wane. They would look elsewhere. I'd look elsewhere too. As if by tacit agreement, we would head in different directions; I to my solitude, they back to their life. In class, I would occasionally raise my hand to speak but was never called upon. Some days, feeling bold, I would make myself heard, answering some obscure question the others could not. I'd be politely rebuffed by the professor. It would be made clear I was out of place. I was not properly enrolled.

I wanted to be angry. But I was not. It just seemed *right*.

And then there was Frances. The summer before, she had been intent on locking down our engagement. My prospects were good. I had a monthly stipend from my father. One day I would take over the family business. Frances and I had been inseparable before I moved to New York. Now, the tone of her letters shifted. From active to passive. From us to her. From talk of the future and our plans, to talk of the present, then only the past.

Finally, a terse letter. She'd gotten engaged to another of her suitors.

I should have burned with youthful indignation and jealousy but those emotions were for those who were truly alive. I was not. Sure, I breathed. I bled. I had even lain in hospital for a couple of days from a reckless injury, a foolish attempt to see if I was immune to death or harm. After being dragged a half block beneath a 1920 Talbot Motor Car, and receiving deep and painful contusions, I realized I was not. The medical staff was polite but distant. They often had to look closely at my chart to remember who I was. They would jot notes, drift away. That was how it had become with Frances. Her letters became notes. She drifted away.

There were plenty of other suitable young women, of course, but I was forever in their blind spots. I would chat with them occasionally at campus mixers or the parties I invited myself to. They, too, were invariably polite, but when they tried to look at me, it was as though it took too much effort. So they looked away. I would too. Conversation would sputter. Their faces would then alight with bright smiles as they saw a friend they knew. Off they'd go.

Always, I felt a measure of relief. It was difficult speaking from shadow.

Later, amid my many and varied studies, I would learn how animals in the wild could smell the sick, the dying, and instinctively avoid them, or leave them behind in their migrations. I wasn't sick, nor dying, but that same instinct was invoked. People sensed something not quite right about me, that I was not fully alive. There was an odd but subtle repulsion.

When my class at Columbia graduated, I didn't attend the ceremony. Rather, I bought passage on a steamer to Europe. Father's business had done well. My stipend had increased. He was not bothered that I never came home, nor did my mother show concern, nor my younger brothers. And the notion I would someday run the family estate as originally planned? It became clear that Ted, two years my junior, would take over. That was fine too.

I would see the world.

The years bled one into the other. I drifted from one quaint European hamlet to another, from one bustling foreign capital to the next, from Belfast to Istanbul, Gibraltar to St. Petersburg, and all places in and between and then beyond. Africa. Asia. India. Australia. South America. I had the monthly stipend wired to even the most exotic of locales. But, always, I was a tourist. An observer. I never sought to engage with the locals, never thought I even could.

After several years, weary of traveling, I returned to New York. That's when I spotted the classified announcement in The Times. I'm not sure why my eyes found that particular ad.

The Society of Those Not Gone Before Their Time:
Have you __not__ suffered a fatal accident or mortal ill-

ness? Whether you did not die recently or long ago,
we offer comradeship, if not commiseration and con-
solation. Every Thursday evening. Brenan's Private
Club off 59th. Downstairs. Enter through back. Knock
loudly. Knock again. Then let yourself in.

3.

The entrance was in an alley at the bottom of a set of stairs, the club ensconced behind a well-polished mahogany door. I knocked, then knocked more loudly, and finally tested the brass doorknob and let myself in. The elegant room was large and well-appointed. I figured it was a speakeasy most nights but tonight the club was reserved. There was a chalkboard just inside the door with the handwritten words: *The Society of Those Not Gone Before Their Time.*

All around, plush leather chairs were occupied by men and a fair number of ladies, reading the evening papers, playing solitaire, or merely sitting with eyes closed, hands clasped, not praying, perhaps just thinking, perhaps dozing. In short, it looked like any gentleman's club, with the exception that not all here were gentlemen, either by gender or station in life.

No one rose to greet me. One or two of the club members gave me a curt nod as if acknowledging an acquaintance that one did not wish to ignore but not talk with either. Just as well, I didn't much want to converse with them, though I did have questions I needed answered. There was a bar to one side but no barman. I hoped the man would soon return so I could order a pint and ask him what this was all about. I waited, clutching the paper with the advertisement.

One of the club's members seated nearby finally noticed me loitering by the bar with my paper. He was stout, well-dressed, well-fed, with muttonchops.

"You must be new. Welcome," he said, not looking up from his paper. "Apologies for not greeting you more enthusiastically. If you truly belong here, you understand why."

I did indeed understand. They were all like me.

"There's no bartender," he added. "We tried that. As you can imagine, we could never get the man's attention, so we made an arrangement with management. Take what you want and settle up later." He glanced at my dapper suit and waistcoat and gave a nod of approval. "I assume you're good for it."

I nodded and pulled myself a pint of ale. Another gentleman glanced at me now too. He was elderly and pale, dressed like a pallbearer. He nodded at the chalkboard by the door.

"What do you think of the latest name for our club?" he asked. "We change it whenever we get a new member," he added, not bothering to hear my answer. "If you belong here, you are *obliged* to provide a new name. It's a tradition."

"Did you found this club?" I asked.

The man looked surprised. "Gracious no. Nobody remembers who founded it, or when. As far as any of us can tell, there have been clubs like this, *societies* like this, all around the world, dating back hundreds of years. Thousands of years, probably. The condition we face is not new." He made an effort to look more closely at me now. He gave me the same look that others did, as though he were trying to see a face that lay in shadow. He seemed to approve. "Yes, of course, you're one of us. You must be. Few others even notice our newspaper ad."

I figured he was right. The living, the *truly* living, would not notice an ad intended for us, their eyes would merely skim over it like a stream slipping past a smooth stone.

"I take it you don't get many here who don't belong?" I asked.

"Oh, occasionally, rarely. Sometimes, it's a person who works for one of the papers where we place the classified ads. Typesetters, that sort of lot. So they have to read the ad. Some work up enough curiosity to come down here. They don't stay long. They are unsettled by us."

I thought again of those animals in the wild that could sense death in others, illness, wrongness. No doubt, the living, the *truly* living, would find this club uncomfortable, like attending a convention of morticians. Looking around, I suspected some here were in that very profession. I was fortunate since I never had to work. I had a stipend from my father's estate, which had grown nicely over the years, and was now dispensed monthly by a banker from a trust fund my father set up. Others *had* to work, though. So they found themselves—sooner or later—in jobs that did not require much interaction with others. They worked on assembly lines. Sorted the post. Counted numbers in the back room of an insurance agency.

Some, no doubt, just drifted. They lived on the streets. Rode the rails. I figured that was why most people couldn't make eye contact with drifters. You pass them on the street, even if you toss a coin, you don't look at them. If you try, you don't really see them, their faces lost in a sort of shadow that wasn't a shadow. They don't look at you either for the same reason.

The living and the half-living don't see eye-to-eye, so to speak.

"For a while, we used a speakeasy password," the elderly man added. "We realized it wasn't needed. *They* don't find this place. If they do, they don't stay. And you're still here."

I nodded. "I'm still *here*." I meant it ironically.

I finished the beer and poured another. I offered to get one for him, then saw he was drinking brandy. I wondered how long before I too was settled in comfortably at this club, with a favorite chair, a snifter of brandy, content to while away an evening in shared solitude.

"How was it for you?" Another man asked. He was dressed casually but exuded wealth. He had a bottle of whiskey set beside him.

"You mean my accident? The one I *didn't* have?"

I thought of telling the man the whole long story but decided not to bother. He was just being polite. I offered an abbreviated version of the events. "A streetcar," I told him. "I was almost struck near Columbia. That's when everything changed for me."

Another gentleman spoke, silver hair, flamboyant attire. He was probably sixty or so. "Streetcars are deadly little beasts, but not deadly *enough* if you get my meaning."

I did. Streetcars were fast enough to kill pedestrians who got in their way but sometimes not quite fast enough to *succeed* in that killing, leaving one in the odd half-life state.

"Ironic, don't you think?" a stout woman asked. She was forty or so, with a bottle of fine port set beside her. Her bold outfit might have suited Molly Brown, The Unsinkable One.

"How do you mean?" I asked.

"They run on tracks, obviously," she replied, as though that answered the question.

But I understood. We each have a life laid out along an unseen track. When we die, the track ends. For some of us—those who were supposed to die but didn't—the track ends but we are left to carry on, lacking traction. We spin our wheels.

"It's just a matter of fate?" I asked.

One of the others, a slender woman of fifty, nodded. "Fate is as good a word as any."

"What about you, sir?" I asked another, a pale man my age. "How did it happen for you?"

He stiffened, annoyed. "Polio. I was deathly ill, then I survived, but then I was *different*. Imagine that? You survive a deadly childhood illness and yet your mother grows distant, as though she doesn't want to see you anymore, as though there was something wrong with you. That can profoundly affect a child, I'll have you know. She lives in Brooklyn, and I here in the city. We never see each other. Neither of us can be bothered to cross the bridge."

He did not elaborate any further but I figured that many in this group had struggled with their affliction for years. No doubt, many put an end to the struggle. They found the nearest streetcar and jumped in front for good, or leapt from a tall building, or plunged into the East River. How many suicides, I wondered, were people just finishing off what fate had left undone?

Others in the room now went on to describe how they had "cheated" death. It was an odd conversation for the men and women of the club were not truly talking to one another. They would sit with newspapers or books or crossword puzzles and occasionally raise their voice to speak but to no one in particular. It was a collection of interwoven *soliloquies*.

A young woman in her late twenties spoke. She'd given birth, a very difficult birth, she said, but her baby rejected her, rejected her breasts, then her husband rejected her too. She came to believe she was a living specter. For a while, the club was *The Society of the Incarnate Ghosts*.

Others in the club explained they had been wounded in the Great War, then recovered, relieved to be sent home. When friends and family rejected them, they begged to re-enlist, to head back to the front lines, but they were refused again and again by the armed services. No reasons were given. Some even tried to enlist in the French Foreign Legion. Rejected there too.

For a while, the club was called *The Society of Rejects of the Foreign Legion*.

For a time, it was *The Society of Fate and the Fated*.

The Society of the Disconnected.

The Society of the Dead Letter Office.

So on, so forth.

After a leisurely evening, no one made an announcement but by tacit agreement the group gathered their belongings and headed for the exit. A few waited for me by the chalkboard.

"What shall we call it now?" one asked me, the muttonchop man. "The choice is yours."

Without hesitation, I replied. "*The Society of the Smoothed Stones.*"

They nodded. No one asked for an explanation. No doubt, they understood. That was the great thing about this group. Everyone here seemed to understand everyone else, even though they said so little to one another. Perhaps that's why they said so little. Thereafter, I met with them once a week for a pleasant evening of shared silence and occasional interwoven soliloquies.

A year passed before she walked in the door . . .

4.

Her name was Abigail. She was a couple of years younger than I and, over the course of the evening as I sat in my comfortable chair swishing brandy in my snifter, I learned her appointment with fate had occurred just a few months earlier. Her family had invested wisely and was spared the Great Crash of Wall Street. Alas, her luck soured. A sharp illness, an unexpected recovery, then a frustrating disconnect from the world.

To her credit, she had quickly guessed what was wrong. She made a point of searching through classified ads, hoping to find others like her. She spotted our advertisement. We were, at that time, *The Society of the Mary Celeste*, a reference to the famous ghost ship, seaworthy but abandoned. We were each like that ship, sailing on but curiously empty of life.

Maybe it was because she had at that point only endured our

affliction for a few months, or maybe her personality was just so strong, but she was unwilling to settle in with the rest of us at the club, content to render our shared soliloquies, content with our fate. She was a spitfire. Some thought she didn't belong. She was an *outsider*. Yet everything she described, her illness, the way people reacted to her, the way she struggled to truly see the faces of others or to be seen by them, it all fit our condition perfectly. The only difference was that she would not accept it.

That night she gave us a new name.

The Society of the Perpetually Unbowed.

I soon learned that the odd plight of those within our sad society, the inability to connect with one another, was not as strong between her and me. Before long, we were having the sort of intense all-night conversations I remember from my schoolboy days. These talks were often interrupted, however, by sessions of lust that would have shocked that innocent schoolboy. Despite our strenuous exertions, no child was conceived, perhaps due to Abie's earlier illness or, more likely, fate would not permit it. No matter. We even spoke of marriage. She wanted it. I was not ready. Fools never are.

In me, Abie hoped for far more than a mere husband, she wanted a co-conspirator, someone who would not go gently into that slumber of nonliving. And I *wanted* to be pulled from that slumber; I truly did. But I had become entrenched in daily ritual. By day, quiet studies on topics of interest to me in one of the many libraries of the city, then dinner, prepared by my house servant. Once a week, an evening at the club. She wanted more, much more. So we bickered. What we argued about most was whether we could change anything if wanted to.

Most of us, after an initial bout of frustration, accepted that we could no longer have a meaningful impact on the world. Some had tried when they were younger and more impetuous. One wanted to assassinate a foreign tyrant who had come to visit New York. He tried but failed. The gun jammed. Others tried less extreme measures. They would set an abandoned building on fire, just to see if they could. The building might indeed burn, but no one would *care*. So, after one or two failed attempts at having an impact, we all settle to our fate.

Abie was not so dissuaded. She concocted a plan. We would begin with an innocent prank. If successful, we would move on to more impactful endeavors. I reluctantly agreed. It was now February of 1930. A major German steamship was coming to New York. The *SS Meunchen*. There would be a brief mention in the society page of the ship docking in the harbor. She had worked at the New York Times before her illness. She knew when the afternoon edition was put to bed. She knew when shifts changed. She knew when the hot lead was briefly left unattended. She knew how to slip in and out, unnoticed. That would be easy. No one truly saw us anyway.

So the plan was that we would sneak into the print facility of the Times during a brief and chaotic shift change. We would make a quick change before the afternoon edition went to print. An innocent prank. One that would surely catch the attention of the sharp-eyed readers of The Times. It would get people talking. We would prove we could make a difference.

We'd then move on to something bigger. Something more meaningful.

So on the morning of February 11, while the afternoon edition was set for press, we snuck into the print foundry of The Times during that shift change. Abie quickly found the intended text. "The stately SS Meunchen this morning docked along the Hudson River." Snickering, we changed *docked* to *sank*. Later that day, we were staggered to learn the *SS Meunchen* caught fire that morning a couple of hours after discharging its passengers.

The ship indeed sank. The five-alarm fire had sent most of the fire equipment in the City rushing to the docks. Not only did the ship burn and sink, the wharf burned too. Only two people were killed, thankfully, but we were rocked to the core.

"Did we *cause* that?" Abie asked.

I had no answer. That week at the club—and it was called *The Society of the Wilting Flowers* at that point—we told the others of our little prank. Many disapproved. It was not our place to interfere with others, with those who were truly alive. Some worried we had now riled Fate, that it would come to finish its forgotten job, it would finish us off, all of us. A few, however, grinned. We had tried to do *something*. That was more than most of us had done in years, maybe ever. *Abigail* had done something, that is. I couldn't take much credit.

Then she asked the others that same vexing question. "Did we *cause* that?"

The consensus was that anything we might succeed in making happen would have happened anyway. For if people were fated to die, as we had been, then ships and machines and other objects large or small were fated as well. We might think we were changing the future, having an impact. Ultimately, we couldn't accomplish anything of significance. It was a deeply pessimistic view that Abie would not accept, but I did. It drove a wedge between us.

That night, as Abie paced about my apartment, agitated, she tried to convince me. "Look, the true heart of our affliction is not what you think it is. It is *not* that we no longer have a slot in life. It is that we believe we no longer have a slot. And because we believe, we use that as an excuse to do nothing, we claim that we fear Fate will *end* us if we try, but that is an excuse to do nothing, to sit and sip brandy, to waste our lives. I admit it is exceedingly hard for us to change things, but not impossible. Somewhere in the world, there is a place we can make a difference."

"I had traveled the world Abie, for many years. There is no such place."

"But you were a tourist, weren't you? An observer. Did you try to make a difference, did you ever seek out those who might *not* see us as speaking from shadow, or who might not care?"

"Of course, I *tried*," I told her. I told myself that too, but without much conviction.

5.

Two days later, Abigail waved goodbye to me from the deck of a steamship leaving from the East River. She was headed to California through the Panama Canal but was destined, eventually, for the Far East. She wanted to find a place where people who had grown up in a different culture might not notice the shadow in our faces. They would not know they were supposed to shun us. A place where we could make a difference. It broke my heart she was leaving but I was far too content in New York. I had my stipend. My apartment. My club.

So I returned to my quiet studies and the weekly meetings of the club. I got the occasional postcard from her. At first, she'd fill up the card, then her writings became briefer, then just a word or two. The last I heard, she had boarded another steamship: the *SS Harvard*. On May 30, 1931, it ran aground in heavy fog off Port Arguello, California. A total loss.

I heard nothing from Abie after that. I presumed she was lost at sea.

Sometime later I learned the *SS Meunchen* had been raised from the Hudson River, towed to dry-dock, repaired, then put back in service. It had a new name. The *SS General von Steuben*. It had, for a while anyway, gained a second life. Eventually, war came again. Despite my age, I tried to enlist. They refused me. In 1945, near the end of the war, I was saddened to read the *General von Steuben*, nee *Meunchen*, had been sunk by torpedoes from a Soviet submarine. This time, there were three or four thousand casualties, mostly wounded soldiers returning home. I wondered how many of them had been meant to die on the battlefield of their injuries but had somehow survived, only to have their lives properly ended when the ship sank.

At least the *SS Meunchen* had found a second life, for a while.

So I wondered, from time to time, whether Abigail had truly died in that California shipwreck. There had been no reported causalities. Perhaps she had used the sinking as an excuse to change her name and identity. Maybe she found her way to the Far East after all.

Had she found *a life* there? I thought of her often over the years. I yearned to travel the world again, to search for her, to search for the place she had hoped to find, a place where those with our affliction were not shunned and ignored, where one could live once again with verve and passion, a connected life. But I was still far too content in New York.

The many years slipped by . . .

6.

March 5, 1970.

Tonight at the club, during a meeting of *The Society of the Left Behind*, we spoke to one another—through our interwoven solil-oquies—of the recent death of the man who had "died" of polio many decades ago and then was rejected by his mother. He had endured the affliction of not living for quite a long time before finally finishing what fate had started. It was an unoriginal suicide, one of many taken off the Brooklyn Bridge. There was a brief and simple notice in the obituary section of The Times. As I was just ready to toss the paper aside, I spotted a far more interesting *memorandum* on the same page. There was no picture, but it described a woman about my age, originally from New York. She was revered in Malaysia for having set up an orphanage, which she had run on her own for many years. The name given was Mrs. Abigail Turner—a very curious choice of a last name, for my last name is Turner as well. Along with her many accomplishments, the article mentioned she had briefly been a member of a social club in New York called *The Society of the Perpetually Unbowed* but had no patience for it.

I will never know why she chose *that* last name. Perhaps, she had wanted to stake out a new life and hastily chose that name as a convenient *nom de guerre*. Or, perhaps, her heart had been broken as much as mine.

I realized then, finally, that I had been a fool not to leave with her back in 1930. I'd been a fool not to search for her later. I had been a fool not to marry her. So I set my newspaper down. I left my snifter of brandy behind. No one said anything to me as I made my way to the exit, slowly, for I am now old. The living world beckons and far too much time has been wasted. I pause now to mark a new name on the chalkboard near the entrance.

The Society of the Never Coming Back.

ARABELLA AND THE STONE OF TARRENTON COUNTY

1774...

T HE STONE BLOCK—SILENT AND massive—mocked him. The townsfolk mocked him too. He could ignore them. He could *not* ignore the rock. Nor could he ignore the fading whispers in his mind. He worried that maybe God himself was mocking him too, for his arrogance, for his presumption, for his foolhardy belief he had been chosen as the tool of a miracle.

"Will the stone be carving itself anytime soon, Simeon?" asked one of the townsmen, jeering. "For the hour grows late, and I have cows to call in from the fields."

Simeon wanted to holler back at the man: *Then tend your kine and leave me be!* It would be better to ignore the man and the many others who filled the town square. Better to focus on the fading whisper. It had been so very clear in his mind. Now, all but gone.

The incantation. The conjuration. The spell. Whatever it was.

He figured there was no name for it, not in any dialect known to Man. For the words—*were they even words?*—were from a divine language. Simeon understood that much, at least. They had come to him in dreams over the last few months. The otherworldly sounds had beckoned in the quiet of his slumbers, and he had done his best to memorize them, absorb them. Each morning when he awoke in his humble cottage bed, he had tried to mouth the words while still fresh in his mind.

Although the words were murky, their importance was crystal clear. His dreams told him that if he whispered the words in his mind, if he got them right, he could call upon a stone to sculpt itself, to become what The Heavens wanted it to become, a sculpture carved without the stain of a man's hands, a man's sweat, without the crude chisel, the jagged adze, the rough hammer.

There would be a purity to the sculpture, and he—a humble and devout artisan—would be the tool to allow the Heavens to turn a crude block of stone into something sublime.

He had told no one of his plan, other than the Duke himself. The Duke, a pious man, had understood and agreed. For several decades Simeon had been the personal artist and sculptor to His Grace, Theophilus Wheate, Duke of County Somerset. The Duke was his patron. He was always generous in securing the stones and paints and canvases Simeon needed. Alas, he was never generous in bestowing upon Simeon a salary, but he had gotten by. A humble cottage. Simple meals. Simeon and his one child had never wanted for more. So when he had confided his dreams to the Duke of the angelic incantation, of how Simeon could cause a mighty stone to sculpt itself into whatever The Heavens commanded, the Duke spared no expense in obtaining a fine stone from a nearby quarry. It stood ten feet tall. White marble. An oblong block with steep, grooved sides. Upon arrival, the stone had been installed in the forecourt of The Duke's Manor.

The resulting sculpture, once complete, would be presented as a gift to His and Her Grace. Alas, The Duke had died. Nearly eighty, strength fading, his passing had surprised no one, but Simeon had so hoped The Duke would live long enough to see the miracle complete.

The Duke must have told The Duchess of the plans for the stone, perhaps a deathbed confession, perhaps a plea to ensure she would continue the bequest. Her Grace, The Duchess Lavinia Wheate, had little interest in art and no patience for a fool who thought he could conjure a stone to carve itself. She demanded the "cursed rock" be taken from her estate. Stout men and stout horses were hired to wheel the heavy block on a sturdy carriage to the central square of nearby Tarrenton Township where it now sat. The stone was his, she had assured Simeon: a gift in perpetuity, but only if it remained in the square, and only if he carved it with his conjurations.

He understood it was meant as a jibe, a mockery. He was to make a fool of himself.

Now the whole Town knew of his plan. Indeed, the whole County knew, for far more had gathered in the square that afternoon than lived in Tarrenton or its surrounding villages and farmlands. They all mocked him. He now wished he were anywhere else.

"Perhaps if you would first carve it some arms and hands, it might finish the job for you."

Another burst of raucous laughter, then yet another, but now the townsfolk were not laughing at him. He spun to see what now captured the town's fickle amusement.

It was Arabella. Simeon's eight-year old daughter.

She had scaled the stone block, her fingers just the right size to fit within the thin grooves of its steep sides, her muscles strong for her age. She stood now atop the stone. No, not stood. She *pranced*.

She stomped. She bounded back and forth. She yelled down at the block. She begged the rock to begin to *change*. She cursed when it did nothing.

The villagers roared with laughter.

Just eight years old, she didn't know better.

"Arabella, come down," Simeon hissed, but she couldn't hear over the jeering crowd.

A couple boys now tried to climb the block too, failing, for none could climb as deftly as his daughter. Simeon shooed them from the stone, as a farmer might drive pests from a barnyard. The townsfolk roared even louder.

Simeon called again to Arabella. He knew she could hear him now, but she ignored him. He wondered if she too were mocking him. *No*, she'd never do anything to embarrass him, not intentionally. She adored him as much as he adored her. She was all he had, her mother having died in childbirth, he never remarrying. Soon she seemed to forget the stubborn stone, and the villagers, her attention drawn to birds flitting about, swooping ever higher into the sky. Like so many children, Arabella begged to fly. She flapped her arms now, as if she might take to the air.

Simeon wished he could fly too, far away.

Her eyes then found his. "Papa, may I go to the clock tower?"

It was her favorite spot in town, a tall church spire at the edge of the town square, the highest point for miles. He understood why she loved that perch. She could be, for a while, higher than the birds, some of them anyway. *Yes, of course*, he nodded. Anything to get her off the stone and out of the square and far from her father's burning and very public humiliation.

But first, how to get Arabella safely down from the stone? The top of the block was well beyond his reach. Arabella answered that question with a quick and reckless jump into his open arms. He caught her and set her down upon the ground and meant to scold her, to spank her, but he saw the simple joy and innocence in her eyes, and he couldn't do that to her.

"To the clock tower with you but be careful." He gave her a little push toward the church, relieved she would cause him no further embarrassment. She scampered away, dodging through the crowd, a few of the boys trying to keep up with her, failing.

Arabella had always been so very elusive.

Simeon tried again to recall the words that were not words. The conjuration. Now, the whispers were gone. Forgotten. He must have gotten it wrong. The incantation had gone awry in a way he could not understand. Or, he had to admit, maybe the dreams were just dreams, mere frolics of the mind, yet they had been so real. Night after night. They could not be ignored.

"Enough of this foolishness!" A brittle voice crackled from behind him. Simeon turned to watch the villagers part as the Vicar strode toward him. "Remove the stone at once."

Was he serious? The block weighed tons. It could not be moved, not without hiring more stout men, more stout horses, another sturdy carriage.

"But, Vicar, the Duchess . . . " Simeon sputtered. "She demanded it be put here. She—"

"I have just come from an audience with Her Grace. Her demands have changed. You are to remove this eyesore. You are never again to attempt any more pagan foolishness."

Pagan? No, the whispers had surely come from The Heavens.

"Have it gone by morning," the Vicar demanded. "And the rest of you . . . " He turned now to the townsfolk. "Have you not homes, have you not farms, have you nothing better to do?"

Shamed, the villagers began to scatter. The Vicar strode away.

The sun was just setting now. A breeze stirred. Soon, the evening would grow chill. Simeon looked to find Arabella and spotted her high atop the clock tower—not looking down at him, nor down at the stubborn marble stone—but once again eyeing the birds of the sky, and the clouds above. He waved, trying to get her attention. It was time to leave the square, maybe the whole town, maybe the whole country. None would forgive his humiliation here.

The breeze stirred more. Not a chill breeze, though. Oddly warm.

Some of the townsfolk paused and looked back at the stone, seeing something there. He saw it now too, a wisp of dust blowing off the top of the marble block. Soon, dust blew off the sides as well. The breeze stiffened, and still more dust blew away.

Simeon realized it was not dust. It was some of the stone. Somehow, the wind itself was scratching at the surface of the marble, teasing bits of it away.

The breeze became wind. The faint plume of dust became a swirling cloud, a growing maelstrom. The dust got in his eyes, in his clothes. Townsfolk downwind of the block scurried out of the swarm of blowing grit. Others hurried back to the square, hundreds of them now, gathering again around the stone.

It was a miracle. The incantation had finally worked. It had never occurred to Simeon that wind would sculpt the stone, but He always worked in mysterious ways. The growing wind swirled close around the marble, a dark and dense whirlwind. There was now so much dust and grit, Simeon could no longer see the block itself. Yet the marble was being sculpted into something, that much was clear. He wondered what The Heavens had chosen to sculpt. A Pietà? An Angelic Countenance?

He glanced back at the townsfolk. Most stood in stunned awe, transfixed. Others cowered in fear. Some stumbled away, terrified. Others fell to their knees. Many—and he had feared this—many now *cursed* him. No doubt, they thought this was witchery. Black magic. Sorcery. The Vicar was among those who cursed him. Yet, once the Vicar saw the final sculpture, once he saw it was a gift from

The Heavens, the man would be shamed by his lack of faith.

Simeon turned back to watch as thick dust spiraled ever higher into the evening sky. Birds swooped and glided around the rising cloud, no doubt enjoying the uplift of the breeze, resting their wings, floating effortlessly. Playing. Dancing. Elusive, like Arabella. Simeon had been so transfixed by the dust and the wind, he had not seen Arabella return. She stood now beside him, staring into the swirling chaos, her eyes rapt in childlike awe.

"What do you think it will become?" he asked her. "What have The Heavens ordained?"

"Papa, don't you understand? It will become what *it* wants to become."

"Arabella, don't be silly. Why would a stone ever want to become anything?"

She grinned but said nothing more so they turned their full attention to the swirling dust and to the stone within the bosom of that dust—a stone that was becoming *something*.

He watched, and she watched, and the whole town watched as the block dwindled.

And dwindled.

What was left became ever thinner. Now, Simeon felt certain he knew what it would become. A crude cross. A thin and humble one. He strained to peer into the swirling dust to find that final sublime sculpture. Thinner and thinner. Then still thinner. Then gone.

The wind stopped. Dust drifted lazily into the darkening sky. The birds flew away.

Simeon was stunned. The stone was gone.

Arabella gave an impish smile. "Of course. I should have known."

He took her shoulders and spun her to face him.

"The truth now," Simeon demanded. "Tell me what you know."

"A confession, Papa," Arabella whispered in reply. "I have a confession. And a promise."

#

1784...

Simeon kept his tears in check as he gave Arabella one last hug while her carriage waited. He shook Beaumont's hand goodbye. He was a good man. He'd make a fine husband. A military man by training, but one more suited to diplomacy. With the end of hostilities and the Peace of Versailles, Beaumont had been offered a post in Paris as an attaché on a diplomatic mission to The Court of Louis XVI. He could have secured a post here in England, but Arabella insisted on Paris. Simeon knew why. He thought again of the day in the town square, and the months and years that followed, and what Arabella had told him that night ten years ago.

It had begun with a simple prayer.

The prayer of a daughter for a father who spent all his time carving rocks, straining his eyes, torturing gnarled fingers that grew ever older. She prayed that the stones might sculpt themselves so he wouldn't have to. She had asked for nothing more than that.

Her prayer was answered, but not by those in Heaven. There were other powers, Simeon understood now. The Heavens were Supreme, of course; he would tolerate no blasphemy to the contrary. Yet it was not sacrilege to accept that other Spirits might wield power too, benevolent power. Gods and Goddesses of the Seas, of the Woods, of the Earth itself. It was those latter ones who had answered her prayer. They had whispered into her mind a conjuration as old as time itself. Arabella had no magic of her own, and never would, but she was a child back then, her mind young and limber and unshackled, so she could hear that otherworldly whisper. In turn, she whispered it to him as he slept. Night after night. Week after week. Month after month.

His mind was not young nor limber and was very much shackled, back then at least. Yet, after many months, he absorbed the shape of those ancient sounds, memorized them in his own crude way. Arabella had been right. The incantation was never to command the stone to carve itself into what The Heavens wanted, but to allow the stone to become whatever *it* wanted. And what would a block of marble, held within the Earth since the dawn of time, wish to become?

The wind, of course.

It would want to rise above the Earth. Drift far and wide. It would want to see the whole of the world. So the stone had gotten its wish. Arabella had gotten her wish too for, from that night on, unburdened by the need to sculpt stone at the behest of The Duke, Simeon had much time to devote to her and she to him. They spent endless hours together. He still sculpted. Mostly, the sculptures were of her. At nine years old. At ten, at eleven, at twelve.

A child becoming a girl. A girl becoming a young woman.

In some, she was a dancer. In many, a bird in flight. He felt the stones never objected to being sculpted into the likeness of Arabella. For she had, with her innocent plea, freed one of their brethren and sistern to reach the sky. Although he didn't understand then, that simple prayer freed her to reach for the sky too, though that would take many years and much hard work.

Simeon had asked her once if she could still remember the incantation. *No, it was not from a language that could be remembered, not by us,* she had told him. For there were words, and deeds too, the human mind was not meant to understand and never meant to remember.

At most, we catch a fleeting glimpse, but the mind cannot hold what the mind cannot fathom. So the townsfolk soon forgot the strange events of the town square, and the Vicar, and The Duchess, all of them forgot that day too. Before long, though, some of the villagers came to Simeon with simple requests. Now that he was free of his obligations to The Duke, perhaps he could sketch a simple drawing of their children, or make a modest painting of their beloved wife or husband, to capture the life of them, and he was happy to oblige. Often, he would trade a sketch for a chicken, or a painting for a grain bushel, and he and Arabella got by.

After a few years, word got out that there was an unusual artist in Tarrenton Township of Somerset County, an artisan with a curious but pleasing philosophy: an artist who believed in art for art's sake, who believed simply in painting and sculpting from life itself, who believed that simple could be sublime. In time, he sold many of the sculptures of Arabella, especially to patrons in London. They had stones delivered to him, and he never wanted for marble.

Then there was the promise Arabella had made.

A simple one, confided by Arabella to Simeon that night ten years ago, that someday she too would fly, like the birds, like the liberated stone itself, ever higher, ever farther, ever faster. This was not a prayer, nor a plea. She had gotten her one wish answered ten years ago. She would beseech for nothing more. This was a promise to herself. She would make it come true.

Always a smart child, Arabella read much and learned quickly and devoted more and more time to kites and aerial contraptions and all manner of windborne gliders. He had plenty of free time to help her build the contraptions and he had enough income from his paintings and sculptures to obtain the needed equipment. There had been many scrapes and bruises as she crashed off the roof of their cottage, or from the higher buildings in town, trying to glide through the air in one of her contrivances, and even a few broken bones, but none that wouldn't heal.

Then came a particularly spectacular crash of one of her gliders while a regiment of the King's Army was passing through town. The dashing Lieutenant Beaumont rushed to the aid of the feisty Arabella, who assured him she needed no help.

In time, the two would become engaged and, seven days ago, they were married.

Just as the stone had swirled away, Arabella would be gone too.

Her lifelong dream would soon come true, Simeon hoped, he prayed. No, he knew it would.

"Papa, you all right?" Arabella asked, no doubt seeing his eyes misting.

"I'll be fine. Hurry now, your coach awaits."

As Lieutenant Beaumont gave Simeon one last sturdy handshake, Simeon wondered whether the young man knew what he was getting into. Simeon did. For Arabella had confided another secret in him as well. She had insisted on a post in Paris for a reason.

In France, there were two brothers. They had made a great and wondrous invention.

The Brothers Montgolfier had shown that one needed no magic to rise above the world. One needed no wings to drift with the birds, and the windblown dust, and see it all.

Arabella meant to meet them, and learn from them, and in time she vowed to construct an aérostatique balloon that would let her go higher, and farther, and faster than anyone ever had.

Arabella would finally rise above the birds and the clouds and see the whole of the world.

HER BEST FEATURE

H ER HAIR WAS GROWING fast now, impossibly fast, rising into the night sky. Thin and fine and shimmering.

She was often told it was her best feature. She always blushed. A blush of embarrassment and of annoyance. For, of course, her hair was *not* her best feature. That was a childish notion, and she was no child. Not a teenager yet but not a mere child. Not anymore.

Her hair grew still longer, swirling higher into the sky. A dozen feet long. Then a hundred.

Then a thousand. Then longer, much longer.

Tugged now by high breezes, her hair spread out, some stretching this way, some that way, growing in all directions, as if to fill a lonely sky.

She realized her body was being pulled upward now. Her hair was drawing her toward the firmament.

As she was drawn ever higher, the breezes tugged at her body.

She knew she should be cold here. She was not. She was sweaty, feverish.

She dared to look down. The town was there, far below, night settling in.

Above, the stars—and other celestial bodies—beckoned. They

terrified her.

Her hair now tried to pull her still higher. It tried to pull her through the sky, and beyond.

She couldn't let that happen. She fought against it. She felt sick, literally ill, nauseated, drenched now in sweat. She could feel the dark cold that lay beyond the sky.

She heard voices from above, from all around. Voices that beckoned. She fought those voices.

The harder she fought, the worse she felt.

And yet her hair still tugged at her, trying to pull her *through* the sky, past it, beyond.

She knew now she needed to rip her hair out to save herself. She tugged hard on her hair, yanked hard. Sharp pain tore at her scalp, at her mind, at her soul. Still she pulled. Harder. *Harder.*

At last, the roots of her long, shimmering hair began to come out through her scalp, uncoiling.

The roots were dark and ugly and writhing. Black and sinister and vile. She nearly vomited.

She pulled even harder. Still more of that filth poured from her, foul and rancid.

But, finally, the last of it came free.

There was a moment of relief, of weightlessness, then she was falling.

She was plummeting fast toward the town below.

She wondered if anyone would be there to catch her. She locked her eyes shut, tight.

She fell and fell and finally crashed into the bed.

The sheets were sopped in her sweat. The blankets were foul-smelling.

She kept her eyes closed, fearing what she might see.

She heard voices around her, familiar voices, friendly voices. They told her *it* was gone. That it was out of her system, that everything was okay now.

Could she believe them?

Keeping her eyes shut, she shoved the blankets away. On wobbly legs and weakened knees she pushed past the doctors, the nurses, her parents, her brother, and made it to the bathroom mirror.

At last, she opened her eyes.

She saw stubble on her scalp. Hair was finally starting to grow back. Now, she believed.

Through all of it, the chemo, the pain, the nausea, she had never given up.

It was out of her system, she knew. Truly gone.

She had fought and she had won.

Simple stubbornness.

It was always her best feature.

SARA SARQUE & THE DEMON EXECUTIONER

PROLOGUE

The thing inside him now sensed the thing inside her.

Cole Cameron could feel the writhing within him, the twisting, the begging to be unleashed. He kept tight hold of that inner leash as he pushed open the weather-beaten front door of the dusty ranch home.

Outside, hot dry New Mexican air. Inside, the weary family waited in a musty living room. A worried father, an anguished mother, a teenage son. A few uncles and cousins. Father Correa nodded to Cole as he entered, relieved. Cole was late but it wasn't his fault. The bus from Albuquerque suffered a flat tire.

Shutting the door now against a gust of desert wind, Cole took in the room. The walls held crosses and icons of the Virgin Mary. Each looked freshly polished, as if that made a difference. The mother worked her rosary with thin, nervous fingers. She and the others eyed Cole with a look he'd seen many times before. Cole was too young, too inexperienced.

Today, like most days, Cole wore plain khaki slacks with a beat-up pair of docksiders and a white long-sleeved button-down shirt. Twenty-eight years old and lanky, he looked like he still ought to be in seminary. The mother, seeing how Cole was dressed, gave Father Correa a puzzled look, then offered Cole a Bible. He ignored it. She made the sign of the Cross. He ignored that too. Instead, his eyes followed a dim hallway to a closed door. No doubt, beyond was the bedroom and the girl and the thing inside her. Cole tried to hide his growing fear. He nodded curtly to Father Correa, squared his shoulders, and girded himself for what was to come.

As Cole headed down the hallway, he heard the mother whisper behind him. "But Father, he has no collar."

"He is not ordained," Father Correa replied.

The family muttered their disapproval.

"You trust *me*, do you not?" Correa asked them. "Then trust me that I trust Cole."

When Cole reached the bedroom door, he glanced back at Father Correa and the others in the living room and wondered if he should warn them to leave the house, to *run*. No, too late for that. If the thing got loose, there'd be no place for them to hide. It knew their scents now. It would hunt them. It would find them. It would kill them.

Cole entered the stale bedroom and locked the door behind him. He eyed the teenager on the lumpy bed. She looked fifteen or maybe sixteen. Pictures of her quinceañera adorned the walls. Her thin wrists were tied by thick rope to a sturdy headboard. Soiled blankets had been kicked away and she lay on stained and soured sheets. Eyes bloodshot, face pale and marked with horrid lesions. Her nightgown was drenched in foul sweat.

Although Cole had seen this many times before, in so many towns and so many cities, in so many countries, in so many *inno-*

cents, it still sickened him and had to fight the urge to retch. He peered then into her eyes. She glared back at him with arrogant and smoldering contempt.

Rather, it was the beast inside that glared. Cole had seen that look many times before too. He had seen the inhumanity and the unhumanity of it. It was the look of a powerful predator at a weak animal it would soon feast on but chose to torment first. It was the look of a thing that believed it was in complete control, an apex predator in the realm of sheep.

It was wrong.

Without a word, Cole unbuttoned his shirt and tossed it aside, exposing his lean physique and bare chest. The arrogance faded. The possessed girl now looked worried—no, *it* looked worried. Her bloodshot eyes—*its* eyes—fixed on Cole's chest. It saw the surging that roiled now beneath Cole's pale skin, the writhing there, the uncoiling.

It knew it was not the apex predator here, not anymore.

#

When the bedroom door was finally kicked open, Cole was slumped in a far corner of the room, still trying to catch his breath. Plaster drifted down from the cracked ceiling. Dust filled the air. A dresser had been knocked sideways and so the family, cursing, had to push hard to shove it aside so they could enter the room, or what was left of it.

They sobbed when they saw the girl had been freed.

Cole glanced at her now. Color was returning to her face, the lesions were healing, her eyes were normal again. The family hugged her and gave thanks to Heaven above. As if that mattered.

Father Correa put a hand on Cole's shoulder. "You okay?"

Cole shook his head no. He found his shirt in the debris beside the bed and tugged it back on. Correa motioned for the family to take the girl to the living room. They did, finally muttering thanks to Cole as they left.

Once they were gone, Father Correa asked again. "Are you *okay*?"

Cole gave him a weary look. "Never again."

"You always say that. Give it time."

"No, Father, *never* again."

"There will be others. You know that. And you are the keeper."

"It almost got loose. What happens then? How many will die?"

From his expression, Cole knew the man had no answer.

1.

Five years later...

Sara was nodding off—her body in a pleasant stupor—when she felt the toe of a shoe jostling her, when she heard the tinkle of her crack pipe rolling away in the darkness. She fought the urge to lunge after it as though it were the most precious thing in the world. Her pestering mind told her there was something far more important she needed to focus on.

"Sara?"

She slit her eyes open and tried to recall where she was.

A woman was looking down on her with a flashlight. At least, she had the decency not to shine the bright light directly in her eyes, Sara thought.

Instead, the beam darted around the bleak surroundings.

Sara brushed the dark tangled hair from her eyes and peered about. She was slumped on a cracked tile floor near the top of a once elegant—now decrepit—central staircase. It took her a moment to recognize the place. It had been a fine hotel long ago. Now, it was a haven for junkies and the homeless, nomads of many kinds. She had crashed here often before. Alongside her, other junkies were curled up in the darkness, passed out. She couldn't recall coming here tonight. She couldn't recall a lot of things these days, except the things she wanted to forget. Funny that. Crack made her forget all those other things and, in that wicked betrayal, forced her to focus even more keenly on the most painful of her memories, her brother Timothy, all that had happened, her long downward spiral since his death.

"Sara, what are you doing *here*? You don't need this . . . "

She recognized the woman now—her old friend Nia from college. Once, a sorority sister. Now, a social worker. They were both thirty but their lives had gone in quite different directions since graduating.

"This is the life you want?" Nia persisted.

Sara squinted up at her again. "I don't need a lecture, Nia."

"I'm pretty sure you do."

"We used to do this shit, together, remember?" Sara reached for the crack pipe, grabbed it. It was cool to the touch and she hoisted it aloft.

"You called me on your cell. Got me out of bed. Said it was urgent."

Oh, yeah. *That.*

Sara now remembered why she'd called Nia. She couldn't think of anyone else to call and she sure as hell wouldn't call the cops. Wobbly, she got to her feet and dusted herself off. Black boots, combat pants, and her beat-up old leather jacket. She was relieved no one had tried to steal the jacket while she was passed out, or the boots. If these junkies only knew how much each was worth.

"This way." She led Nia to a pair of side doors.

"You know if it's an overdose, you need to call 911."

"I need someone who's not strung out to tell me if this is real."

Sara pushed past the pair of double doors into what was once a stylish ballroom with high ceilings, now dark and grimy. Broken

windows along a far wall offered a view of other gritty buildings in what was now a bleak commercial district near downtown
Los Angeles. Outside, the sounds of late night in DTLA. Sirens
whined in the distance. Scattered traffic moved on the streets below. What was it, 3:00 am, maybe later?

Along a sidewall of the spacious ballroom, a set of stairs led to a
mezzanine platform high above the floor. Sara nodded to a shape
moving near the base of the stairs. Nia shined her flashlight.

A junkie—a young guy named Walter who Sara knew from
the streets—had his back to them. Shirtless, his neck and arms
were twisted in a grotesque and inhuman way. Limbs were not
supposed to bend like that. At least, not in the stone-cold sober
world. Sara wondered if this was all a drug-filled delusion. Nia
would surely be pissed if this was not real.

Nia gasped. "What the *hell*?"

"So this *is* real? You're seeing this too? I was afraid it was real."

Nia shined her flashlight beam on the man's back. He had
wounds there, or maybe lesions. They looked like the sort of welts
one might get from nasty bedbugs or skin diseases, but Sara understood these were not bites and he was not sick. The man, Walter,
turned to peer back at Sara and Nia. He stared into the bright beam
of the flashlight, unblinking. His lips drew back into a sneer, the
arrogant look of a predator. Sara shuddered.

"What's he on?" Nia asked, her voice hushed. "Something new?"

"You're kidding, right? For God's sakes, Nia, that is *no* drug."

Sara felt around her neck and then under her blouse for the small
crucifix she always wore on its fine gold neckless. She twisted it now
nervously in her fingers and watched as Walter lurched his way up
the stairs toward the mezzanine. With each step, his arms and legs
jerked and twitched, like a pale mannequin controlled by a palsied
puppeteer.

He reached the mezzanine platform and balanced just at its edge.

"Stay back from there!" Nia warned.

The warning was pointless, Sara knew. Whatever controlled Walter meant for him to plummet off the platform, like a lemming from a cliff.

The man was *possessed*. Sara was now certain of it. She'd seen more than enough horror movies to know what possession looked like. She'd seen enough true horror in the real world to know that all that Old Testament shit must be real. Demons must be real. The Devil must be real.

How could the world be the way it was otherwise?

This was the proof of it.

Maybe if she wasn't so strung out, she'd be skeptical like Nia. Crack had a way of cutting through the pointless barriers the sober mind put up.

"Let him go!" Sara yelled. "His name is Walter and he never hurt anyone. Find someone else to screw with!"

The demon within the man sneered again, then turned and calmly let Walter plummet off the high platform. Nia screamed.

Sara wanted to do something, *anything*, maybe try to catch him, maybe break his fall, but she couldn't get her legs moving. So she watched in stunned silence as he slammed hard into the floor. The sound of it, like a bag of mud and bricks hitting solid ground, was sickening. Blood spurted from his nose and mouth. Sara finally got her legs moving and hesitantly made her way to him, trying hard to shake off the effects of the crack she'd taken earlier, trying hard to focus. Walter was still alive, barely.

Nearby, Nia pulled out her cell phone and was trying to call 911.

"No signal," Nia declared and moved closer to the windows.

Sara then saw, or thought she saw, a flicker explode from Walter's chest and hurl toward Nia. Too fast to make out. Sara tried to follow it with her eyes, but Walter suddenly clutched her wrist, digging his bony fingers into her. His eyes rolled back and he struggled to form words. His lips and mouth twitched awkwardly like a man having a stroke.

Words finally emerged from his throat, yet the words seemed disconnected from the twisting contortions of his mouth.

"Cole Cameron. Exorcist. Find him," the voice told her. "Father Correa. Find him *first*. He'll help. Our Lady of the Angels . . . "

Walter slumped back and his eyes faded and Sara understood he was now dead. She turned finally to look at Nia. A shaft of bright moonlight through the high windows fell across her face. Sara gasped. Nia's eyes were bloodshot. Her mouth was tightening into a leer, her expression turning cold and cruel. She was getting that same arrogant look Walter just had.

"Not you now too?" Sara didn't hesitate. She strode over to Nia and punched her hard in the mouth. Nia collapsed to the grimy floor, out cold.

Sara could hear the shuffling feet of other junkies as they approached the ballroom. She couldn't let them see Nia this way. Who knows what those assholes would do to her unconscious body? She grabbed Nia and dragged her into a large side room. In the dim light, Sara spotted a sturdy pipe running along one of the walls. It looked to her like renovation work had begun here some time ago but was abandoned. She found leftover electrical tape and tied Nia's wrists to the pipe, then taped over Nia's mouth, leaving her nose free to breathe.

"Sorry," Sara whispered to Nia. "I never would've called you if I'd known this would happen. I'll find someone who can get that *thing* out of you. I promise. Or I'll figure out how to do it myself." Sara fussed with her crucifix again, then slipped it back under her blouse. "I always knew this shit was real. Demons. And angels. I *knew* it."

Sara knew, also, how badly she needed to believe in Heaven and Hell and in angels and demons, especially angels, but she couldn't dwell on that now. She returned to the spacious main ballroom. A couple of junkies stood over Walter. She recognized both but didn't know their names.

"He dead?" asked one, a wiry young guy with a frayed Lakers jersey.

"Of course he dead," said the other, an older junkie with thick scratched glasses. "You see breathing?"

"What do we do?" asked the younger guy.

"We call Raphael," Sara announced, startling them.

The younger guy gave her a sharp look. "I hate that pusher. We need to get an ambulance or something."

"No one's calling 911," the older man spat. "We'll have cops stomping all around here."

The younger junkie nodded toward the broken windows that opened out onto the city. The street below was a few stories down.

"We could just toss him—"

"Show some respect!" Sara barked. "We're *not* tossing Walter out the window."

Sara pulled out her cell phone and moved to the windows to get a clear signal to make a call.

"Okay, Sara, *whatever*," the younger guy said, rolling his eyes. "You deal with this shit. We got no time for this."

Junkies had nothing but time, she knew, but she wouldn't argue the point. The hoped to get Raphael himself and not one of his men. There was no time to waste.

2.

Sara paced beside the body of the dead junkie.

She had covered his head and chest with her leather bomber jacket out of respect and so she wouldn't have to look at the badly twisted neck, the pale white skin, the dead eyes. She checked the time yet again—5:45 a.m., the February morning still dark outside—and paced some more.

Finally, Raphael strode in. Hispanic and heavily tattooed, he was in his thirties or maybe forties. Sara had never asked him his age. She didn't want to insult him. He wore what looked to Sara like a cross between a stylish modern tuxedo and a jet black 1940s zoot suit. She had to admit, the man had style. In his left hand, he worked an old black wooden yo-yo. She had never seen him without it. He was forever bobbing it up and down on its black string without even looking at it. He never did any sophisticated tricks, just up and down, out and back, as though its rhythmic motion calmed and soothed his mind. She could always tell when he was annoyed because he would abruptly snap the yo-yo back into his hand and clench his fist over it. He was with two of his men. She recognized them: Victor and Tony. Both were musclebound and none too bright, but likable.

Raphael spotted Sara's leather jacket and the dead man beneath it. As she feared, he snapped the yo-yo back into his palm and glared at her.

"What's this bullshit? Sara, when you said *urgent*, I thought you needed more product. Thought it was a big buy."

"Sorry, Raph, I'll make it up to you. I didn't know who else to call. You can take him away?"

While Victor and Tony stared at the dead body, Sara noticed Raphael was now peering around the rest of the ballroom and into the adjacent rooms, scanning for anything else that might mean trouble. It was funny, she thought, but cops and pimps and pushers shared that same look, always scanning for clues, for trouble, for the next threat. She didn't want him to spot Nia, so she hurried forward and grabbed her leather jacket off of Walter, letting Raphael and his men see the twisted neck.

"What the *hell*?" blurted Victor.

"Can you see to it he's found by someone who can deal with the body?" Sara asked Raphael. "Somewhere respectful. Not a dumpster."

"Girl, you know I'm all about respect," Raphael replied.

She made the mistake of glancing toward the door leading to the side room. He noticed.

Raphael nodded to Victor and Tony. "Put the decedent in the trunk. We'll leave him behind the morgue." He turned to Sara. "There's a loading dock there. They'll find him later this morning. He'll be taken care of."

Victor and Tony hauled the body out.

Once they were gone, Raphael motioned to the side room. "What are you hiding back there, Sara?"

"You don't want to know."

"Oh, I always want to know *everything*."

Raphael pushed past her and strode into the side room. Sara reluctantly followed, tugging on her jacket.

"Isn't that the social worker? Nia?" Raphael asked when he saw the poor woman, still bound and gagged and tied to a sturdy metal pipe. "Thought she was a friend of yours."

"She is," Sara replied. "I *had* to tie her up."

"Because . . . ?"

Sara shook her head. "I can't explain."

Raphael glared at her. "You can. And you will. And you will do so now."

"She's *possessed*. Okay?" Sara told him. "There was some sort of *demon*, and it was in that dead guy, Walter. Then it got into Nia. I need to find a way of getting it out before it kills her."

Raphael gave her a look like she couldn't be serious.

"Yes, a demon. From Hell," Sara added. She nodded to a Virgin Mary tattoo Raphael had on his neck. "You believe in God, right? In Heaven? In angels? The Virgin Mary?"

Raphael didn't reply. He resumed bobbing his yo-yo up and down while eyeing Nia.

"If you believe in Heaven, you believe in Hell," she persisted. "If you believe in angels, you believe in demons. I always have. Haven't you?"

"Why are the hot chicks always the craziest?" Raphael rolled his eyes. "Whatever. I'll deal with the dead man. Pay me later. *You* deal with your friend."

As Raphael headed for the exit, Sara called after him. "Do you know when they open the doors to *Our Lady of the Angels*?"

Raphael paused and looked back at her. "The church?"

"Cathedral," she corrected.

"Why the hell would I know that?"

#

Sara loitered outside the massive and modernist *Cathedral of Our Lady of the Angels* until its front doors opened at 7:00 am sharp. A few parishioners were waiting outside as well. Sara let them push their way in first, then tentatively entered. She hadn't been inside this cathedral or any other in years. Following the death of her brother Timothy, she never felt worthy to enter a church. She knew that was misguided—the opposite of how it should be—yet that was how she felt.

Sara approached a nun, who was busy setting up a table to accept donations from visitors.

"I need to see Father Correa," she asked the woman.

"A Father? Wait please. I fetch one."

The woman's accent was thick and Sara wondered if she understood Sara wasn't here to speak with just any priest. "Father *Correa*," she repeated.

"A Father. Yes. Patience, please." She motioned toward a chapel set off from the main nave of the cathedral, then hurried off.

"Not just any Father but . . . "

162

The woman didn't seem to hear her, so Sara shrugged and made her way to the chapel. It offered a couple of spacious confessional booths and she stepped inside one, closing its wooden door behind her. As she waited, she realized she was fussing and fidgeting, an all too obvious nervous habit that told the world she was a junkie. As she worked to calm her fidgets, she spotted movement beyond the thick confessional screen.

"My child, when was your last confession?" the priest asked her.

"Father, I confess every day, every hour, every minute to every sin I ever committed," Sara told him, flatly. "There are a lot."

"When was your last confession to a priest?"

"I find it more convenient to confess straight to God. But that's not why I'm here."

"Then what's on your mind, child?"

"You are Father Correa, right?"

"Here I am but the ears and voice of God. What troubles you?"

"I'm looking for a guy named Cole Cameron. He's an exorcist, I think. Am I right? I need him."

There was a long pause beyond the screen.

"Where did you hear that name?" the priest asked.

"From a dying junkie. Look, I don't have time to explain. My friend Nia is possessed. Really, truly possessed. Don't tell me it's not real. That it's my imagination. That I need to see a psychiatrist. Because this shit is *real*."

"The dying man spoke?"

"A voice came from him. But I don't think it was him. It was an angel or something. Shit. I don't know. It gave me your name. And that other name. Cole Cameron."

After a long pause, the priest spoke again: "543 South 14th. It's a sanitarium run by the Sisters of Saint Mary. You'll find him there."

"Sanitarium?" Sara asked. "He's a priest there?"

"He is no priest. And he will refuse to leave that place. So if you truly need his help, you must find a way to entice him to leave."

"Entice?" Sara thought that was an odd choice of word for a priest.

"The young man is stubborn."

"But he can help me, right? He can get that *thing* out of my friend?"

"You can trust him, but only so far. Beware his noble weakness."

Noble weakness? "Look, can he get *it* out of my friend or not?"

"He's done that sort of thing many times before."

"That's all I need to know," Sara declared and left the confessional. She hurried to the cathedral's exit.

She passed a young priest waiting near the donation table. He eyed her expectantly. "Miss?"

She pushed past. She had no time for any pleas for donations.

On the steps of the cathedral, she called Raphael with her cell phone. "I need your help again. And yes, I'll pay. You know I'm good for it."

When he asked how much, she assured him whatever it would take. She meant it. It was her fault Nia was possessed. She'd do whatever it took to fix that. She already had one death on her conscience today. She would not allow another to be added to her growing list of regrets.

She ended the call and headed on foot to meet up with Raphael. As she made her way briskly along the sidewalk past clusters of addicts and stoners and other homeless, she mulled over how she would convince this man—Cole Cameron—to leave that sanitarium and help her. She would *not* "entice" him, whatever the priest had meant by that. She'd explain about Nia and get him to help her. He was an exorcist, after all, and had done *that sort of thing* many times before. If he refused? She needed a Plan B.

There always had to be a Plan B. She spotted a scruffy young stoner hunkered in a side alley inhaling deeply from his bong, the thick smoke of the weed swirling within its tarnished glass tube, and she got an idea.

3.

Sara climbed from Raphael's Lincoln Town Car as Victor pulled the massive vehicle to a stop across a quiet street from the Sisters of Saint Mary sanitarium, or *Sanatorium*, as its discrete entry sign read. Raphael and Sara had ridden in the back of the plush car. Tony was upfront with Victor.

She was thankful the car wasn't gaudily pimped out like some drug dealers favored. The black vehicle's windows were darkly tinted. Its tires were high performance ones, and so anyone paying close attention would understand the vehicle was no standard limo. It was equipped for fast getaways. Hopefully, such would not be needed this morning.

"Get the shit ready, okay?" Sara reminded Raphael as the man absentmindedly worked his well-worn black yo-yo.

"We'll be ready," he replied. "But the meter is running, just saying."

Sara tried to calm her fussing and fidgeting as she strode to the sanitarium's entrance. She would need another hit soon, but for now she had to keep her mind clear and her reflexes sharp, or at least as clear and sharp as they could be with so much blow stacked up in her body.

In the lobby, she told the Sister at the check in desk she was there to see Cole Cameron. The nun, whose name-tag read Sister Abie, eyed Sara's outfit—her aged leather jacket, the cargo pants, the combat boots—with a look that might have been disapproval or maybe envy. It was hard to judge facial expressions when coming off a high.

"Sorry, Mr. Cameron doesn't wish to see anyone. He hasn't for years."

"But Father Correa sent me," Sara explained.

"Father *Correa*?" The Sister perked up. "He must be feeling much better. That is news Cole will welcome. Maybe he'll want to see you after all. And the doctors do say Cole should engage socially."

Sara puzzled over this. She had just spoken with Father Correa earlier that morning, but the Sister made it sound like he'd been ill for some time. The priest must have recovered enough to return to the cathedral. Good for him. Perhaps miracles do happen.

The Sister set a *Back in a Moment* sign on her desk, then escorted Sara down a long white corridor lined with open skylight windows. Sara eyed the wide windows as she followed the nun along the quiet and antiseptic hallway. Sara hoped she wouldn't need to use the "shit" she'd mentioned to Raphael but the open skylight windows would do nicely if she did.

"Keep your distance from Mr. Cameron, of course," the nun told her. "And try not to smudge."

Smudge? Before Sara could ask what she meant, Sister Abie opened a side door and motioned for Sara to enter.

"Cole, there is welcome news about Father Correa," the Sister announced.

Sara entered the room and stopped cold. The ceiling, walls, and floor were lined with blackboard slates. Cryptic chalk writing covered every square foot of the room. Up, down, and all around her. She threw a puzzled look back at the Sister but she was already heading back to her station.

A lanky man in his early thirties—Cole Cameron, she presumed—was erasing some of the cryptic text with his left hand while simultaneously re-writing the same text with his right hand. It looked to Sara like some ancient runic language. Whatever it was, Cole was writing and re-writing it over and over again. He wore a loose white shirt and baggy pants. His brown hair was crudely cut, just short enough so it would not spill across his eyes as he worked. His pale skin looked like it hadn't seen the sun in years and, if you dressed him up in elegant black clothes, he'd fit right in at a DTLA goth club. Here, though, he just looked crazy.

While writing the cryptic text, he whispered something repeatedly under his breath that Sara couldn't make out.

Okay, so the guy has gone insane, Sara concluded. *Great.*

She eyed the rest of the room. There was a simple cot set to one side. A tray with unfinished breakfast waited on the cot. There was also a wooden table with a stack of musty old tomes and reams of hand-written notes. Through a side door, she spotted a bathroom. It too was lined with blackboard slates filled with the same obsessive runic script.

Sara moved closer to Cole, taking care not to smudge the chalk words beneath her feet.

"I'm Sara. Sara Sarque. Father Correa said you'd be reluctant to help me. He didn't say you were bat shit crazy."

"Does that mean I'm crazy like a bat? Or crazy like shit?" Cole replied without turning to face her. "As the case may be, neither."

"He sends his regards," Sara added, not knowing what else to say.

"Unlikely. I have become profoundly disappointing to him. Besides, I thought he had a stroke."

"He seems to have recovered."

Cole paused his writings and gave Sara a long, lingering look. She wondered whether that was because he liked what he saw—most men did, a simple and often annoying fact of life she'd dealt with ever since she was a teen and men began to assure her she could 'model' if she wanted—or whether he just disapproved of her outfit, the leather biker jacket, the combat boots. She worked again to tame her fusses and fidgets. He noticed and sniffed the air.

"Great. A *junkie*," Cole sighed. "Trust fund prima donna? I guess we all have our demons, right? All too often, self-inflicted."

A spike of anger flared in her at the trust fund *prima donna* insult. She was anything but. Yet now was not the time to get into all of *that*.

"My friend Nia . . . " Sara began, trying again to calm her fussing hands. "She's a good person. Not like me. She's *clean*. There's a thing inside her. I'm told you can get rid of it. That you're some sort of exorcist."

Cole snorted. "Father Correa tell you that?"

"No, it was a dying junkie. He was possessed. Or *had* been. The demon had just fled his body into Nia, but I don't think it was him talking. It was an angel or something speaking through him."

"There are no angels," Cole said flatly.

Sara wanted to ask why an exorcist living in a sanitarium run by nuns would think there were no angels, but she would not point out that bit of hypocrisy. She didn't want to get into an argument with this odd man.

"Then maybe it was the demon somehow still talking through the guy," Sara told him. "Giving me false hope. Screwing with me."

"Demons don't talk," Cole replied. "You were high and hallucinating. Find a shrink. And stop poisoning your body."

"Nia is for real possessed. I've got her tied up. It'll *kill* her if we don't do something. Soon."

Cole's eyes narrowed at the word "we" and looked like he might have a snarky reply but instead resumed his cryptic writing.

"There was an *arrogance* in its eyes," Sara added.

Struck by what she said, Cole ceased his writing.

Sara stepped closer to him now. "Like a predator that toys with its victim before finally killing it. You've seen that look before?"

The expression on Cole's face changed from skepticism to resignation. "I cannot help your friend."

"She will *die*."

"We all do, eventually," Cole told her. As if to make the point, he erased a wide swathe of the cryptic runes, then began to rewrite them.

Anger flared again inside Sara but it would do no good to get into a yelling match here. Instead, she approached Cole, trying to conjure up a warm smile, an inviting smile, an *enticing* smile, trying to get close enough to put a friendly hand on his shoulder. He backed away from her.

"Did the Sister not say keep your distance? You'd be wise to do so."

"Am I supposed to fear you?" Sara asked.

"Not me." Cole opened his white shirt to show her his bare chest. Something seethed and churned just beneath his skin.

Startled, she stumbled back. "What the *hell* is that?"

"A thing more powerful than whatever possesses your friend," Cole told her. "A thing that can *never* be unleashed again. I doubt I could pull it back inside me. Trust me, you don't want it let loose upon the world."

Sara puzzled over this for a moment, then understood. "I get it. You've got a demon *inside* you. It can attack the other demon, right? Drive it back to Hell. It's the real 'exorcist', not you."

"Clever girl," Cole replied, then resumed his cryptic writing. "But they're not from Hell. There *is* no Hell. There is no Heaven. There is another realm and they come into ours to feed. It's called a *tar'dor*. They feed on us. Our souls. They don't hate us. No more than we hate the lambs we eat for dinner. *Tar'dor*s hate one another. They fight for dominance. And territory. We are that territory."

Sara eyed the endless writings on the walls and the floor. "This is all to keep it trapped here with you. Some sort of spell?"

Cole sighed. "There are no such things as spells. It's a *command* from an ancient language. And it's not to keep it imprisoned here."

He tapped the wall. "It's to keep other demons from finding me. If others find me, they'll come to test their strength against the strength of the beast inside me. They will try to take its territory. I cannot allow that."

"So that's why you won't leave this room," Sara said, more to herself than Cole.

"I can never leave," Cole declared. "It wouldn't take long, maybe just days, maybe just hours, and other *tar'dors* would find me."

"What happens when you sleep? Won't it—"

"It remains leashed within me."

"When you're awake, it's awake?" Sara asked and Cole nodded. "It could kill the thing inside my friend Nia if you just let it?"

"Sister!" Cole yelled to the door. "We are done here." He then looked to Sara, his eyes sympathetic now. "My advice, stay far from your friend. Maybe it will spare her and find someone else to feed on. Someone deserving. Let it cull the herd."

Someone *deserving*? Anger again threatened to boil inside her. Who could ever deserve that sort of death, a demonic death? She would not wish that upon anyone.

Sister Abie arrived and beckoned from the door for Sara to leave.

As Sara exited the room, Cole called to her. "Did something really *talk* to you? And give you *my* name? An angel?"

"You said there are no angels," Sara replied brusquely. "We're on our own."

Sara followed Sister Abie along the corridor toward the lobby.

"That's far longer than he has permitted anyone to speak with him for years," the Sister told Sara. "If you come back tomorrow maybe he'll agree to talk a bit longer."

Sara said nothing but eyed the open skylight windows again.

Time for Plan B.

4.

When Sara returned to the parked Lincoln Town Car, Raphael and his two men—Victor and Carlos—were still seated inside, smoking. Cigarette butts were piled on the street beside the car.

"Plan B, then?" Raphael asked.

Sara nodded.

Raphael motioned to Tony who, without a fuss, handed Sara a smoke bomb and lit it for her. Also, without any fuss, Sara carried the sputtering smoke bomb across the street to the sidewalk alongside the sanitarium and lobbed it through one of the nearby wide skylight windows into the corridor she'd been in earlier with the nun. She stood back and waited.

After a moment, fire alarms screeched inside the sanitarium. She waved for Raphael, and he and his men joined her, grinning. Bored by the wait in the car, they were probably ready for a little action, a little mischief and mayhem. Raphael had put his black yo-yo aside and instead clutched a soggy cloth in his hands. Sara led them into the sanitarium.

Inside, thick smoke filled the lobby and the adjacent corridor. Raphael and his men watched with bemused enjoyment as various Sisters in their habits scurried to and fro, helping patients exit their rooms amid all the smoke. Sara squinted through the smoke and spotted Sister Abie who was trying to fetch Cole from his room. He refused and so the Sister hurried further down the hall to get help. Sara then sprinted to Cole's room, with Raphael and his men close behind her.

Cole seemed to be doing his best to ignore the chaos. He continued to write his cryptic inscriptions, muttering to himself. Raphael stepped in behind Cole and jammed the wet cloth over his mouth. Cole collapsed. Sara was pleased the knock-out compound worked quickly. She then led the way as Tony and Victor carried Cole to the lobby exit amid the thick smoke.

Soon, they were back on the street. In short order, they had Cole safely in the trunk of the Town Car and were driving off nonchalantly. Fire trucks passed them on their way to the sanitarium. Sara glanced back, puzzled by the amount of smoke now pouring from the building.

The smoke bomb should have sputtered out by now.

#

When they got back to the derelict hotel, Nia was still taped securely to the pipe but now she was awake. Her eyes were bloodshot. Her flesh was pockmarked with lesions. The thing inside her must be awake too, for Sara saw that Nia's expression had the same arrogant look she'd seen before in Walter—the look of a predator who believed it was at the top of the food chain. Sara placed a chair about ten feet from Nia. Victor and Tony carried Cole in, still unconscious, and propped him up in the chair.

"Smelling salts," Raphael said as he handed Sara a small vial. "Use them when you're ready. They work fast."

"You're not staying?" Sara asked.

"Love to. But I've got business to attend to. Call me later. Let me know if you raise the Devil. Or send the Devil back to Hades. Or whatever the hell you're planning on doing here."

As Raphael and his men left, Sara overheard one say, "crazy rich chicks, what can you do?"

Crazy? Guilty as charged, Sara conceded.

Rich? Not so much anymore.

Sara eyed Cole, slumped in the chair. She was sorry she had to kidnap him, but if he hadn't been so damned stubborn and had just come along, certain *complications* could have been avoided. On the drive over from the sanitarium, Sara had checked the news on her cell phone. The smoke bomb wasn't supposed to cause a fire, just a lot of smoke, but it *did* trigger a fire. The news said the sanitarium had a lot of old non-fire-resistant insulation that had never been replaced. No one was injured but the sanitarium was gutted. *Shit.* That was not what she wanted. She would make it up to Cole somehow. And the Church. *Somehow.* But for now she had other problems.

Two junkies shuffled into the room, curious about what was going on. Sara recognized them. One went by the name Camo because he always wore camouflage hunting gear. The other was a younger guy named Lester.

"Sara, what the hell is this shit?" Camo asked as he eyed Nia. "What the hell is wrong with her?"

"You should both leave," Sara told them. They didn't. "Don't say I didn't warn you."

Sara couldn't waste time trying to convince them to leave. Nia needed her help and needed it now. Sara had to get the thing inside Cole to do, well, whatever in the hell it was supposed to do. She broke the vial of smelling salts and held it under Cole's nose. His eyes fluttered open.

Confused, he looked around.

"What the . . . ? Where am I?" Cole sputtered. He spotted Nia tied to the pipe, saw her bloodshot eyes, her possessed look. "*What?* No!"

It looked to Sara like Cole was fighting to keep hold of the thing inside him. Then he lost the battle or maybe just changed his mind. His eyes rolled back and something exploded out of his chest toward Nia. It grew rapidly in size as it did.

In the dim room, Sara couldn't get a clear look at it. She caught glimpses of fangs and claws and insect-like limbs. She saw it only in strobe-like flashes of chaotic images. It wasn't flashing the way a television screen might flicker with a bad signal. It was as though the demon itself was winking in and out of existence, or maybe this was some sort of weird and otherworldly camouflage, a demonic trick to fool and confuse its prey.

As it pounced toward Nia, the demon inside her lashed out in defense. Sara saw that creature only in strobe-like flashes, as well. It too was an unholy combination of claws and fangs and strangely jointed limbs. Yet it was different from the other demon. Smaller. Maybe a different *breed* of demon, Sara figured.

The fight was furious. Roars and unholy screeches echoed throughout the room. Sara and the two junkies watched, frozen in shock and fear, as the two demons fiercely attacked one another, then counterattacked. They slammed into the walls and some-times the high ceiling, buckling the woodwork, bringing plaster raining down from above.

First one, then the other, seemed to gain the advantage. As they fought, Nia's demon pounced into Lester, and when it leapt again it took the man with it. He was hurled violently across the room and slammed hard against the far wall, his neck snapping, killing him instantly.

Sara was too shocked even to scream.

The demon inside Lester rebounded out of his dead body and leapt to the other side of the room with Cole's demon now in chase. Cole's demon—the bigger of the two—dove into the other junkie, Camo, and he too was flung now across the room. His arms and legs bent and snapped as he was hurled through the air, killing him even before his body crashed into a far wall. The man now crumpled lifeless to the floor.

In the manic chaos, Sara realized a cop had entered the room, gun drawn. She figured he'd probably been patrolling out on the street and heard all the roaring and crashing and hurried up-stairs. The burly deputy gasped at the unfolding chaos. One of the demons careened toward him and he fired his weapon at it, missing badly. The loud gunshot stung Sara's ears and reverberated throughout the room.

The deputy then became possessed, first by one, then by both of the ferocious demons. As they fought within the officer, his body buckled and contorted and rose off the floor, then he was slammed hard back to the ground, killing him too, a sickening sight. The two demons now leapt out of him and tumbled across the floor, still locked in combat, still visible only in maddening strobe-like images, head-ache-inducing flashes.

At last, Cole's demon defeated the other. In the flickering chaos, it was hard for Sara to tell exactly how it won the fight, but the demon that had possessed Nia now whimpered, sagged lifelessly, and then, in a final flash, disappeared entirely.

Cole's demon, still flickering in that maddening churn of reality and unreality, glanced back toward Cole and then bounded toward one of the broken windows that looked out upon the city.

Sara watched, bewildered, as Cole raised his hands toward it.

"*Auwk mym doth be en thay!*" Cole yelled.

To Sara, the words sounded medieval, maybe Old English or Old German or something more ancient. Whatever it was, it caused the demon to stop short of the window. It flickered there.

"*Auwk mym doth be en thay!*" Cole repeated.

He strode forward, his hands still stretched out toward the creature, trying to draw it back to him, clearly struggling to do so.

Sara hurried to Cole, hoping she might somehow help.

The demon lunged at *her* now. She leapt back, barely dodging its snapping jaws, then leapt back again when it lunged a second time. She turned blindly to run but slammed headlong into a wall. Trapped, she spun back to face the thing. It was right in front of her now, strobing like mad, its wicked snapping fangs mere inches from her neck.

"*Auwk mym doth be en thay!*" Cole yelled at it.

The flickering demon was pulled back toward Cole, then seemed to find new strength and lunged at her yet again. This time it jumped *into* her. She felt dizzy and disoriented. Her vision was now strobing on and off.

"*AUWK MYM DOTH BE EN THAY!*" Cole bellowed.

The demon was yanked out of her, as a dog on a leash might be yanked back, an unseen leash. In a few more strobe-like flashes, it was drawn back inside Cole—shrinking somehow at the last moment—and was absorbed into his chest, disappearing into him. For a second or two, Cole's eyes had the arrogant look of the demon, then returned to normal.

"Was it . . . ? Was it *in* me?" Sara asked, her heart pounding, her lungs heaving. She tried to catch her breath. Her dizziness finally cleared.

"It was in you for a moment. But you'll be okay," Cole told her, then looked about the room. He eyed the dead men with despair.

So did Sara. Their mangled bodies, their broken necks, reminded her of the night her brother Timothy had died. She felt sick.

"How did I get *here*?" Cole demanded.

Sara was too shaken to answer.

Cole dabbed his fingers on his chin and sniffed at the knock-out drug residue left there. He glared at Sara with a look of betrayal.

"You *drugged* me? You brought me here? I *warned* you!"

Sara finally caught her breath and pushed past Cole to get to her friend Nia. She spotted a bloom of red growing on Nia's shoulder. The bullet from the deputy must have struck her. Nia was unconscious now.

"Carlos! Carlos! You all right?" a man hollered from the nearby ballroom. Sara figured it was another deputy. "I called for backup!"

The deputy charged in and stopped cold when he saw the dead bodies. At first, he didn't seem to even notice Cole or Sara or Nia as he hurried to his fallen colleague. Then he spotted Cole approaching him with his hands out, trying to apologize.

"Sorry. Nothing I could do," Cole said, almost weeping now. "There was just *nothing* I could do."

Furious, the deputy drew his sidearm, his finger twitching now on the trigger. Sara stepped in behind him and clubbed him with the chair. He slumped to the floor, knocked out cold. Sara tossed the chair aside and hurried to Nia. She shook her gently, trying to revive her.

"Nia?" Sara asked but got no reply.

Cole joined her and inspected the bullet wound. "Not too bad. She'll be okay."

Sara nodded, relieved, then heard sirens wailing on the streets outside the building. "We've got to get out of here. I know a place where we can—"

"*We?*" Cole sputtered. "You go where you want. I need to get back to my room." He sniffed the air. "Others will find me. Soon."

"The smoke bomb I used caused a fire. It wasn't supposed to, I swear. The sanitarium was gutted. You can't go back. Sorry."

"Are you kidding me?"

"And there's this." She pointed to a device on the uniform of the deputy she knocked out. "Body cam. It probably got a clear look at you."

She checked the other deputy and was relieved his bodycam had been shattered in the attack, so it probably didn't capture her face.

Stomping boots approached the room. Police radios crackled.

Sara grabbed Cole and hauled him to a hidden opening formed from loose panels in a far wall of the room. She pulled him through the opening and replaced the panels just before a SWAT team swarmed into the room, weapons drawn. She could see them through a crack in the wall panels.

"Officers down! Officers down!" the team leader barked. "Lock the building down! No one enters. No one leaves."

Sara watched as some of the team tended to their colleagues

and the dead junkies. Others hurried to Nia. "This one is alive. Paramedics!"

Sara turned to face Cole, expecting him to be furious at her. Instead, he was staring down into darkness. She looked down too.

Shit! She and Cole stood on a ledge within an old service elevator shaft that descended into darkness. The shaft itself was not the problem. She had used this escape route a few times before when cops had raided the building. The problem was there had been a sturdy ladder on this side of the shaft leading down to the next level. It must have broken away at some point. There was another ladder on the far side, but it looked flimsy and they would need to work their way around the shaft on a narrow ledge just to get to it. Beneath them, loomed a four-story drop.

5.

Cole stifled a gasp when he saw where Sara had led him. They stood side by side on a ledge staring down into darkness.

The SWAT team could be heard working in the adjacent room, tending to the dead bodies and to Sara's friend. Cole was relieved her friend, at least, had survived but was furious that this impertinent woman—Sara Sarque—had kidnapped him and brought him to this derelict building. He'd been lucky to draw the *tar'dor* back inside him. It had been nearly five years since he last unleashed the beast. This time, like that time, the only reason he had the strength to draw it back was the other creature weakened it in the fight. He could feel his *tar'dor* nursing its wounds.

He threw Sara an angry look that said *What the hell do we do now?* He needed to escape the police and find a safe place—a room where he could write the ancient blocking commands on the walls, the floor, the ceiling, as he had at St. Mary's. Otherwise, other *tar'dors* would find him.

A jail cell would be a disaster. Those other beasts would come to test their strength against the strength of the one within him. Many people would die, other inmates, guards. Still more would die if his *tar'dor* then got loose. Even worse, if anything could be worse, was that there'd be proof then of the existence of the supernatural creatures. Security recordings, numerous eyewitnesses. It would all go viral on the Internet. The world was not ready—and *never* would be ready—to learn of these demonic beasts.

All this flashed through his mind as he stared down into the dim elevator shaft. The shaft itself was made of old concrete, crumbled in places, with rusted rebar exposed. Each level had a narrow ledge like the one they were balanced on now. Rusted metal ladders on opposing sides of the shaft connected each level, but many rungs were missing. In some places, the entire ladder from one level to the next was gone.

Sara elbowed him and pointed to a flimsy ladder on the far side of the shaft and motioned for him to follow her. Was she insane? He shook his head, giving her a very firm *no*. She ignored his protest and worked her way along the narrow ledge to the other side of the shaft, then began to climb down the ladder there. For a junkie, a *prima donna* junkie, she seemed rather nimble, though her hands shook at times and she paused to quell those shakes. Maybe that was just fear from the climb. But maybe the shakes were from the drugs that, no doubt, still coursed her junkie veins.

What was she on? Cole wondered. Crack? Heroin?

There was another crackle of police radios in the adjacent room. Cole had no choice but to follow Sara. He worked his way cautiously along the ledge to the far ladder, then awkwardly began the descent, clutching the rusted ladder tightly. Before long, his arms were shaking. He always tried to stay in shape in his room at St. Mary's—daily pushups and deep knee bends—but that had done little to prepare him for *this*. His foot suddenly slipped off a rusted rung and he barely caught himself. Sara glared up at him from below, as though he was trying to plummet to his death.

But rung by rung, he made it down one level, and then another.

Two stories down, Sara waited for him on a ledge near where a wall panel was missing. The ladder on their side of the shaft was missing too, so they needed to get beyond that opening to reach the ladder on the far side.

Through the opening, he could hear police officers interrogating homeless who lived in the building, or maybe they were other junkies like Sara. The police were loudly demanding to know what they had seen. They demanded to know who had killed the deputy and the others.

Sara, who was balanced ahead of him on the ledge, peeked through the opening, then darted past to the far side of the shaft and waved for Cole to step closer. Now, he could peek into the adjacent room. He waited until the police were looking the other way, then slipped past the opening to join Sara. At the last moment, he ducked to avoid scraping his scalp on metal rebar, which threw him off-balance. He teetered now on the ledge.

Sara reached out and pulled him safely to her. For an awkward moment, their bodies were pressed together. He hadn't been this close to anyone in years. The nuns at St. Mary's knew to keep their distance from him. But now he was pressed up against Sara, kissing close, and he couldn't deny how very attractive she was. Lovely eyes, bee-stung lips, messy dark hair. *No!* He was mad at her. He couldn't be *attracted* to her. Anyway, girls like her never went for guys like him. He was a lanky seminary school dropout. She was . . . well, a *BTG*, a beautiful troubled girl. A hot mess.

Embarrassed, he pushed away from her. She smirked at his awkwardness and then led the way down the next ladder of the elevator shaft. The muscles in his arms and legs throbbed, but he made it down the last couple of floors. There, along with broken sections of rusted ladders, was the old service elevator. They climbed down through its roof and finally emerged near a loading dock on the ground floor of the building.

The loading area was a large and dusty space. A wide door led to an alley behind the building. Cole spotted an armed deputy pacing the alley. The man was far enough away so Sara and Cole could talk quietly without being heard. Sara nodded to the elevator shaft they just climbed down.

"Not afraid of heights, are you?" Sara whispered.

"Not my favorite thing," Cole hissed back.

"Yeah, not my favorite thing either, trust me." She flexed her hands as if to calm shaking nerves from the climb down the shaft.

She wasn't fooling Cole. Those were drug shakes. During the years he had performed "exorcisms" with Father Correa, the jobs took him all around the world, into countless dark and dirty neighborhoods, countless dark and dirty tenements. *Tar'dors* seemed to favor junkies and others who dwelt in those sad realms. It was their way of culling the human herd.

Sara pointed to the deputy in the alley. "We got to get past him."

"Then what?" Cole asked.

"Then don't worry about it. When you hang with junkies, you learn routes to avoid cops." She glanced about and spotted some old ragged clothes piled up nearby. She eyed Cole's white outfit from the sanitarium and tossed him some of the ratty clothes. A trench coat. Worn pants.

"Put these on," she told him.

Cole winced at their foul smell. "You can't be serious."

"Where we're headed, you need to blend in."

"Look, I don't know where *you* are headed. But I need a room where I can write on the walls and the ceiling and the floor. Otherwise, *others* will find me. And you. You've seen what they do."

"I know just the place. But to get there, you need to blend in."

"Where is that *place*?"

"Don't worry about it," she grinned.

He very much worried about it, but if she knew how to get away from this building, which was swarming with police, to reach a safe-haven, he would have to stick with her. First chance he got, though, he would ditch her. She had gotten him into enough trouble already. He looked forward to ditching her—the geeky guy for once turning the tables on the hot mess. So Cole grudgingly tugged the ragged clothes on. As he did, Sara pointed out a large abandoned storage locker near the back alley door. The locker's door was open but looked like it could be closed and latched.

"I'll lure the cop over there. You scare him into the locker with that beast of yours," Sara whispered.

"I'm *not* letting it out of me again," Cole hissed.

"You don't have to. Just let him see it surging within your chest, like you showed me back at the sanitarium."

"Then what?"

"Then don't worry about it," she winked.

Before Cole could protest, Sara headed toward the alley where the deputy was still pacing back and forth. As she did, her steady walk turned, step by step, into a sultry swagger, as though she were drunk or stoned. What was that girl up to?

6.

Sara tousled her hair, unzipped her leather jacket to reveal a bit of fetching cleavage beneath her blouse, and wobbled seductively toward the deputy, giggling like a drunken sorority girl. She hated to have to use her feminine wiles but they did come in handy sometimes.

"Miss, you need to remain inside," the deputy told her. "Detectives are getting statements from everyone in the building."

"Whatever for?" she purred.

"There was a murder. Several. They need to know if you saw something."

"I did. It's just inside."

She beckoned and he followed her, pulling out his flashlight. She led him toward the open locker but he balked at the loading dock entrance.

"I can't leave my designated zone. I'll call for assistance."

"Sheesh. It's just *right here*," Sara purred again and she beckoned him closer to the vacant locker until he stood beside it.

Cole stepped out of nearby shadows and tugged his ragged coat open, like a pervert exposing himself. But what he exposed was that unholy *thing* surging just beneath the skin of his chest.

The deputy gasped when he saw it. "What the . . . ?"

Sara shoved the deputy into the locker and slammed the door shut, latching it closed. He began pounding on the door, raising a racket. Other cops would hear and come running, so she sprinted away down the alley, running as fast as her combat boots would allow, Cole close behind her.

Ahead, there was a torn opening in a chain-link fence. She led Cole through the fence into a vacant dirt lot, then to a maintenance access shaft. Its iron cover had long ago been taken off, probably stolen. A rusted sign read Underground Irrigation/Flood Control Channel. She'd taken the route many times before. She glanced back at the alley to make sure they were not being followed, then hastily climbed down the shaft using metal rungs bolted to its sides. These rungs were only in slightly better shape than the rungs in the elevator shaft, but they held her weight.

Reaching the underground channel, Sara used her cell phone flashlight to peer about, looking to see if they were alone here. They seemed to be. Cole muttered and wheezed as he clambered down the rungs behind her, his chest heaving, trying to catch his breath from the run.

"I see you're in *great* shape," she teased. "How long did you hole up in that room at the sanitarium?"

"Not nearly as long as I should have," he replied, tartly.

"Yeah, sorry again about burning it down. But the news said the place was a fire trap. Should have been demolished long ago."

"So you did me and all the nuns a favor?"

"You can thank me later," she replied with a smile, then led Cole along the dark concrete flood channel.

A stream of water trickled along the center of the wide underground channel. Garbage and debris were piled up on both sides. Soon, they reached a long section where the concrete ceiling of the channel was partially open to the sky, letting light in so she could shut off her cell phone flashlight. From further ahead, voices echoed back along the channel.

Cole caught up with her and peered nervously ahead.

"Just homeless folks, Cole," she said. "Vagabonds. Harmless."

"That's not what I'm concerned about."

"You're worried about other demons finding you? You were serious about that?"

"I'm serious about everything," Cole replied. "You should've figured that out by now."

"Just part of your charm," she said with a wink. "You must be the life of the party."

"Screw you."

"That's not going to happen. The way you smell, no woman will *ever* want to screw you again," she teased. "Assuming any ever did."

Cole rolled his eyes at her little jibe, then paused to sniff his foul-smelling coat. "The odor should help. The main way *tar'dors* find us—and find other *tar'dors*—is through smell."

"*Tar'dors*?" she asked.

"That's their ancient name." Cole sniffed the coat again. "The smell might keep them from finding me and my *tar'dor*."

"Me and my *tar'dor*? Good grief. You make it sound like a pet."

"It's a vicious heartless killing monster. But it has been inside me for ten years. That's longer than most marriages last."

"So divorce the thing."

"I've spent the last five years trying to figure out how to destroy it—or force it to return to its own realm—but I don't know how. No one knows how. So I keep it trapped inside me."

"How exactly do you do that?"

"I visualize a locked chamber. A psychic place inside my mind, inside my body. In it, writings cover the floor, ceilings, and walls, the same language you saw in my room at St. Mary's. But these commands—"

"You mean spells," Sara cut in.

"There are no such things as *spells*," Cole declared, pronouncing the word as though it were something foul one might step in. "These commands—"

"They're words with supernatural power. Sure sounds like spells to me," Sara said. "And you can call these things *tar'dors* all you want. But they sound a lot like demons to me. And they look like vicious demons."

"*Anyway*," Cole continued, impatiently, "in that inner chamber, I visualize a leash. And a door. A very sturdy leash. A very sturdy door. The walls of the chamber are lined with the leashing command."

"*Auwk mym doth be en thay*?" Sara asked, repeating what she heard him yell again and again back in the derelict building.

"Yes. But here's something remarkable I discovered years ago. All I need to do is mentally recite that command and the ancient runes form on the walls of the chamber in my mind, as if they write themselves," Cole explained. "I can feel the creature pacing even now. It throws itself against those walls, against that door, straining at its leash. It does that too often."

"Here's something I don't get. When that demon comes out of you, it's huge. Eight feet tall at least. So—"

"How can it fit inside me?" Cole cut in. "I don't know. What I do know is that *tar'dors* don't abide by the physics of our world. Neither does the psychic chamber I create with my mind. So it's not like it shrinks down to fit inside a little chamber in my chest and then expands when it gets out. The chamber is somehow both larger than me and smaller than me. It gives me a headache thinking about it, so I don't think about it. I just accept it."

Sara wondered if she too could visualize an inner chamber in her mind to hide things away. She thought of maybe locking away her most painful memories, especially of her brother Timothy, of a night two years ago, of how they had locked eyes for a moment as he perched atop a high balcony, drugged out of his mind, how he had turned, and then . . .

No, it was unfair to Timothy and a cop-out for her to lock those memories away. After his death, friends told her that forgiving herself would not mean forgetting. She would not alllow herself to either forgive *or* forget.

"Sometimes, you open that inner door?" Sara finally asked Cole.

He nodded. "And it has become so very hard for me to pull the thing back in when I do."

"Sara, that you?" a man called from ahead. "You got some shit for me? *Good shit*."

Close ahead was a homeless encampment. Here, the channel was partially open to the sky with easier access to downtown streets.

"Sorry, Clarence. Not today," Sara said when they reached the encampment. "I've got cash for you though."

Sara dug some money from a pocket of her cargo pants and handed it to the homeless man.

"Get yourself a good meal," she told him, then nodded to others living there, "and share it."

"Who's he?" the man growled, peering up at Cole.

"He's no one," Sara told him. "You take care now."

She quickly led Cole farther along the underground channel. Here, more junk and debris was piled about.

Cole glanced back at the man and gave Sara a look.

"Don't worry about him. Clarence sees himself as the leader of that little encampment and he doesn't want anyone else joining their group. Like your *tar'dors*, men can be rather territorial too, unfortunately."

Cole eyed his own ragged and smelly clothes and nodded. "Guess I look homeless now too," he grumbled as they continued along the channel.

"So, you ever going to tell me how you got that demon in the first place?" she asked, trying to change the subject.

"You ever going to tell me how you became a junkie in the first place?" he replied.

"Nope."

"Ditto."

"You don't like me much, do you?" she asked, teasing him again.

"Sara, you *kidnapped* me," Cole replied, suddenly angry. "You torched where I lived. Now those two junkies back in that old building are dead, and a cop too! All because you wouldn't leave well enough alone."

"Well enough alone? My friend Nia was *possessed* by a demon."

Cole didn't reply, which was good, since she'd probably punch him if he said anything more about "leaving well enough alone." She'd never forget how Nia had looked, the lesions on her skin, the inhuman arrogance in her possessed eyes. She hoped Cole had been right about her gunshot wound and she'd be fine, but what did he know about gunshot wounds? She would help Cole for now. She owed him that. She *had* kidnapped him and burned the sanitarium to the ground. But then she'd track down Nia at whatever hospital she'd been sent to and make sure she was truly okay. Cole peered back the way they had come, worried about something.

"What?" she asked but Cole didn't answer.

Then she saw it. *Him*.

Clarence, her homeless friend, was somehow crawling along the concrete ceiling of the flood channel just above them—scurrying like a crab, arms and legs contorting in ways no human limbs ever should. It was a sickening sight. She grabbed Cole and turned to run. Too late. Clarence launched at them and struck Cole, knocking him hard to the ground.

The demon inside Clarence lashed out at Cole.

7.

Sara stumbled back as Cole's demon, his *tar'dor*, launched itself from his chest at the attacking demon. As before, she saw only strobe-like glimpses of the two beasts. Since they were in close quarters, the two demons—Cole's and the one in Clarence—didn't fully leave their hosts to claw at one another. As they snarled and fought, Cole tried to push himself away from his attacker so his own demon had more room to fight, but Clarence, panicked now, grabbed hold of Cole's coat. It reminded Sara of how a drowning man would cling to another, pulling both under.

Sara searched amid the debris in the channel for a weapon. She grabbed a metal pipe. It was heavier than she expected but she hoisted it above her head. In the dim light of the tunnel, it looked to her like the demon in Clarence was biting and snapping close to Cole's throat, and yet Cole still could not free himself. She swung the pipe, hard enough to knock Clarence out, she hoped, not hard enough to kill the poor man.

With a sickening thump, the pipe thudded into Clarence's head and he slumped motionless to the ground. His demon suddenly disappeared, or jumped away, or *something*. She couldn't tell. Still clutching the pipe, she looked around for the creature, ready to swing the weapon again.

"Where'd it go?" she gasped at Cole.

"It's still *inside* him," he replied, climbing hastily to his feet. "Remember what I said? If I'm unconscious, *it's* unconscious. It's one of the few times they're vulnerable."

"Then why stay inside us? Why bother to *possess* us?" Sara asked. "They can jump around. I saw it back at that old derelict hotel."

"They need our energy. Literally. It's like us being underwater," Cole said. "We don't last long without oxygen. Our souls are their oxygen. To enter our world, they must enter through one of us."

As Sara tossed the metal pipe aside, Cole hunkered down near Clarence. "What are you *doing*?" she asked.

"This is unpleasant. But I can't let this man come to with a demon inside him. He'll die. Others too."

Sara watched with morbid curiosity as Cole gave his demon just enough leash to feed on the demon inside Clarence. She saw strobe-like glimpses of claws and teeth. There was no roaring or screeching this time. It looked to Sara more like a lion quietly shredding the carcass of a dead animal. When it was over, Cole wiped his mouth, as though he had just eaten too. He had a sated look in his eyes.

Cole then checked Clarence to make sure he was still breathing, that his heart was still beating. "He'll be okay. He'll have a nasty headache, though, from the way you clobbered him."

"Before, you told me that if you ever had to release your demon again, you wouldn't be able to pull it back in."

"I doubt I would," Cole replied. "But here I didn't let it completely out of my body. The longer the leash, the harder it is for me to pull it back."

"If it ever does get away from you, what'll happen?"

"It'll either possess someone else and go on another killing rampage or return to its own realm and then—"

"But isn't that what you *want*?" Sara cut in. "For it to return to where it came from?"

"*And then* . . . return once again to our world to kill. Just like a bear that has gotten a taste for human food, it will return again and again."

Sara mulled this over.

"So you see my dilemma, Sara. I can't let it off its leash. I don't know how to destroy it. And if I can't find a safe place in which to shield myself, like I did back at the sanitarium, other *tar'dors* will find me and attack."

"Those other demons can possess anyone, anytime?" She recalled how Cole's had been inside her for a moment back at the derelict building.

"I doubt any would leap into you while you're close to me. They prefer to possess someone farther away, *then* launch their attack."

"But you can't say for sure?" Sara asked, worried.

Cole nodded.

"Then how do I keep one from possessing me?" she asked.

"Okay, Sara, listen and repeat: *Loch lym soth bewen ma-thay.*"

"That's what you were whispering back in your room?"

"It's also what I wrote on the walls of that room. If you whisper it to yourself—even silently in your own mind—it should help keep them from finding you and possessing you."

"Should *help*?" Sara prodded.

"There are never any guarantees with these creatures."

Sara gave it a try. "*Loch lym soth* . . . what?"

"*Loch lym soth bewen ma-thay,*" Cole corrected.

"*Loch lym soth bewen ma-thay,*" Sara repeated shakily, then with greater confidence. "*Loch lym soth bewen ma-thay!*"

"By George, I think she's got it," Cole said, drolly. "I really think she's got it."

"Yeah, very funny. I get that joke. From *My Fair Lady*."

"See, I'm not so serious all the time," Cole replied.

"*Loch lym soth bewen—*"

"*Silently*, within your mind is fine," Cole reminded her. "And not *all* the time. You're permitted to think other thoughts too, should you occasionally have any."

Before Sara could fire back a snarky reply, voices approached along the channel. Cole looked worried.

"Probably some of Clarence's friends from the encampment," Sara said. "They'll take care of him." She and Cole lifted the man up and propped him along a side wall, then hurried down the channel away from the voices.

"You seem to like to club guys on the back of the head," Cole said to Sara once they were out of earshot of the others. "How worried should I be to turn my back on you?"

"Very," Sara replied with a little smirk. "Hey, do you see them the same way I do? Just flickering glimpses?"

The strobe-like flickering reminded her of when she would go out dancing at night clubs, with their bright strobe lights flashing on and off, the faces of other dancers there for a moment, then not there, then there again. She always liked that strobe effect, as if it transported her to another world. With these creatures, it was just sickening. Unholy and inhuman.

"All I see are flickering glimpses too," Cole told her. "I'm not sure why we see them that way. Maybe, because they come from another world, our minds struggle to comprehend them the same way we struggle with optical illusions. Our brain tries to reject what we see, but can't."

"That other world isn't Hell?" she asked.

"Depends how you define Hell."

As they walked on, Sara mulled over the hell that Cole had been living in the last five years, isolated in that room at the sanitarium, writing and rewriting ancient spells on the wall. He claimed there was no way of destroying the demon inside him but maybe he'd stopped trying to find a way. Father Correa had spoken of Cole's *noble weakness*. That was probably it. Cole believed he was making a noble sacrifice by remaining in that room and forever holding the unholy beast within him.

Although Cole might have given up hope to destroy the creature, the voice she heard emanating from the dead junkie Walter gave her hope. Clearly, forces were at work that Cole was unwilling to acknowledge. Maybe it wasn't an angel that had spoken to her but it was *something*. That something might be the key to destroying Cole's demon. She had promised to find Cole a safe place to hide out and she would. But then she'd go and talk to Father Correa again. There must be some way of destroying the creature or banishing it from our world so it would never return.

"What are you thinking about now, Sara Sarque?" Cole asked, seeing her lost in thought.

Sara ignored the question. Ahead, she spotted the exit they needed from the flood channel and sprinted to it. A set of iron rungs led up an access shaft. She climbed quickly to its metal cover and put her shoulder into it to leverage it open. She lifted it just enough to peer into the surrounding alley. It looked deserted. At least, she saw no one in the one direction she could look. There was no way to tell if there was anyone in the opposite direction, maybe a cop or security guard. They had to risk it, so she pivoted the cover out of the way and hastily climbed through.

8.

Cole followed Sara up through the access tube into a grimy alley behind a brick building that stood a half dozen stories high. He was relieved the alley was vacant. No one was lurking there to spot a couple of fugitives emerging from underground. Sara led him to a dented metal door at the rear of the grubby building. He figured this was where she meant for him to hide out. It looked seedy, but if it offered sanctuary, he would gladly take it.

He needed to surround himself again with plain walls upon which he could write the ancient blocking incantation to shield himself and his *tar'dor* from others. He couldn't allow another blood bath like the one that morning, the mangled bodies, arms and legs and necks twisted and broken. He recalled the first terrifying time he'd seen carnage like that. It had been ten years ago at the seminary academy when he and his friend—his *best friend* at the time, another student by the name of Marek Meyers—were experimenting with incantations and everything had gone so very, very wrong. Poor Marek. He then became world-famous for all those deaths, the notorious "Seminary Slayings," and was sentenced to life in prison for murders that were never truly murders.

"We should be safe here," Sara said, breaking his train of thought. "From cops at least. Then we figure out how to kill that thing inside you. Once we've done that, I'm going to find Nia to make sure she's okay and—"

"There is no *we*," Cole cut in. "I just need a room. And a lot of black felt tip markers. Find me a place I can hide in for now, you owe me that, then we part ways. I'll contact the nuns. They'll find a more permanent place for me to live."

"That's still your plan? Just curl up in a cubby hole and write those inscriptions on the walls all day and all night? That's no life."

"Says the girl who curls up in a flophouse and takes drugs all day," he replied tartly.

Sara winced at this. It looked like she might fire back a snarky reply, but a slot in the door abruptly opened. Two eyes peered out.

"Cliff," Sara spoke into the slot. "I need to see Raphael. It's urgent."

"Who's he?" a man asked through the slot, his voice deep.

"Cole? He's cool. Well, he's an *asshole*. But you can trust him."

After a long pause, the door finally opened. Sara entered quickly. Cole lingered in the alley. "What *is* this place?"

Sara grabbed him by his ragged coat and yanked him inside.

Cole found himself in a large bland room with a service elevator at one end and a table and a heavy safe at the other end. There were drugs and cash on the table, *lots* of drugs and cash. The guy who let them in, Cliff, was a hulking fellow. He looked like a defensive tackle or maybe a pro wrestler. A couple of other men, both armed, guarded the cash and drugs.

Cliff smelled the stench of Cole's ratty clothes. "Shit? Sara, you bring some foul *vagrant* in here?"

"He's not. He's *clean*. We had to borrow those clothes. Long story." Sara turned to Cole. "Strip."

"What?" Cole asked, shocked.

"Take your clothes off," she demanded.

Cole looked to Cliff and the other men, hoping they would all burst out laughing at the joke. They didn't. They really wanted him to strip.

"Here?" Cole asked, then spotted a side door that might lead to some privacy. When he stepped toward it, the armed men blocked his path.

"Yes, *here*," Cliff said, his deep voice rumbling. He motioned to a trash can in the corner. "Throw that foul shit away. *All* of it."

Cole fumbled with the buttons on his grubby trench coat.

"You got something he can wear?" Sara asked Cliff.

Cliff nodded to one of his men, who stepped into the side room. Cole meant to wait for some fresh clothes but—

"*Now!*" Cliff barked at Cole, "I won't ask again."

Cole got the message. He kicked off his shoes and pulled off the rancid clothes. He expected the others to turn their backs to give him some privacy. Only Sara turned away. Once Cole got all his clothes off, underwear too, he saw Sara peek to get a look at his butt. Cole was lanky, but at least his physique had filled out some since he was in seminary school.

Buck-naked now, Cole shoved the ratty old clothes into the trash can. Cliff motioned for him to stand in a far corner of the room. Reluctantly, he did, holding his junk, burning with embarrassment. One of the armed men grabbed a fire extinguisher out of a closet and blasted Cole with white fire extinguisher powder. Cole coughed at the fumes but grudgingly turned around so the man could spray him on all sides. A dry shower, of sorts.

"You'll thank me later," Cliff told Cole, "when you're not plucking lice from your crotch."

Cliff pressed the service elevator call button and the elevator door slid open. Sara, grinning at Cole's embarrassment, strode into the lift. Cole grabbed his shoes off the floor with one hand and followed her, still holding his junk with his other hand. The other armed man finally returned with fresh jeans and a plaid shirt and tossed them to Cole.

As the door closed, Cliff gave them a wry smile. "Thank you for your patronage. Customer satisfaction is our highest priority."

As the elevator rose, Cole tugged the jeans on. "No underwear?" Cole muttered. "Just jeans and a shirt?"

Sara smirked. "Ladies love a man who goes commando."

"What exactly is this place?" Cole asked as he finished dressing.

"Don't worry about it."

"I'm getting really tired of you saying that."

The elevator lurched to a stop at the top floor of the building. The door opened into a musty hallway that led to another door where another hulking bouncer nodded to Sara. He let them into what looked to Cole like a modern-day opium den. Hookers and their customers lounged about on threadbare furniture, smoking cigars and cigarettes. He saw loads of coke and other drugs on coffee tables and end tables. The décor seemed to date from the 60's or 70's. Cracked windows offered jagged views of downtown.

Snapping a black wooden yo-yo into his palm, a tall and elegant Hispanic man rose from a nearby sofa and gave Sara a warm smile. "Sara dear, I presume you've come to reconcile your account." He turned to Cole and shook his hand. "And Mr. Cole Cameron. Sorry we didn't get a chance to meet earlier. I'm Raphael. Any friend of Sara's is a friend of mine."

Before Cole could object that Sara was *not* his friend, she cut him off. "Raph, things went pear-shaped. Can we talk in private?"

Raphael led them through a far door to a large corner office. There was a massive desk with a big mirror on the wall behind it. Two of Raphael's men were watching a big flat-screen TV that was mounted to another wall. They both seemed to recognize Cole too. He realized that Raphael and his men must have been the muscle who helped Sara kidnap him from St. Mary's. She couldn't have done that all by herself. He wondered what indignities he suffered when they hauled him to that derelict building. He hoped he wasn't just tossed in the trunk of a pimp-mobile.

"Boss, you got to see this," one of the men said, nodding to a breaking news broadcast on television.

A male TV reporter reported breathlessly that there was "one officer dead at the scene, with reports of other victims." The broadcast showed an exterior view of the derelict building where the deputy and the junkies had been killed. "This man is wanted for questioning," the reporter intoned, and now the TV showed bodycam video of Cole, his face visible. "Along with what appears to be a young woman. Both fled the scene." The TV then showed shaky bodycam video of Sara—too blurry to make out her face.

Raphael glared at the TV, then pulled a shiny Colt 45 from his desk and aimed it at Cole. His men drew handguns too.

"You brought a cop killer, *here*?" Raphael hissed at Sara.

"Cole didn't kill anyone," Sara insisted, waving for them to lower their guns but they held their weapons steady on Cole.

"So what the hell happened?" Raphael demanded.

"Since you won't believe a word I say without proof," she nodded to Cole, "show them what you got."

Cole hated that he now had to reveal his secret inner beast to these men but, if he didn't, things might go even more "pear-shaped" soon. So he tugged open his shirt. Raphael and his men tensed up on their guns, as if Cole might be hiding a weapon. They relaxed when they saw just a bare chest. Their eyes then went wide as Cole gave his *tar'dor* enough leash to writhe just beneath his skin. For a moment, he let it surge from his chest a foot or so toward them, providing a strobe-like glimpse of snarling teeth.

Raphael and his men stumbled back, stunned. Cole pulled the creature back inside him and let his chest return to normal.

"Holy shit!" Raphael blurted, nearly dropping his Colt 45.

Sara motioned again for the men to lower their guns. "You don't want to shoot it," she said. "That'll just make it mad. Right, Cole?"

Cole nodded nervously as he buttoned his shirt back up.

"That thing got loose," Sara explained. "*It* killed the cop. And a couple of others. It wasn't Cole's fault."

"Sara, when you talked before about demons and possessions and exorcists, I thought you were tripping." Raphael motioned to the door. "No way you stay here with that unholy *thing*."

"There are security cams and traffic cams all over town," Sara replied, exasperated. "He'll be spotted. That's why I brought him here."

"I just need a room with bare walls to write on," Cole told Raphael. "It doesn't have to be big. You must have plenty of rooms where your 'gentlemen clients' take those hookers and—"

"Out!" Raphael waved his gun again.

Cole and Sara reluctantly headed for the door.

"Wait," Raphael said. "That thing you did where you let it surge under your skin, does that have to be under your chest?"

Cole shrugged, not understanding what the man was getting at.

"If you could do that over your face instead of your chest, you could disguise yourself, right?" Raphael told him. "For a while. Enough to avoid being seen on security cameras, at least."

"It might work," Cole replied. "Never tried it before."

"Try it now," Sara told him.

Cole puzzled over exactly what to do. Then he hit upon an idea. The mental chamber he used to keep the *tar'dor* locked inside him didn't have to be a square room and it didn't have to be in his chest, where he usually visualized it. The chamber could have any shape and be anywhere within him. So he visualized the chamber moving up into his head, behind his face. In his mind, the chamber moved. He visualized the chamber's door taking on the shape of his face, and it did. He then shifted the door forward so it aligned with the contours of his face. Now, the tricky part. He needed to open that door just a bit to let the *tar'dor* surge slightly outward.

Cole looked at himself in the mirror and gave it a try. Nothing happened. He tried again. This time a roiling boiled up on his face, completely changing his features, like a weird funhouse mirror.

"That's sick!" yelled one of Raphael's men.

"Wicked!" shouted the other.

Cole mentally snapped the inner door shut. His face returned to normal.

"Wow!" Sara said, grinning. "Just *wow*. That was so cool."

Cole was secretly thrilled he'd impressed Sara, but he couldn't let her know. He was still mad at her, after all.

Raphael set his gun down and led Cole to the door. "Good luck.

But, Cole, if you do get caught by the cops, remember: you were never here. I don't know you. And I don't believe in any of this supernatural bullshit. It's not good for business. Just saying."

As Cole left the room, he saw that Sara was lingering behind. Her hands were shaking again.

"I need a moment with Sara," Raphael told Cole and then politely closed the door, leaving Cole waiting in the drug den.

As Cole paced awkwardly about, a few of the hookers and those *gentlemen clients* he had mentioned gave him bemused looks.

9.

"Why did you come here?" Raphael asked Sara bluntly the moment the door was shut with Cole left on the outside.

"I didn't know he was on the *news*," Sara replied, hoping that answer would satisfy Raphael.

"Sara, why come *here*?" he persisted and locked his eyes on her.

Sara knew she was busted. "I'm running dry."

Raphael grinned and fetched a bag of coke from a cabinet. When Sara reached for it, Raphael pulled it back. "Settle up first."

"You know I'm good for it," Sara replied. She wasn't sure she was anymore.

"What I know is you could be killed any moment—very unpleasantly—if that *thing* gets loose. And dead clients don't pay."

Raphael reached into his desk and pulled out a keypad device. He spun its display to face her. "Wire transfer from your off-shore account? Or crypto this time?"

Sara sighed. "Wire transfer."

She eyed the display with concern. "That much?"

"It does add up," Raphael replied, with another grin.

Sara entered her bank account number, hoping she still had enough in that account to cover the amount. Her funds wouldn't last forever. The device beeped approvingly.

Raphael checked the display to confirm the transaction. "Always a pleasure, Sara."

"Hey, you got a fake ID Cole could use?" she asked.

"You know I've got *everything*. I'm your one-stop shop."

He opened a drawer for her. It was filled with dozens and dozens of fake driver's licenses. Some for men. Some for women. All ages and ethnicities and hair colors. Mostly California, but some from other states too. She rummaged through and found one for a guy named Terry Walton who looked kind of like Cole. Similar age and hair color and skin tone, at least. It was better than nothing.

"You need one for yourself, Sara?"

"Nah, I've had my own for a few years now." She dug her fake ID from her pocket to make sure she still had it with her. It had her actual photo but with a phony name—Cathy Smith.

"Then I'll just put the one ID for Cole on your new tab."

"Nothing's ever free from you?" Sara asked.

"Business is business," Raphael grinned.

As Sara headed for the door, he called after her.

"Why are you sticking with him, Sara? You two an item now?"

"Cole? An *item*? Oh, *hell no!* He's not my type. But it's my fault he's in this mess. Besides, there's more to it than just demons. Cole says there are no angels, but . . . " She chose not to explain why she needed to believe existence didn't end at death, that the soul carried on, that maybe her brother Timothy was somehow helping her, guiding her, forgiving her.

"But?" Raphael persisted.

"I'd better go before Cole gets into too much trouble out there." She stuffed the bag of coke in a pocket of her cargo pants and left.

In the main room, a tall transgender hooker was teasing Cole, her hands all over him, and he was red-faced with embarrassment.

"Cole, leave the poor girl alone and fetch the elevator," Sara told him. Before he could protest, she darted into a nearby restroom.

Inside, the sink counter had a tray of little spoons and straws. She quickly laid out a line of coke from her bag and snorted it. Her body craved crack but this would work for now. She paused then to check herself in the mirror and fix her hair. As she did, she silently whispered the blocking incantation Cole had taught her—*Loch lym soth bewen ma-thay.* She could not allow herself to be possessed by one of those vicious demons.

She left the bathroom and found Cole at the service elevator, holding the door open for her, impatient. They hopped in and she pressed the button for the hotel lobby, one floor above the back alley entrance they had first come through. As the elevator rattled down the shaft, Cole gave her a look of obvious disapproval. No doubt, he knew she had just scored some coke and had boosted herself in the bathroom.

"You recognize this place?" she asked him, nodding to a placard above the bank of elevator buttons that read *Moderne Hotel.*

Like New York's famous *Chelsea Hotel,* the *Moderne* was of the same vintage and notoriety, a rundown venue with a long and ignominious history. It was favored by those living on the edge of society, aspiring authors, actors, and playwrights, drug dealers and drug abusers, bohemians of all kinds. It now rented its rooms by the week.

Cole shrugged a no. "As long as it's got rooms to rent and you've got a credit card, I'm sure it'll be fine. Then we part ways."

The elevator door opened on a lobby furnished with dusty sofas and chairs. A motley collection of guests lounged about.

Cole headed to the reception desk. "Sara, you *can* pay for the room, right? And I need black markers, lots of them."

"Cole, you can't be serious. We need to get that *thing* out of you. We need to kill it. So let's go and talk to Father Correa. Maybe he can help. Or he'll know someone who can." She didn't wait for an answer and sprinted through the main lobby to the front exit.

"What, no!" Cole called after her. "Sara!"

On the street out front, she spotted Raphael's Town Car parked in its usual spot in a nearby loading zone. She was relieved to see that the usual guy who tended to the car, an elderly gent named Sal, was there buffing the car's fenders. He would be no trouble.

Sara jauntily approached him. "Sal, keys in the car?"

"Sara! Always a pleasure to see you," Sal beamed.

"Raph wants me to run a quick errand," Sara told him. "Back in a jiff." She kissed Sal on the cheek and hopped in the driver's seat.

Cole, bewildered, climbed into the passenger side.

"An *errand*?" Sal stood beside the car, flustered, clearly not knowing what to do. "Mr. Raphael, he never *told* me that—"

"Does he tell you *everything*?"

Before he could answer, Sara gunned the engine and roared off.

As Sara drove, Cole fumbled for a seat belt.

"Did we just *steal* this car?" he asked her.

"Borrowed," Sara corrected. "He'll get it back."

"Raphael strikes me as a man you don't want to piss off."

"Don't worry about it," Sara replied, peering in the rear-view mirror to make sure they weren't already being followed by Raphael's men in one of his many other cars.

She then spotted a traffic camera mounted above an intersection ahead. She pointed it out to Cole and he distorted his face as they passed through the intersection, making himself unrecognizable.

"That is so cool!" She beamed. "I'd love to be able to do that."

"Look, I'm happy to see Father Correa. If *he'll* see me," Cole told her. "And the Sisters at *Our Lady of the Angels* should be able to find a place for me to stay since *you* obviously won't. The archdiocese has properties all over the city. But I don't see how Father Correa can be of any help."

"Why not?" Sara asked.

"Remember those old books in my room? Those had been his. It was the world's last remaining research on *true* demonology. Not the bullshit of Dante. Not Fallen Angels and Devils and Satan. Real demonology."

Sara turned a corner heading toward the cathedral.

"If there had been any clue in *any* of those books on how to get rid of the damned thing, he'd have found it years ago. Or I would have. Or—"

"Cole, stop being so pessimistic. *Sheesh.*"

Sara turned another corner and the massive modernist cathedral loomed nearby. She parked the Town Car just across the street. She checked her phone and saw a number of increasingly stern messages from Raphael. The man was indeed *pissed* she had "bor-rowed" his car. He'd get it back soon enough. She shut off the phone and would now keep it off, not so much because of Raph, but she didn't want police tracking her if they somehow ID'd her from earlier that morning when the deputy was killed.

She and Cole hurried into the cathedral, with Cole doing his best to shield his face from tourists who were snapping pictures of its stylish entryway. Inside, she looked about for someone to ask to find Father Correa. She spotted the same young priest who tried to talk to her before.

"We need to see Father Correa," she told him.

"I'm sorry, the Father fell ill a while ago. Perhaps I can help."

"Ill? He's not here?"

"He suffered a stroke. He's been in a rest home for some time."

Sara was stunned by this. "But I . . . "

She looked to Cole who seemed baffled as well.

"He's not recovered after all?" Cole asked the priest.

"The doctors say there's little hope of recovery," the man replied.

Sara eyed the side chapel with the confessional she'd been in earlier. "But I swear I . . . " She had spoken with Father Correa that very morning.

"Which rest home?" Cole asked. "I'd like to pay my respects."

"Our Lady of Rest," the priest replied. "It's over on 10th street."

Sara spotted a security guard eyeing them and was worried he might recognize Cole from the news. She tugged Cole to the exit.

Soon, they were back in the Town Car with Sara driving. "I swear I spoke with Father Correa. In a confessional. This morning."

"You were in a *confessional*? So you never *saw* him?" Cole asked her. "No clear view."

"No, but he said it was him. Why would anyone lie about that?"

"Then . . . what is going on?" Cole asked.

"Maybe it was like that voice I heard coming from the dead junkie," Sara told Cole. "Something was speaking to me from *beyond*. So I only thought there was someone on the other side of the confessional."

"But there are no angels," Cole said, firmly.

"And demons never talk, right?" Sara replied.

She would accept Cole's claim that demons never talk—they were vicious beasts after all—but she refused to believe there were no angels.

After several more turns, she pulled the car to a stop at the Our Lady of Rest nursing home. As she and Cole made their way to its entrance, she paused to eye a row of sculptures of chubby little cherubs who peered down from above its front door, smiling benevolently, and she wondered if she truly was being watched from above or, if not above, from *somewhere*.

10.

Sara strode to the reception desk of the nursing home where a dotty older receptionist smiled up from her crossword puzzle.

"And you folks are?" she asked as she set the puzzle down.

Before Sara could answer, Cole cut her off. "I was a seminary student under Father Correa. Then we worked closely at the Catholic Linguistic Institute. I'm hoping to say hello."

The receptionist smiled warmly. "Ah, yes. Well, I'm afraid he doesn't talk much anymore." She squinted up at Cole. "Have you visited before? You look so very familiar."

A TV flickered silently behind her in a waiting area. It showed a news broadcast about the deaths at the derelict building that morning, with Cole's face shown as a "person of interest" in the investigation. Sara was relieved when the broadcast then switched to the weather.

"Yes, no doubt from a prior visit," Cole told the woman.

Good, Sara thought. Cole can lie too. It might come in handy.

The receptionist looked to Sara. "And, young lady, you are?"

"My fiancée," Cole quickly added.

Sara had to stifle a smirk. Cole was a more brazen liar than she was, for she wore no engagement ring. And, of course, the notion that a woman like her would marry a square like Cole was *absurd*.

"Well, congratulations," the receptionist beamed. She pointed to a pair of elevators. "One flight up. To the right."

As Sara and Cole headed to the lifts, the receptionist called after them. "I do hope he still recognizes you."

Once the elevator door closed, Sara smirked. "Fiancée? You wish."

Reaching the second floor, Cole and Sara headed down the hallway, reading nametags on doors until they found the right room.

Father Correa, who looked to be in his seventies, was propped in a wheelchair in a brightly lit room. Sara winced when she saw his face. Sagging features, unfocussed eyes. The man must have had a major stroke.

Cole teared up as he hugged the old priest, then knelt beside him. "Father . . . Miguel . . . I am so sorry," Cole said. "I heard you had a stroke. I had no idea it was so bad. I should have visited before. I am ashamed."

Sara teared up a bit now too.

Father Correa looked at Cole. There seemed to be a flicker of recognition in the old man's eyes. "Cole?" he whispered.

"My situation has gotten worse," Cole replied. "Much worse."

"Is it time for lunch?" Father Correa asked, his mind no doubt drifting.

Cole gave Sara a defeated look.

Father Correa then suddenly straightened up in his wheelchair. His head tilted back and his mouth opened.

Words came out. "Marek. He will have your answers," a voice said. "Go to him. Soon. He waits."

"See!" Sara exclaimed to Cole. "That's not *him*. That's an angel or—"

Cole schussed Sara. "Marek Meyer? But he is—"

"Use these names," the voice said. "Cathy Smith. Terry Walton. They will be on the list. Go soon. He waits. He knows."

Cathy Smith? Terry Walton? Sara was stunned to hear those two names. And Marek Meyer—*the* Marek Meyer—the notorious psycho killer?

Father Correa slumped again and resumed his vacant expression.

Sara grabbed Cole and pulled him to his feet. "Marek Meyer?" she demanded. "Marek *Martin* Meyer?"

Cole nodded as if that were no big deal.

"The Seminary Slayer? *That* Marek Martin Meyer?"

Cole nodded again.

"You *know* him?" Sara was gob-smacked.

"Yeah, we have a bit of a history. Best friends, once."

"The guy who slaughtered eight students?" Sara recalled the endless news stories from ten years ago. The seminary students had been brutally murdered, limbs snapped, some with their heads twisted fully around. The police said they had never seen anything so brutal. So *inhuman*.

"Not him," Cole said. "It was a *tar'dor*."

Sara understood. Those murders had indeed been inhuman. It had been one of the demons that killed those students. *Holy shit!*

"And we're supposed to visit *him*?" Sara sputtered.

"Seems so," Cole said with maddening nonchalance and turned to leave.

Sara grabbed him again. "Wait! First off. Cole, you need to acknowledge that *voice*. That was a voice from *beyond*. That was an angel. Or something. Don't tell me we're *both* hallucinating now."

Cole nodded. "It wasn't Father Correa, that's for sure."

"And demons don't talk," Sara said.

Cole nodded again.

"So now we're supposed to go and meet with Marek Martin Meyer," Sara declared. "You know he's in a maximum security prison, right?"

"That must be what he meant by the list," Cole replied. "It's got to be the approved visitor list at the prison. He's incarcerated at a max security facility up near Lancaster. We'll need to get fake IDs with those names."

"Yeah, funny thing about that." She dug in her pocket and pulled out the two fake IDs. "I took the liberty of getting you a fake ID at Raphael's. Figured it might come in handy. I've had one of my own for a few years now. We junkies prefer to travel incognito."

She handed Cole the IDs.

"Cathy Smith? Terry Walton?" Cole sputtered as he read the names. "How could that voice *know*? How is this possible?"

"Right? I mean how is *any* of this possible?" Sara asked. "Yesterday, I was just a little junkie girl minding her own business. Now the weirdest of weird shit is happening. The *weirdest*."

She took the IDs from Cole and stuffed them back in her pocket.

"I guess we're taking a road trip," she said, heading for the door.

Cole followed her and they made their way down the hallway to the elevators. Sara spotted the elderly receptionist standing at one end of the hallway and gave her a friendly wave. The woman didn't wave back. She just stared at Sara and Cole. The hair on the back of Sara's neck rose. She turned to Cole and now spotted an orderly at the other end of the hallway. He too was just standing and watching. Swaying. Staring.

But the fear didn't really grip her until she saw the look on Cole's face, the look of dread, the look of growing panic.

11.

"Sara, get down on the floor!" Cole yelled, hoping the two *tar'dors* would come only after him and leave her alone.

The receptionist and the orderly were both charging now, converging from opposite directions, moving faster than any human could move. Their arms and legs were twisting and folding at grotesque angles. Cole could hear bones breaking, tendons and ligaments snapping. When a *tar'dor* was in attack mode, it didn't care if it killed its host's body, which would be discarded.

Sara dove to the floor at the last moment as the orderly charged at her, the *tar'dor* inside that man's disjointed body emerging now to attack. At the same time, the *tar'dor* possessing the receptionist emerged from that poor woman's body to attack from the opposite direction.

Cole had no choice but to unleash his own beast. It exploded out of him in defense. The fight was furious and chaotic. Otherworldly roars. Deafening screeches. Cole saw only strobe-like glimpses of teeth and claws and strange insect-like limbs. Other patients in the rest home peered out from their doors, bewildered and terrified. Sara stumbled to her feet and waved for them to get back. Shocked, most did. She hustled to push an oblivious elderly man who didn't see the danger back into his room.

Cole saw that neither of the two attacking *tar'dors* were especially powerful on their own. Together, though, they put up a ferocious fight and Cole's *tar'dor* was badly bitten and lacerated. Still, it finally succeeded in killing the demonic beast that had possessed the orderly, then the one from the receptionist. The dead creatures slumped, flickered briefly, then disappeared. Cole's demon then charged away down the hallway.

"*Auwk mym doth be en thay!*"

Cole repeated the command again and again as he struggled to pull his *tar'dor* back inside him. Finally, he managed to draw it back and lock it within the inner psychic chamber, but it was exhausting. Cole slumped to the floor beside the bodies of the receptionist and the orderly.

Sara hurried to Cole and pulled him back to his feet. "We've got to get out of here, Cole! Everyone's going to call 911."

Cole had never felt so exhausted after a battle before and wondered if it truly was exhaustion from working to pull the *tar'dor* back inside him, or whether the injuries to the creature were taking a toll on him too, as though they were in some sort of symbiotic relationship. He wondered how he had managed yet again, as in the derelict building, to pull the beast back into him. Was it just that the creature had been weakened by its injuries? It almost seemed as though something was helping him, something unseen.

Now was not the time to try to figure that out. Sara was right. They needed to get out of here before police swarmed the building. He let her help him to the elevator, then down to the ground floor, then out to the car. He collapsed in the passenger seat.

#

They rode in silence for a long while without Cole paying much attention to where they were headed. He kept thinking of the two innocents at the rest home who lost their lives. Sara, too, seemed shaken by their deaths. As they drove, Cole regained his strength.

"You okay?" Sara finally asked.

"It gets harder every time," he replied.

Cole looked around and saw they were on a freeway heading north past the San Fernando Valley. "We're heading *where*?"

"To see Marek Meyer, of course. It's about an hour's drive to the prison." She handed him the fake ID. "You're Terry Walton, remember?"

Cole squinted at the ID. "I don't look all that much like this guy. The hair color is right but—"

"I've visited friends out there before," Sara cut in. "The guards mostly just make sure the IDs match the names on the visitor log."

"I don't think it'll be that easy," Cole replied.

Sara looked at him. "That trick you did before . . . Can you control it?"

He eyed the fake ID. "If you expect me to make my face look like this guy's, forget it."

"No, not that. Just make your features a little less distinctive. A little blander. Human facial recognition is all about picking up on a few key distinctive features," she explained. "Bland goes unnoticed."

"You know this, how?" Cole asked. Sara Sarque, the *prima donna* junkie, seemed far more knowledgeable than he first assumed.

"Don't worry about it," she grinned.

"Yeah, that never gets old."

Sara dug a makeup compact with a mirror from her jacket pocket and tossed it to Cole. "Give it a try. You've got some time to figure it out."

Around them, the traffic started to thin out as sprawling suburbs gave way to rural areas.

"So, Cole, there's something I've been wondering about. Why

did you show me your demon back at the sanitarium this morning? You let it surge beneath your chest. You could have kept it hidden inside you."

"I was trying to *scare* you away, obviously."

"You weren't. Cole, you were trying to impress me. Admit it."

Cole laughed nervously. "You are so full of yourself, Sara. Why would I want to impress *you*, little Miss Junkie?"

"Okay, sure. *Whatever*, but I know you were."

She was right, Cole knew. He couldn't help himself. Guys like him rarely ever impressed women like her. So he showed her his secret. It was a mistake. If she hadn't seen the *tar'dor*, she might have just left him alone and none of this would have happened. He'd still be back safe in his room.

"Marek Martin Meyer!" Sara suddenly declared. "I'm going to meet the notorious Marek Martin Meyer. Well, Cole, you do know how to show a gal a good time." She winked at him. "So how is it you know Meyer?"

"Don't worry about it," Cole said drolly.

"Hey, only I get to say that. Besides, I can tell you're dying to dish some dirt on him, so start dishing."

Cole shrugged. "Okay, if you really want to know . . . The story begins with the Fall of Constantinople in 1453."

"*Gawd.* Constantinople?"

He looked at her. "You want the story or what?"

"Give me the Cliff's Notes version."

"Okay, here goes. Constantinople was sacked by the Ottomans that year. But that's not important. What's important is there were ancient texts in a cathedral there on mysticism. Texts unknown to the Church in Rome."

Cole could imagine the panic back then as priests ran from a medieval cathedral that had been set afire, clutching their precious scrolls, escaping on horse-drawn carts just before Ottoman soldiers arrived.

"Those scrolls," Cole continued, "were rescued and sent to Rome. A priest named Father Ignatius had the task of translating them into Latin."

Cole closed his eyes and could visualize the priest hunkered beside a sputtering candle, translating the scrolls into leatherbound notebooks, the same books in his room at St. Mary's until Sara had torched the place.

"What the priest found was remarkable: a language he said pre-dated all others."

"The language on the walls of your room?" Sara asked.

Cole nodded. "The writings spoke of a *latus mundi,* a side world. A place of bestial demons. *Tar'dors* is the name they were given in that ancient tongue. Sara, you've seen what those creatures can do."

As Cole told the story, he also worked on his "bland disguise." He peered into the compact mirror and, after several tries, he started to get the hang of it. He could calm the roiling beneath his skin so that his facial features would become bland and generic. Non-descript and forgettable.

Cole set the compact down and looked at Sara. "Long story short: Father Ignatius was excommunicated. He took the texts to Bulgaria where they were eventually buried by a massive earthquake. Flash forward five and a half centuries. Two seminary students and their tutor found the texts."

"The students were you and Marek Meyer?" Sara asked. "And the tutor was Father Correa?"

Cole nodded. He recalled the day vividly. He and Marek were both still in their early twenties back then. Young, earnest, collegiate. They'd been digging through rubble when they came across the cache of old leatherbound texts. Father Correa had hurried over to see what they had found and together they spent days poring over the Latin translations.

"And . . . " Sara prodded, as Cole was lost in his thoughts.

"And Father Correa didn't believe any of it. Not back then. Demons from another realm? Ancient commands that could summon them and control them? He scoffed at such nonsense. But Marek and I believed. We hatched a plan to invoke a *tar'dor*, one we could control, one we could use to vanquish other such creatures. To assassinate them. Execute them." Cole looked over at Sara. "The *keeper* was supposed to be me. But Marek went ahead one night on his own. He wasn't strong enough. He couldn't leash it within him. Eight innocents died in that seminary dorm that night. It would have been more except the *tar'dor* made the mistake of leaping into me."

Cole shuddered at his memories of that night. Bodies of the other seminary students, many of whom had been his good friends, were strewn along the dorm's hallway, its walls splattered with blood, a scene of horrific carnage. Marek had been standing at the far end of the corridor, terrified, panicked. The demon was inside him, surging under his chest. Marek was trying—and failing—to recite the ancient commands to hold onto it.

The *tar'dor* within Marek had then burst from his chest and charged toward Cole. It was the first time Cole had ever seen one, at least to the extent a person ever could see one. All he saw were terrifying strobe-like glimpses of the creature, flashes of insect-like limbs, sharp talons, a bristly and hairy carapace, a vicious snapping maw, fangs like jaundiced razors.

Cole shuddered now at those horrific memories. "I'd already memorized the leashing command. So when it pounced into me, I trapped it within me, in that psychic chamber I told you of. That was ten years ago."

"The spell, I mean the *command*, to leash it is *Ach mim* something something, right?" Sara asked. "I remember you yelling it over and over."

"Auwk mym doth be en thay," he corrected her.

"So Marek Meyer went to prison for killings committed by a *tar'dor*?" Sara asked. "The same one now inside you?"

Cole nodded.

"Why doesn't he just conjure another? There are many more of them, right?"

"The ancient command to invoke a *tar'dor* can only be used once by a given person to become a keeper," Cole explained. "Marek can try again and again to leash some other *tar'dor* inside him. None will obey the command. He shot his wad, so to speak."

Sara turned off one highway onto another and followed signs pointing the way to the prison.

"Besides, Marek willingly pled guilty," Cole explained. "Those deaths were on his conscience. Still are. He does his penance in prison."

"So then you became an exorcist?"

"Father Correa was my handler. He researched cases of *alleged* possessions all around the world to find ones that were true possessions—cases where a *tar'dor* had entered our world. It usually happens several times a year. And, of course, the victim's families always thought it was a demonic possession. The Devil. Satan. *Beelzebub.* They were always shocked and disappointed when the 'exorcist' who showed up—me—was not a priest. But we got the job done. My *tar'dor* never failed to defeat the other one. I'm not sure how Marek did it, but when he called a *tar'dor* into our world that first night, he got the most powerful one of all."

"Over time, it became harder to control?" Sara asked.

"After I nearly lost control of it on a job in New Mexico, I swore to never unleash it again. But Father Correa talked me into it. A month later, in a village in Guatemala, it got loose."

He shuddered at memories of bloody carnage.

"I *finally* got it back under control—but not until a dozen villagers were slaughtered. We barely escaped the country as the local police hunted us. So, I got that room at St. Mary's and spent the last five years there trying to figure out how to either destroy the creature or take it back to its own realm and leash it there so it can never return."

"Sounds perfect!" Sara exclaimed. "Let's make that happen."

"If I only knew *how* . . . " Cole sighed. "Father Ignatius wrote of something called *Amin-aer-ing*. Loosely translated: *spirit walking*. I think it might be the key to taking the beast back into its realm to leash it there so it can never return. But Ignatius wrote most of his notes in code to avoid the Church inquisitors who believed his work was blasphemous. Over the years I could eventually decode all of it, but still no clue about how to spirit walk. I think there must be some special command to recite, but I have no clue what it is. Of course, I could just let the creature go free and it would eventually return to its realm. But not until many, many had died. And, as I said before, it would just keep coming back into our world to hunt again."

"That voice. It said 'Marek will have your answers. Got to him. He waits.' Does that mean Marek has figured out the spell, or command, or *whatever* it is, to take that thing back to its own realm?" Sara asked.

"Maybe. Hopefully. But I'm baffled by whatever that voice was."

"Because demons don't talk and you don't believe in angels."

Cole tested his facial disguise one last time, and it worked well enough to turn his features into a bland and unremarkable face. He handed the compact mirror back to Sara. "Okay, I told you my story. Now it's your turn. How did an obviously smart girl like you become a *junkie*?"

"Oh, look! We're here." Sara pulled the car into the dusty prison parking lot. "Saved by the bell."

12.

The prison was set amid flat stretches of sagebrush in the high desert north of Los Angeles. Sara joined a short line of cars at the entry station to the visitor parking lot. Beside her, Cole was fidgeting with worry.

"They probably scan license plates," Cole told her. "What if Raphael reported this car stolen?"

"Not his style. Men like Raphael *never* call the cops."

As each vehicle stopped briefly at the entry station, guards thrust mirrors on long poles under the cars to spot any explosives or contraband hung underneath. Car trunks were popped open and briefly inspected.

"There's nothing in the trunk to worry about?" Cole asked.

Shit. Sara hadn't thought about that. "Too late to check now."

She was waved forward and she and Cole rolled their windows down. Guards peered inside the car with flashlights. One guard motioned for her to pop the trunk. While silently saying a quick prayer, Sara pulled the trunk release and waited as the guard opened the trunk and looked inside.

Finding nothing, the guards waved them toward a visitor's lot. Relieved, Sara pulled into a spot and, just before climbing from the car, she remembered the bag of coke in her pocket. She hid it in the glove compartment as Cole gave her a look.

It was a short walk to the entrance. As she eyed the bleak prison, she felt she deserved to be locked up here, not for her own recreational drug use—what she chose to put in her body was her own damn business—but because she had given her brother Timothy the coke that led to his death. She hadn't known it was laced with LSD. That was small consolation for the tragedy that unfolded, his long fall from her high balcony.

Sara shook off the painful memories as she and Cole entered the building and lined up behind other visitors at a metal detector. A guard was checking IDs against a list on a clipboard. Other visitors soon began to queue up behind Cole.

"Give me a bland face," Sara whispered to Cole as they waited.

Cole worked his disguise trick and she watched as his face became bland and forgettable. The trick worked well but she worried that, once the guards were all looking at him, his nerves might get the better of him.

She had an idea. She dug her metal cigarette lighter from her pants pocket and slipped it to him. "Put this in your pocket."

Cole eyed the metal detectors. "But it'll trigger the—"

"Exactly. Draw their attention to the lighter, not your face."

They were up next so Sara strode forward and handed the entry guard her fake ID. "Marek Martin Meyer," she announced loudly and proudly. "We're here to see Marek Martin Meyer."

"Good for you," the guard replied, rolling his eyes.

The guard checked the name, Cathy Smith, on her ID against the clipboard list and waved for Sara to step through the metal detector. She passed through without incident.

"I'm here to see Meyer, too," he told the guard quietly as he handed the man his fake ID.

As the guard looked down to check the fake name on the ID against the visitor list, Sara saw that Cole was struggling with his disguise. For a moment, the fangs of the demon inside him emerged from his face.

Sara gave Cole a sharp look and he worked to try to get his disguise under control, but he was still struggling with it. Just as the guard looked up from his clipboard, Cole tossed the metal lighter onto a nearby tray. It clattered loudly there, distracting the guard. By the time he looked at Cole again, he'd gotten his disguise back under control.

"Almost forgot," Cole said, pointing to the lighter. "I'd hate for that to set off the metal detector, am I right?"

"No lighters inside," the guard said flatly.

"Oh, well then." Cole tossed the lighter in a waste bin. "I can get a new one later. I mean, that was a nice one but—"

"Next!" the guard barked, annoyed now with the delay.

Cole stepped through the metal detector to join Sara and his face returned to normal. They followed signs to a Visitation Room.

Before long, Sara and Cole were sitting on one side of a long wooden table in a large room patrolled by guards. Inmates and visitors were spaced out along the table, talking to one another. There was no plexiglass barrier and no closed-circuit phones to talk through, which was nice. But the inmates all had their wrists locked to metal bars on their side of the table.

Most of the convicts looked hard-core, with arms sleeved with gang tattoos or other ink. This was no minimum security prison for white-collar offenders. The prison was Level 5. Max security. Its inmates were hard-core felons, murders. But, as Sara eyed them, none were as famous or notorious as Marek Martin Meyer. He was the Charley Manson of this prison.

She spotted Marek being escorted in by guards. He was the same age as Cole, early thirties. He looked out of place among the others. No tattoos. Clean cut. He still looked like a seminary student. Cole had a certain weather-beaten look about him from all his world travels, and his many battles with demons from the other realm. Marek had spent all those years locked in here, getting pudgy, staying pudgy.

When Marek arrived, he gave Cole and Sara a warm smile and waited politely as a guard locked his wrists to the metal bar on his side of the table.

Once the guard stepped away and was out of earshot, Marek leaned toward Cole with a big lopsided grin. "Hey, Cole. I mean

Terry. Thanks for coming. What's it been? Ten years?"

Cole seemed puzzled by the friendly greeting.

"Yeah, sorry I never visited," Cole muttered. He then nodded to Sara. "This is—"

"Sara, of course. I mean, *Cathy*," Marek added, loudly whispering her fake name. He winked as though it were all a joke.

Sara was baffled. She glanced at Cole. He looked confused too.

"Cole, relax. The guards watch but don't listen." He turned to Sara. "You are even more lovely in person. I'm so glad you came."

"You know me?" Sara asked, trying hard to figure this out.

"Marek, what's going on?" Cole asked. "We heard a weird voice from Father Correa. *Marek will have your answers.*"

Marek grinned. "In case you haven't figured it out, that was *me*."

"What?" Cole sputtered.

"That voice you heard coming from Father Correa, that was me." Marek turned to Sara. "Sorry, Sara, it wasn't the voice of an angel. Just me."

"The other voices, too?" Sara asked. "The voice I heard in the confessional?"

"Yeah," Marek shrugged, like a schoolboy confessing some minor infraction. "I guess I got your hopes up about higher powers and angels and all that. I didn't mean to. If Cole here didn't block off his room with all those incantations, I could have gone straight to him."

"How'd you know about my room?" Cole asked. "And how did you . . . ?" He trailed off, lost in thought.

Marek turned to Sara. "Cole's a smart guy. He'll figure it out. He's always been just a step or two behind me."

"Spirit walking!" Cole exclaimed, and nearby inmates and visitors looked over at him, annoyed. A guard glared at him too. Cole lowered his voice. "Marek, you finally figured out how to do that?"

Marek nodded and Cole looked thunderstruck.

"Sara, Father Ignatius believed there's a way for people—well, some of us anyway—to project our spirits from our flesh and—"

"Eavesdrop," Sara cut in, understanding now.

"Yes," Marek nodded. "That's part of it."

"And talk *through* others," Sara added.

"Sometimes," Marek replied. "The dying. Or those already half dead."

"Father Correa?" Cole asked, finally regaining his composure. "You spoke *through* Father Correa?"

Marek nodded, sadly. "His stroke was so bad that he's already half gone. It broke my heart but it allowed me to speak through him to you."

Sara recalled how Father Correa had been slumped in his wheelchair, then bolted upright. She understood now that a spectral version of Marek—invisible to her and Cole—must have slipped inside the old priest, much the same way that a *tar'dor* demon can slip inside a person. Marek had then spoken through Father Correa. That was why the voice had sounded so strange, as though it was not his voice, for it wasn't. Marek must have done the same thing with the junkie Walter as he lay dying.

"Marek, how did you finally figure out how to spirit walk?" Cole asked with curiosity and obvious envy.

"In a way, Father Correa's stroke opened that door for me," Marek began. "It seems that ten years ago he had found *another* manuscript in the ruins in Bulgaria. One he kept from *us*, Cole. After his stroke, when he was moved to that nursing home, someone must have gone through his belongings and found the old manuscript. Probably staff from the Linguistics Institute. The manuscript got scanned into the Institute's archives." He turned to Sara to explain. "All documents of the Institute are made public for researchers around the world to download as needed."

"And you get Internet access here?" Sara asked.

"I'm a model prisoner. They let me work in the prison library. I get an hour of Internet time there each day. The prison librarian loves me since I'm the only inmate who doesn't try to get around the porn filters." He chuckled. "Anywho, I found the scans of that manuscript."

"They were enciphered?" Cole asked.

Marek nodded. "An especially nasty code. So it took me a while to decode the whole manuscript, but once I did, I found the ancient command for spirit walking." He turned back to Sara. "That's our word for it. Or astral projection. In the ancient tongue, it is called *Amin-aer-ing*."

"So you could leave your body in your prison cell here, then travel anywhere?" Cole asked, in awe.

"I even entered the other realm," Marek explained. "That was a *big* mistake. There are no words to describe the horrors there."

Marek seemed shaken just thinking about it.

"After I returned," Marek continued. "I realized I somehow had allowed more *tar'dors* to enter our realm. More than usual, anyway. I can sense when one has entered our world and go to investigate." Marek again looked to Sara. "So I was there, *watching*, when that guy, Walter, was killed by a *tar'dor* and then your friend Nia was possessed by it. I'm so sorry about that. But I figured if I could get you to fetch Cole from the sanitarium, his *tar'dor* could kill it."

Sara recalled the creepy voice that had spoken to her. *Cole Cameron. Exorcist. Find him. Father Correa. Find him first.*

"You were there in that derelict building? You were watching us? Watching *me*?" Cole asked, annoyed.

"More than watching, Cole. I helped you get your *tar'dor* under control when it tried to get away."

Sara remembered how Cole had called out those ancient words. *Auwk mym doth be en thay.* He had struggled to pull his demon back inside him. It had nearly gotten free and killed her.

"I stood alongside you, Cole, helping. Because, you're right, you *can't* control it anymore. It's grown too powerful for you."

Something still didn't make sense to Sara. "Wait. In the confessional, there was no one there to talk through, right? Father Correa wasn't there. There was no one in the confessional but me."

Marek nodded. "That's a lot harder. *Visual* projection."

"You figured out *that* too?" Cole asked, not hiding his envy.

"Mostly. That's a step beyond mere spirit walking—manifesting a visible presence so people can *see* your spirit, some of it anyway. It takes far more effort. But, Sara, I was able to make you see movement on the other side of the confessional screen and let you hear a voice. *My child, when was your last confession?* I'm getting better at that sort of visible manifesting, but it's still much easier to talk through the dead or the dying."

"The fake IDs? You were eavesdropping at Raphael's?"

Marek nodded. Cole looked at both of them, puzzled.

"Sara held the fake IDs in her hand back at Raphael's office. So I got a peek at them and remembered the names. I thought it would be a clever idea to have those two names put on the visitor list here."

"But wait," Cole said, "Here's what I still don't understand. Why go through Sara? If you wanted to talk to *me*, you could have just—"

"I *tried* to spirit walk into your room at the sanitarium but all those incantations you wrote on the walls to keep *tar'dors* out also kept me out," Marek explained. "I needed *someone* to get you out of that room. I needed someone strong-willed to *haul* you out."

"Strong-willed?" Sara laughed. "That's a polite way of describing me, I guess."

"Sorry I had to drag you into all this, Sara," Marek told her. "But I needed to convince you that you needed to kidnap Cole. To do that I mimicked Father Correa's voice in the confessional. You wouldn't have gone to get Cole if the dying voice of some random junkie told you to."

"No junkie is *random*," Sara replied.

"Sorry, poor choice of words," Marek told her. "Besides, if I didn't send you to Cole, you'd just have been another dead victim of that *tar'dor*."

"That wasn't the only demon though," Cole noted. "There've been others. There was one in the underground flood channel."

"I was there, too." Marek turned to Sara. "Ordinarily, it's rare for *tar'dors* to enter our realm. Maybe just a half dozen a year. Now, far more are coming. That's why I need your help, both of you."

Cole shook his head no.

"Sara, did Cole tell you he has not just any *tar'dor* inside him, but the most powerful ever to enter our realm?"

"Yeah, and he won't shut up about it," Sara replied.

"Whose fault is it, Marek, that I have that *tar'dor* inside me?"

"Water under the bridge, Cole."

"*Water under the bridge*?" Cole glared at him. "Marek, I've been stuck holding that *demon* inside me for ten years!"

The guards heard the loud talk of "demons" and smirked.

"It's time to take it back to its realm and *destroy* it," Marek said.

"You know how?" Cole asked.

Marek nodded. Before he could say anything more, two police officers marched into the room and headed straight for them.

"Oh shit," Sara swore under her breath.

"Your IDs please," the first of the two officers—his name-tag read Officer Samson—said when he reached Sara and Cole.

Sara sheepishly pulled out her fake ID. Cole took out his too. The two officers—the other was named Tucker—glanced at the names on the IDs, then slid the two IDs into an evidence bag.

"Are you two aware," Officer Samson began, "that it's a violation of federal and state law to use false identification to enter a correctional facility?" Cole looked horrified. Sara just shrugged. Samson then continued, officiously, "and are you aware, Mr. Cameron, that you are wanted in connection with the murder of a law enforcement officer, and others?"

Cole looked like he was ready to pass out.

"Cole Cameron. Sara Sarque," Officer Tucker announced. "Hands behind your back."

Cole gave Sara a panicked look as they were both handcuffed.

13.

Sara feared Cole would panic as the two were marched to a pair of squad cars in the dusty prison parking lot. The deputies—Samson and Tucker—read them their rights. Cole looked like he might pass out.

As she was led to one car and Cole to the other, he called to her, distraught: "Sara, you've got a good attorney, right? For both of us?"

"Cole, relax," she told him. "We've got the best lawyer ever. A real nasty one. Fangs and claws and wicked teeth."

Officer Tucker chuckled. "Lady, every lawyer I met is like that."

"Just don't use him, Cole, until we're back downtown."

"Sara, I can't do that! You *know* I can't!"

"No choice," Sara said as they were put into separate squad cars.

Before long they were out on the highway heading back to the city. Sara had told Cole that *he* needed to relax but now she was the one struggling to calm herself, her hands fussing and fidgeting. It had been too long since her last hit. She should have had some coke before entering the prison. She thought now of Raphael. His car would, no doubt, be searched and then impounded for they would find the bag of coke in the glove compartment. He'd be furious. "Borrowing" his town car was bad enough, but letting it fall into the hands of the local 5-0 would be unforgivable.

She fidgeted more and struggled to get comfortable. It was hard. The handcuffs that locked her wrists behind her back dug into her forearms.

"You've got to listen carefully," a voice said.

At first, she thought it was the deputy driving the car who had spoken, but it wasn't. The voice came from the backseat where she sat, yet she was alone. Then she spotted a faint shape shimmering in the air beside her. It was shadowy and elusive and faded in and out.

"Marek?" she whispered, realizing he must be spirit walking from the prison.

"I can't sustain my image for long," Marek replied, his voice faint.

As Sara watched, he struggled to maintain the image, then it faded completely. "Marek," she whispered, a bit too loudly.

Tucker eyed her in the rearview mirror, puzzled.

"Sara, it'll be easier if I just project my voice, okay?" Marek whispered, his voice emanating from the air beside her.

"Of course," Sara whispered back, hoping the officer wouldn't hear through the plexiglass that separated the front and back of the squad car.

"Cole told you I lost control of the *tar'dor* ten years ago," Marek's voice told her. "That's not how it happened. Cole took it before I had a chance to leash it inside me. I had just drawn it in and was working to form an inner psychic chamber to hold it when Cole ran up to me. *'Let me take it!'* he yelled. I told him, *'No, Cole. I can't let you do that.'* He then *pretended* to check on one of the student victims. Instead, he grabbed a thick textbook that had fallen nearby and clubbed me with it. While I was still dazed he recited the command to pull the *tar'dor* into himself."

Sara was surprised by these revelations but not shocked. That seemed like exactly the sort of thing Cole would do.

"He couldn't stand that I'd be the keeper," Marek told her, his voice still emerging from thin air. "He had to make that sacrifice himself. That's his noble weakness, Sara. That's why he can't be trusted, not completely."

"Shit, really?"

"I accepted the blame for all those deaths," Marek went on. "We both couldn't. He had the creature in him by then, so he had to remain free from prison so he could use it to vanquish other *tar'dors*."

Sara mulled this over. It was a tricky situation. She couldn't fully trust Cole, but she couldn't really trust Marek Meyer either.

"Cole will probably tell you the only reason I wanted you two to visit me in prison was so I could steal the *tar'dor* back from him," Marek told her, his voice fading briefly, then coming back louder. "I couldn't do that even if I wanted to. Cole would have to choose to give it to me."

"So what do we do?" Sara asked.

"When you get back downtown, I'll make sure you get free," Marek replied. "Grab Cole and head underground." His voice was fading again.

"Okay, but then what?"

"Then you and Cole need to—"

Marek's voice cut off completely now.

"Marek?" she asked. "Marek! We need to do *what*. Marek!"

Deputy Tucker turned to glare back at Sara. "Lady, save the crazy for the shrinks. It's wasted on me."

Sara ignored him and peered ahead. Before long, they'd be at L.A.'s downtown central jail. Then, shit would hit fan. And fan would hit back.

14.

As the two squad cars neared the downtown jail, Cole was struggling to control his *tar'dor*. He caught a reflection of himself in the plexiglass barrier between the front and back seats. His face shifted as his *tar'dor* fought to emerge. There was a brief flicker of fangs. Officer Samson, who was driving, must have caught a glimpse in the rearview mirror. Cole could see the man shake off what he'd seen.

"*Auwk mym doth be en thay,*" Cole whispered to himself. "*Auwk mym doth be en thay.*" He kept repeating it.

Skyscrapers loomed all around. He was sweating badly now, a nervous wreck. He couldn't allow the thing to get loose. Not now, not here, not anywhere. He knew Sara wanted him to release the creature enough to shock and frighten the cops so they could escape but it was just too risky.

Samson pulled the car to a stop at the rear entrance of the main DTLA police station and jail. The other squad car with Sara stopped behind them. Suddenly, Marek's shadowy image flickered to life beside Cole.

"Marek? That you?" Cole asked. He figured this must be one of those visual manifestations Marek had talked about back at the prison. It was creepy. Clearly, he was struggling to maintain the projection. It flickered.

"Cole, you've got to unleash your *tar'dor*," Marek's told him.

Unleash it? Cole was trying his hardest to keep it inside him. "I can't. I won't be able to pull it back."

"I'll help," Marek told him. "But you *can't* be locked in a jail cell. Others will come. Unleash yours while you still have a chance!"

Cole knew he was right. Other *tar'dors* would find him in jail, eventually. They'd possess other inmates or guards, then attack him. The carnage would be awful. Cole glanced back and saw Sara being pulled from her squad car. Her wrists, like his, were handcuffed behind her back.

Samson opened the rear door of the car Cole was in and he climbed clumsily from the vehicle.

Sara yelled: "Cole, unleash it! Do it now!"

Cole knew he had no choice. He unleashed the beast.

There was a sudden strobe-like blur of fangs and claws and unholy limbs that launched toward Deputy Samson, knocking him back across the ground. Cole reached out to psychically yank the demon back before it could possess the startled man. As he did so, Cole saw that Marek now stood beside him, his projected image at least, and he was helping Cole try to control the creature. Still, the thing was bounding around wildly, like a ferocious dog fighting at the end of an unseen leash.

"What . . . the . . . *hell*?" Deputy Tucker sputtered, staring at the unfolding chaos.

Sara used the distraction to slam Tucker into the side of his vehicle, knocking his head hard against the fender. He slumped to the ground unconscious. Sara, still cuffed, bent down beside him to tug a key from his belt, then sprinted away.

"Cole! This way!" Sara yelled as she crossed the street.

Cole needed to get control of the *tar'dor* first. The creature was still careening around, strobing wildly as the beasts always did.

Deputy Samson yanked his sidearm from its holster and fired wildly at the careening demon, the bullet harmlessly striking a brick wall. The beast then leapt toward the officer again. Terrified, Samson fumbled his gun to the ground and stumbled back from the creature in shock. Cole and Marek together yelled the leashing command—*Auwk mym doth be en thay!*—and together they managed to draw the *tar'dor* back inside Cole. Marek's image then abruptly disappeared.

Cole stumbled and staggered after Sara. He caught up with her on the other side of the street. Glancing back, he counted a half dozen police officers charging from the building. He and Sara took off down a side alley, both running awkwardly with their cuffs on. He hoped the key she pulled from the officer's belt was a handcuff key, otherwise they'd not make it far. Ahead, Sara ducked around a corner. When Cole caught up with her, she was panting for breath and clutching the key.

"Cole, quickly now, put your back to me," Sara told him.

He did so and she used the key to unlock his cuffs. She was surprisingly deft at this, and he wondered how often she'd been arrested before, how often she had escaped before. Now freed of his cuffs, he used the key to try to unlock hers, but he was clumsy and nearly dropped the key. One of the pursuing officers charged around the corner.

No choice. Cole unleashed his *tar'dor* again and it surged toward the deputy. The man staggered back around the corner, terrified. Cole yanked the demon back inside him. It was easier this time. Maybe Marek was here, invisible, helping him. With his hands shaking with nerves, Cole tried again to unlock Sara's handcuffs and finally succeeded. She tossed them aside.

"Where to?" Cole asked her. "We can't hold them off forever."

Marek flickered into view, beckoning them to follow him along another alley. "The underground flood channels are this way!"

Sara shook her head no. "I've got another place in mind."

Cole hesitated, not knowing whom to follow.

"Trust me!" Sara yelled. "I know my way around here."

She grabbed Cole and pulled him toward a different alleyway.

Together they sprinted along the alley until they reached a dead end. Cole looked around as he tried to catch his breath. A modern residential skyscraper loomed high above them. A sturdy rear door led into the building. Sara pulled a small keychain from her pocket

229

and tried to unlock the door, but the key didn't fit.

"*Damn!*" Sara exclaimed. "They must have changed the lock!"

"'Trust me,' she said," Cole replied, exasperated.

He looked frantically around the alley. No way out except the way they'd come, and the cops were closing in from that direction.

"We are so *screwed*," Cole muttered.

Sara, though, quickly put her back to the locked door.

"Unleash it!" Sara told him.

"What?"

"Do it! Unleash it! Let it charge me!"

Marek appeared beside Cole, his image flickering. "Do it. I'll help."

Cole suddenly understood what Sara had in mind. Clever girl, he thought. He faced her, took a deep breath, and unleashed his *tar'dor*.

It launched toward Sara but at the last moment she ducked, and it slammed into the door with ferocious force, knocking it off its hinges.

Cole and Marek worked to yank the demon back inside Cole as Sara shoved the broken door aside. Marek then flickered away and Cole followed Sara into the parking garage of the residential skyscraper.

"You two are getting better at corralling that thing," Sara said, as she hustled through the garage.

"I doubt even the two of us will be able to control it much longer," Cole replied as he tried to keep up with Sara as she wove her way between parked cars toward an elevator lobby. The cars were mostly high-end: Mercedes, BMWs, Porsche, etc. He wondered who lived here. Maybe it was a rich boyfriend who'd given her that rear door key that no longer worked.

Cole caught up with Sara in the elevator lobby. There was a set of main elevators on one side. Another lift, marked PRIVATE, stood opposite. Sara punched in a keycode to call the private elevator.

Cole started to ask who she knew who lived here, but Sara put a finger to his lips and nodded to the garage behind them. The pursuing officers could be heard searching for them. He and Sara anxiously watched the elevator indicator lights as the voices of the cops grew ever closer.

Finally, the private elevator door opened and Sara and Cole hustled in. Its door closed just as two officers charged into the elevator lobby behind them. Cole could see that the luxurious elevator served only a few of the floors of the building. Garage, Lobby, Penthouse. Sara stabbed the Penthouse button and the elevator began to glide smoothly upward.

"You know someone who lives *here*?" Cole asked.

Sara ignored the question as she eyed the blinking floor indicator lights, as if willing the elevator to move faster. The lift finally opened onto a short hallway with plush carpet and a couple of stylish doors. She hurried to one, unlocked it, and led Cole into an elegant condo. It was a palatial loft that seemed to encompass fully half of the top floor of the building.

Floor-to-ceiling windows offered an expansive view of downtown Los Angeles. A wide balcony jutted over the street far below. Cole wondered how high they were. Twenty floors? Thirty? Sara hustled to a security panel and entered a code to disable an alarm.

"This place is *yours*?" Cole sputtered.

Sara didn't answer and instead darted into the kitchen. Cole meant to follow but he spotted a set of awards and framed articles from magazines mounted along a wall. He read some of the titles: "Entrepreneur of the Year Award given to Sara Sarque"; "Founder of High-Tech Startup is Latest Multi-Millionaire"; and "Facial Recognition System Wins Awards for its Inventor."

"I guess you're not some trust fund *prima donna* after all?" Cole called to her but, if she heard him, she ignored that question too.

Sara then returned with a handful of sports drinks and energy bars. She pushed past Cole and nodded for him to follow. As he did, he passed a fireplace and lingered at photos on the mantle of Sara and a young man.

The pictures were arranged as a shrine. A photo of a cemetery headstone had the name Timothy Sarque. The engraved dates showed he had died a couple of years ago. Cole figured he must have been Sara's brother. Probably her younger brother, judging by the photos.

"Cole, we don't have time," Sara said as she waited for him near a far wall of the loft.

"If this place is *yours*, why do you—"

"Why do I live the junkie life? We all have our inner demons, Cole, yours just happens to be real."

Cole eyed the balcony with worry. "Is there some other way out? We can't stay here long. The cops are probably on their way up already."

"Then shut up and get over here," Sara told him.

He finally joined her where she stood beside an unadorned side-wall of the loft. She pressed a hidden button along the wall.

A panel opened, revealing a metal vault door with a security access scanner. She leaned in and let the device scan her face.

The vault door then slid quietly open.

15.

Sara darted past the vault door into her panic room and dumped the provisions on a side table. She grabbed the bewildered Cole and yanked him into the room. The thick metal door clanked shut securely behind them. She eyed the bank of security screens mounted along one wall of the room. They showed images of the parking garage, the private elevator, the penthouse level hallway, and the loft condominium itself.

One of the screens showed two deputies ascending in the elevator. They must have used the police/fire override to access it. The images were sharp enough to read their name badges: Wilcox and Santos. The one named Wilcox was lugging a large black iron battering ram. The lift soon reached the penthouse level and the officers charged into the hallway. They pounded on the hallway doors until her bewildered neighbor—who owned the other loft on the penthouse level—opened his door. After a few words were exchanged, he pointed the deputies to her front door. It took them only a few swings of the battering ram to shatter the door's lock.

Sara hastily entered commands into her security panel. "I'm resetting the alarm," she told Cole. "It'll slow them down a bit."

With the front door breached, the deputies pushed their way into the loft, instantly triggering the alarm. They jammed their fingers in their ears at the piercing screech. In the panic room, the alarm could be heard through the walls but was heavily muted, just a distant-sounding wail.

"They'll get the super to shut off the alarm," Sara told Cole. "They'll figure out, soon enough, that there's a hidden panic room."

"Sara, just how bad are *your* demons?" Cole asked, as he eyed a side table that held some of Sara's used drug paraphernalia. Old crack pipes, empty bags of blow. He took a close look at her face and seemed worried.

She hadn't realized it but she was sweating a lot. It wasn't just the mad dash from the jail. She was suffering withdrawals. Even Cole could see that. She ignored his question and looked around the panic room.

"Marek? You here?" Sara asked the air. When Marek didn't appear, she turned to Cole. "Marek told me he's losing the strength to project his image from prison. If he can't appear to tell us what to do, we're screwed."

Cole eyed the drug table again. "You'd come in here to dope up?"

Sara shrugged. "Before, sure. When I wanted to hide from the world. Now, I just hide in plain sight. I go where I belong. I *belong* with junkies."

"It has to do with the guy in the photos? Timothy?" Cole asked.

"My baby brother," Sara replied with a sigh. "Tim was eighteen when he died. But a baby brother is always a baby brother."

Sara decided there was no point now in keeping her past from Cole. "Look," she began, "a little bit of fame and a lot of success went to my head. When my start-up hit big, I lived the entrepreneur rockstar life. Parties. Drugs. *Lots* of parties. *Lots* of drugs. The party ended when I made the mistake of giving some blow to Tim. It was laced with LSD."

"He died of an overdose?" Cole asked.

"No." Sara nodded to a security screen that showed the loft balcony that jutted out high above the streets far below. "He died jumping off that balcony one night, strung out of his mind, thinking he was Spiderman, thinking he'd shoot out a spidey web and swing gracefully to the ground."

"I'm so sorry to hear that," Cole replied. "One might think a person would use a tragedy like that to get off of drugs."

"Yeah, well, one might *think* a lot of things, Cole. One would usually be *wrong*," she spat, then adopted a softer tone. "Even before my brother's death, I read a lot of Sylvia Plath. You know her most famous quote?"

"The one where she says 'dying is an art' and, like everything else, she does it exceptionally well?" Cole asked.

"There's more to it. She went on to say she does it so it feels like hell. So it feels real. She said she had a *call*. Cole, I feel that call too."

"A slow-motion suicide, that it?" Cole asked her.

Before she could answer, Marek flickered into view beside them.

234

"Sorry I'm late. Been trying hard to manifest myself. It's been a struggle, but once we get into the other realm, it'll be easy for me to stay with you," Marek told them. "For now, it's really hard."

As if to prove the point, his image flickered and faded. When he finally returned, he spotted the energy bars and sports drinks on the table.

"Good idea," Marek told them. "Load up on calories. Your bodies will need that energy when we're in the other realm. First though, you've got to understand a couple of things. When you're spirit walking in this world, *our world*, you can jump to other places instantly."

He grabbed hold of them and whispered something and—

Sara suddenly found herself in a small prison cell.

She was there with Cole. He looked like a shimmering ghost. She peered down at her own arms and legs, shimmery too. It was pretty cool, she thought. A spectral version of Marek stood alongside Cole. Lying before them on a cot was Marek's flesh and blood body, unmoving.

"Thankfully, I have no cellmate," Marek's projection explained. "Otherwise, who knows what he'd be doing to my unconscious body? I can't have those sort of . . . distractions."

He grabbed Sara and Cole and in an instant—

Sara found herself back in the panic room, slumped on the floor. Cole was lying beside her. They got up and brushed themselves off. She felt some fresh aches and pains.

Marek's spectral image gave them an apologetic look. "Sorry. I should have mentioned it's a good idea to lie down first before spirit walking."

Cole rubbed a sore elbow. "Yeah, that might have been worth mentioning."

Sara eyed the security monitors. The deputies had gotten the main burglary alarm shut off and were searching the loft, guns drawn. As she watched them, Sara realized she was now sweating even worse than before. She felt weak and hungry. She grabbed a sports drink off the table and slugged it down, then she tore into an energy bar and devoured it.

"Okay," Marek began, "when we get into that other realm, we will—"

"My body will crave other stuff soon," Sara cut in. "Crave it *badly*. So you will have to forgive me, but I really need to do this." She pulled a bag of coke from a stash in a cabinet and was ready to snort some when Cole knocked it away, spilling it all to the floor.

Cole stomped on the powder, kicked it about, ruining it.

"What the *hell*?" Sara gasped. "Cole, I *needed* that."

Cole glared at her. "Well, I *need* someone who's not drugged out of her mind. We have work to do, a creature to destroy."

"Save the lover's quarrel for later," Marek told them. "Listen to me for two goddamned seconds, okay?" He spotted a black marker on the table. "Sara, grab that. Anything you're holding will go with you into the other realm, and we'll need that marker."

"What for?" Sara asked, putting the pen in a pocket of her pants.

"Don't worry about it," Marek replied. "Just bring it."

"See?" Cole asked Sara. "See how *annoying* that is."

"Listen you two! In the other realm, there's no jumping instantly from one place to another," Marek told them. "So we'll have to travel by foot and it'll be dangerous. And this last part is really important: if you die there, you die *here*. If you die here, you die there. So try to avoid either."

"Okay, so we go into that other realm, then what?" Sara asked.

"Father Ignatius wrote about a place—a *pit*—where even the most powerful of *tar'dors* can be destroyed," Marek explained.

"Sounds good," Cole said. "But how long will it take us to get to that pit?" He was eyeing the security monitors with worry.

Sara checked the screens too. Many more cops had now entered the loft. "They'll find this room," Sara said. "They'll need to cut through the vault door but they'll get in. Eventually. No panic room is impenetrable."

"Then let's stop wasting time." Cole turned to Marek. "How do we get to the other realm?"

"First off," Marek began. "Lie down before you fall down."

Sara and Cole both quickly got down on the floor.

"Repeat after me," Marek said. "*Ahm me enna be ahm nhe.*"

Sara and Cole both repeated the incantation. "*Ahm me enna be ahm nhe. Ahm me enna be ahm nhe.*"

Sara gasped as she emerged from her own body, which remained on the floor, unconscious now. She peered at her spectral arms and legs. She liked this *spirit walking*. As the spectral version of Cole rose from his body, she saw that his demon—his *tar'dor*—rose too, its strobe-like image was visible inside Cole's own spectral image. It was fighting to break free.

"You've still got to hold it inside you, Cole," Marek warned.

"*Auwk mym doth be en thay,*" Cole said and the demon receded within Cole's spectral image and was no longer visible.

"Very, very weird," Sara said, then something else puzzled her. "Marek, can *anyone* recite that spell and spirit walk?"

"No, it doesn't work that way. I can do it because I had a tar'dor in me once. Cole can too. He's been a keeper for years. There's something about having a tar'dor within you, even briefly, that helps unbind your spirit from your flesh to enable you to leave your body," Marek explained. "You can do it too, Sara, because one jumped into you back in that derelict building. Remember? I was there and helped Cole pull it from you."

Sara had all but forgotten that. She recalled now how she'd suddenly grown dizzy with the thing inside her. Her vision had been strobing on and off, just for a moment or two. She wondered now if her mind had *made* her forget, rejecting those memories as too alien, too *inhuman*.

"Anyway, I have a whole theory about how ancient shamans and medieval sorcerers had true spirit walking powers and they originally came from *tar'dors* but—"

"But we have no time for *that* now," Cole cut in. "Let's get on with it. I can't hold the creature inside me forever. So what do we do *now*?"

"Now, we walk through walls," Marek said matter-of-factly.

Marek strode briskly toward the closed metal vault door of the panic room and walked right through it. Sara tentatively followed. She closed her eyes as she stepped into the door, fighting the instinct that said she'd bang her head against its hard metal. When she opened her eyes again, she was in the main part of the loft. She turned to watch Cole as he joined them.

Marek continued on to the balcony. Sara paused to look more closely at the police officers. She was standing right in front of them but they didn't see her. As she watched, one of them, Deputy Wilcox, found the hidden button for the panic room's outer wall panel and pressed it. The panel slid open, revealing the vault door. Behind the door, she knew her body and Cole's too were slumped on the floor, unconscious. Whatever they needed to do in the other realm, they had to do it before the police cut through the door. Maybe they had an hour. Maybe less.

"Let's call SWAT," Wilcox told the other officers. "They're good at cutting through shit like this." Wilcox looked up at a video camera that was mounted high on the wall. "We *know* you're in there. Might as well come out now. We'll get the door open soon and we'll drag you out."

Sara flipped him the finger, then joined Cole and Marek on the balcony, twenty stories above street level. She had not set foot out here since the night Timothy died. Marek peered down from the balcony. Sara was reluctant to get close to the railing. Cole seemed reluctant too.

"Marek, what are we doing *here*?" Sara asked. "Isn't there some spell we recite to get to that other realm?"

"It's not a spell, it's a *command*," Marek replied. "But, yes, there are more ancient words to recite. And we've got to jump too."

"What?" Sara stepped back. "That was not part of the bargain."

"Father Ignatius's notes were clear," Marek told her. "You've got to recite the ancient command and then prove you're worthy of entering the other realm. This jump will do nicely."

"You're *serious*?" Cole asked. He seemed as reluctant as Sara.

"Yeah, screw that," Sara said, backing away from the railing.

"This is what we *need* to do," Marek declared.

He beckoned Sara again to the railing. She shook her head no.

"Sara, just repeat the command—*Ahm-mehna-mahn*—and jump."

"Sara's got issues with this balcony, Marek," Cole told him. "Maybe we should leave her behind and go on without her?"

"No, I can do this," Sara said. "I can *do* this." She edged to the railing and peered down at the street far below. "Truth told, I have thought so many times of taking this jump. Never had the courage."

"Then say the command and let yourself go," Marek told her.

He grinned as he repeated the command "*Ahm-mehna-mahn. Ahm-mehna-mahn*" and nonchalantly let himself fall from the balcony.

"Sara, you don't have to do this," Cole told her.

"Of course I do." Sara closed her eyes. "For Timothy," she whispered, then repeated the words. "*Ahm-mehna-mahn. Ahm-mehna-mahn.*"

She hurled herself off the balcony.

16.

Cole watched as the spectral form of Sara plummeted from the balcony. Part way down, she seemed to disappear. He hoped that meant she made it to the other realm. He edged now closer to the railing.

Although he knew his flesh-and-blood body was still back in the panic room, he had to fight against every self-preservation instinct to force himself to jump from the balcony. He peered down at the street twenty floors below and gathered his resolve.

"For . . . ," Cole whispered to himself, "For . . . Sara," then he recited the ancient command. *"Ahm-mehna-mahn. Ahm-mehna-mahn."*

He leapt from the balcony.

Gravity grabbed him as if he had actual weight, but he was too busy fighting blind panic to puzzle over the physics of spectral projections. The building's many floors raced past him, blurring as he gathered speed.

The world then began to darken. He could no longer see the building or the street below. Yet he kept falling, faster and faster. He knew he must have already plummeted well beyond where the street was. Yet he continued to fall, continued to accelerate. Eventually, he could start to make out *something*. He raced past it so fast it was hard to focus on, but it looked like he was in some sort of roughhewn shaft, like an old mining tunnel, or maybe a natural cavern. Stone of some sort.

He suddenly realized there must be a *bottom* to the shaft, which he'd hit, eventually, and hit hard. There were no such things as *bottomless* shafts. Or maybe this was Hell. Maybe he had already died and this is what Hell was—falling forever in terror without ever striking bottom.

Cole shut his eyes and screamed.

#

"Are you with us?" a voice asked.

Cole blinked his eyes open and looked around. He found himself on the floor of a large round chamber with rough stone walls. The ceiling above looked solid. There was no hint of the shaft he'd plummeted down.

"Are you with us?" the voice repeated, and he realized it was Marek.

He saw that Sara was in the chamber too. "You okay?"

Cole nodded and got up and dusted himself off, gathered his composure. He peered at Sara and Marek. Here, they looked solid. Flesh and blood. Not spectral projections. He eyed his own arms and legs. Same thing. He poked himself in the arm, hard enough to hurt, and it *did* hurt.

"How is this possible?" Cole asked.

"In this realm, specters look real because they *are* real here," Marek explained. "The *tar'dors* too. Hurry now. Time is wasting."

A dim stone passageway led from the chamber and Marek hurried into it. Cole and Sara rushed to catch up. Cole puzzled over the fact he could see anything at all here for none of them carried flashlights, but the tunnel they were in and the chamber they'd just left were both illuminated by an odd and otherworldly glow. The physics of this realm—if it even was physics—was clearly different from the familiar world left behind. He felt as if he was breathing musty air, but was there truly any air here? Or was his mind just confabulating that—making this unearthly realm seem normal because the human mind could only process *normal*?

As they hurried along the passageway, Cole eyed the rough-hewn walls. It looked like they were formed of stone stalactites and stalagmites, all packed close together. He stopped to take a closer look. They were not stalactites or stalagmites at all. They were claws and fangs and limbs.

"What the hell?" Cole sputtered. "These are—?"

"Yes, *tar'dors*. Ancient ones," Marek replied.

Cole gasped. If these were indeed *tar'dors*, then thousands of them were lining the walls, jammed together like bats in a cave.

"Fossilized?" Sara asked.

"Dormant," Marek said.

Cole looked closely at one of the dormant creatures again, and it *shifted* slightly, like a sleeping bat twitching a wing. But this was no small bat. The dormant *tar'dor* was at least seven feet tall.

"They're still *alive*?" Cole asked.

"Time is wasting," Marek said and pressed on.

Cole and Sara gave one another a look, then hurried to catch up to Marek. The farther they went along the passageway, the walls looked less and less like stone and more and more like sleeping *tar'dors*. What before had looked like rock now looked more like flesh. More of the dormant beasts twitched in their slumber, rustled their limbs, sniffed the air.

One opened a malevolent eye as they passed it.

"They smell what's inside you, Cole," Marek explained. "They smell a powerful *tar'dor* with the stench of a human. And they smell a human with the stench of a *tar'dor*. They *will* awaken. Hurry now."

"This is madness!" Cole turned back the way they had come. "We need to get out of here. My demon can't defeat all these!"

"Cole, don't be a fool. There's no way back," Marek told him. "Not that way."

"Then how do we get back?" Sara asked.

"There's another chamber like the one we landed in but with a shaft leading up," Marek explained. "The same command we spoke to come here will take us back. First, we need to find the pit Father Ignatius spoke of. A shaft that heads *down*. Bottomless."

Marek now broke into a trot and Sara followed. Cole hurried to catch up, then sprinted ahead of them. The sooner they found that pit, the better. He charged around a bend and nearly collided with something standing in the middle of the passageway. Shocked, he saw it was a dead woman. She looked young, maybe no more than twenty or so.

She stared back at him. Her flesh was pallid. Her eyes were black pools of empty darkness. Her neck was disjointed, obviously broken. Cole spun away from her but now found himself face-to-face with an elderly man. Also dead. He was missing an arm and much of his shoulder, maybe bitten off. His other arm and both legs were broken and dangled uselessly, yet somehow the man stood, wobbling.

Cole stumbled away and fell to the ground. He scrambled backward and bumped into something else. He turned slowly to see a dead torso with arms but no legs, no head. The torso looked like it might have been that of a middle-aged man once but with his legs and head chomped off.

It raised a pale hand toward Cole, as if in accusation.

Cole spun away to face the other two horrors. They both now raised their pale arms toward him. Was it truly an accusation? Cole wondered. Or were they just pointing out an intruder here, one who didn't belong?

17.

Sara heard Cole gasp from around the bend in the passageway. The damn fool had raced ahead. Did he not realize they needed to stay together in this unholy Hell? She and Marek sprinted to reach him. They found Cole, terrified, surrounded by horrific dead souls. They *must* be souls, she thought. In this realm where specters looked real, where specters had flesh and blood, dead souls must look real too. Whatever they were, she nearly vomited at the sight of them. Dead, mutilated, chewed apart, some missing arms, legs, one without a head. No one deserved that fate. *No one.*

Marek stepped forward and the dead souls backed away, giving him space. He helped Cole back to his feet.

"They're harmless, I think," Marek told him. "They fear you, Cole, more than you fear them. Rather, they fear what's inside you, Cole. They sense it."

"What are they?" Cole asked.

"The souls of those killed by *tar'dors*. They're trapped here."

"Forever?" Sara asked.

Marek didn't answer. Instead, he eyed the "dormant" *tar'dors* packed within the walls with growing worry. Many were twitching.

"We need to keep *moving*," Marek told them. He grabbed Cole and pushed him forward and the two broke into a run.

Sara hurried to catch up. As they rushed down the long passageway, more and more of the dormant demons along the walls twitched and rustled. Ahead, she spotted what looked like the end of the passageway. Beyond, there seemed to be a large chamber. Eerie light emanated from it.

After another fifty yards or so they finally reached that chamber.

It was vast—the largest cavern Sara had ever seen. She joined Marek and Cole at a wide ledge overlooking the vast space. It was a mile wide, at least. She couldn't clearly see its far side or even its ceiling. Both were lost in hazy darkness. The ledge they stood on seemed to circle the entire chamber, although it too became lost in the hazy darkness.

Along the wide ledge, other dead souls wandered. As with the ones seen before, these too had been chewed apart. On the floor of the chamber, still other dead souls were lurching about or crawling feebly across the stone floor. In the distance, she spotted some *tar'dors* prowling among the dead souls. Here, in their realm, the *tar'dors* didn't flicker and strobe. As she watched, it looked like some fought others for dominance, then pounced on the dead souls and chewed on their prey.

"What godless hell is this?" Cole muttered.

"*Tar'dors* will gnaw on the souls of the dead long after they're dead," Marek explained. "Like a dog with a bone. Maybe there's still a little life force in there to feed on. Who knows?"

Sara was speechless at the cruel enormity of what she saw.

"This way," Marek said as he headed off to the left along the wide ledge. "We must hurry. They will sense our fresh souls."

Sara saw how some of the creatures had stopped their gnawing. Now, they gazed ominously in their direction.

"How far to that pit you spoke of?" Cole asked.

"Another mile, I think," Marek told him.

"Just how big is this realm?" Sara asked.

"Endless, I suppose," Marek said.

Sara puzzled over this, for something didn't quite make sense to her. "So . . . in this endless realm, the only place to destroy a *tar'dor* is not all that far from where we entered? Seems like a rather lucky coincidence."

Cole glared at her. "Isn't that *good*? Do you want to have to go farther? Stop wasting time with stupid questions. I need to kill the *tar'dor* inside me. I can't hold it much longer." Cole hurried after Marek.

Sara followed as they made their way along the wide ledge. They passed more dead souls who stared at Cole. Marek led them into a long passageway that was much like the first one they'd been in. Its walls were lined with dormant demons that rustled and shifted and began to awaken.

"How much farther?" Cole asked. He was struggling now to keep up with Marek and seemed to have gotten a stitch in his side.

"Just keep *moving*," Marek pleaded. "Ready your *tar'dor*. I fear we'll need it soon."

Sara too was now struggling to keep up with Marek. She squinted ahead, her vision becoming blurry. She was sweating and shivering. She fought off dizziness. Marek came back to help her.

"Why am I so *cold*?" she wondered aloud.

"How long since your last hit?" Marek asked.

"*Shit!* I forgot. Far too long," Sara replied.

"We've got no time for this!" Cole yelled.

"Cole, some of the inmates I know at prison were junkies," Marek said. "They told me severe withdrawals can trigger seizures. Heart attacks."

"All the more reason to keep moving," Cole said. "Let's destroy the damned thing and get the hell out of here and get back to the panic room."

"Cole's right," Sara said. "Let's keep moving. I'll be okay."

They hurried along the corridor. Ahead, one of the dormant demons awoke and pried itself from the wall. It unfolded its limbs and blocked the passageway. This was the first time Sara had gotten a clear and close-up look at a *tar'dor*. It was horrific. A maw of yellowed rotting fangs. Sharp talons. Hairy insect-like limbs. A pair of malevolent and jaundiced eyes.

Cole stopped when he saw it, terrified, and stumbled back.

Marek grabbed him and shoved him ahead to face the malevolent creature. "Cole, unleash your *tar'dor*! It must kill that thing!"

Sara peered back the way they'd come. Behind them, yet another demon was unfolding itself from the wall. They would be surrounded soon. Before she could warn Cole and Marek, Cole unleashed his demon. It launched out of him and attacked the creature that loomed ahead of them.

Cole's demon—his *tar'dor*—was every bit as horrifying as the other creature, but his was even bigger, stronger. The fight was ferocious. A blur of snapping fangs and talons ripped the air.

Attack and counter-attack.

At last, Cole's demon defeated the other, snapping its neck, but the fight had wounded his demon. Yellow-red blood spilt from its wounds. In pain, it lunged toward Cole but didn't attack him, nor Marek. Instead, it charged directly toward her.

Shocked, Sara ducked. It leapt over her. Just above her, Cole's *tar'dor* slammed hard into the other demon, the one stalking them from behind. Sara struggled to crawl away as the two creatures snarled and clawed and fought just above her, but she was trapped as their sharp claw-like legs pounded and pistoned the ground all around her. As she struggled to escape, she was splattered with some of the foul blood of the creatures. Cole's demon finally won, its fangs sinking deep into the neck of the other creature, which slumped dead, pinning Sara.

Cole and Marek were now frantically repeating the leash incantation, trying to pull the *tar'dor* back into Cole. *Auwk mym doth be en thay! Auwk mym doth be en thay!* It tried to bound away down the passageway, back toward the main chamber. The wounded beast fought hard to get away, but Cole and Marek managed to draw it back into Cole. Sara understood. They needed to destroy the creature, not let it go. If they let it go, it would eventually return to the human realm to possess and kill more victims.

Cole and Marek now came back to where Sara was pinned and worked to pull her from beneath the dead beast. Once she was freed, the three of them sprinted ahead along the corridor. As they ran, still more of the demons lining the walls began to awaken and rustle their limbs.

18.

Cole charged headlong down the passageway, with Marek and Sara at his side, and finally reached a large round chamber with a gaping pit at its center. The room—formed of rough-hewn stone—looked to be about a hundred feet across and had a domed ceiling. Here, there were no *tar'dors* lining the walls or prowling about, but there were other horrors. Dozens and dozens of dead souls lurched and twitched as they made their way around the pit. These too had mangled bodies, missing limbs. There were dead pools of blackness where their eyes should have been.

These souls seemed oblivious to him and Sara and Marek too.

That was a relief at least.

Cole edged forward and peered into the pit. A stone shaft extended down into echoing darkness, seemingly bottomless.

"This is it? The death pit?" Cole asked.

Marek nodded, then turned to Sara: "The marker, please."

Sara dug around in her pockets to find the pen she'd brought from the panic room. She tossed it to Marek. He hastily began writing on the stone floor, just where the passageway entered the chamber. The sounds of awakening *tar'dors* echoed from that corridor—the rustling of their limbs, the scraping of their talons across the stone floor.

As Cole watched, Marek wrote the blocking command—*Loch lym soth bewen ma-thay*—along the floor using the ancient runic symbols. He then quickly wrote the same symbols along the sidewalls and across the top of the entrance. Once they fully encircled the entryway, the runes began to glow. Cole watched in awe as the runes then extended out from the stone and stretched across the entryway like the strands of a glowing spider web. They intertwined with one another to form a shimmering barrier.

"That should hold them," Marek declared. "For a while, at least."

"Then let's *destroy* the one inside me," Cole begged. "How do we do it? Another ancient incantation?"

Marek nodded and worked his way toward the far side of the pit.

As he did, he called back to Cole: "We'll recite a special command together. Your *tar'dor* will be drawn from you toward me. When it's over the pit, release it. It'll plummet into the bottomless pit. Gone for good."

It took Marek a minute or so, pushing his way past the dead souls who wandered about, but he finally reached the far side of the pit.

Cole saw that Sara was now slumped on the floor, shivering. Suffering. Poor girl. She squinted over at the dead souls.

"Why so many *here*?" she asked.

Cole shrugged. "Who knows? Maybe they think this place is safe for them since it's deadly to *tar'dors*. Maybe they're working up the courage to jump into the pit. Obliteration is probably better than endless suffering."

Marek called to Cole across the bottomless pit. "Repeat after me, Cole: *Auwk mym goth amathay!* We need to say it together. *Auwk mym goth amathay!*"

Cole repeated the guttural-sounding command along with Marek. "*Auwk mym goth amathay! Auwk mym goth amathay!*"

Cole's *tar'dor* was drawn out from within him. But it was not pulled out over the pit as Marek had claimed. Instead, it was clawing toward Sara.

Cole fought to pull it back within his body. "*Auwk mym doth be en thay! Auwk mym doth be en thay!*"

It worked and the *tar'dor* was drawn back inside him.

Marek made his way back toward Cole and Sara.

"Father Ignatius must have been wrong!" Marek called to them. "It's not working. But I have another plan. I hoped it wouldn't come to this."

The growls of other *tar'dors* now came from the entranceway. Several of the ferocious beasts fought to get past the shimmering barrier Marek had created. Cole saw that the barrier was holding but the demons were not giving up. They redoubled their fight.

Marek threw Cole a look of worry, then peered into the pit.

"Cole, give me your *tar'dor*. Let it possess *me*, as it had ten years ago. I'll hurl myself into the pit. It will be consumed. We both will."

"No, there must be another way!" Cole yelled.

"Look, I'm never leaving that prison anyway," Marek pleaded. "Let me do this. Let me atone for my mistakes."

Nearby, slumped on the floor, Sara shivered, even worse than before. It seemed to Cole as though she was now struggling just to remain conscious. Back in the panic room, her body must be going through severe withdrawals, maybe life threatening ones.

"Cole, can you trust him?" she asked, her voice weak. "What if Marek just wants it for himself?"

Cole hadn't thought of that. Was this just a ruse to get Cole to give Marek the *tar'dor*? That was the only way one keeper could transfer a *tar'dor* to another—voluntarily. Marek had no hope of ever becoming the keeper to some other *tar'dor*, so it was the one inside Cole or none. And Marek *had* betrayed Cole ten years ago when he broke their agreement and tried to summon the demon into himself. Maybe Marek had been biding his time in prison, waiting for a chance to take the *tar'dor* back and, with it, gain control of the creature's ferocious powers.

"Cole! Ignore her," Marek begged. "Sara's not thinking straight. She's in withdrawal! Give me the demon before it's too late. I'll end this *now*. I'll end the hell you've been in for ten years! I'll hurl myself into the pit to kill it."

"No. I'll end this," Cole declared. "I'll hurl myself into the pit." He moved closer to the edge.

"No!" Sara pleaded. "Don't do it!"

"Cole, don't be a fool!" Marek yelled. "You still have a life to live. I don't. Life in prison with no chance of parole. Let *me* destroy it."

"Cole," Sara called to him, shivering. "It won't take long for Marek to escape prison with that demon inside him. You can't let him have it. You can't sacrifice yourself either. There's got to be a better way. You . . . "

Sara trailed off. She had spotted someone or something among the dead souls. Cole looked but saw nothing different, just the same hapless souls that had been lurching their way around the pit the whole time.

"Sara?" Cole asked. "What do you see?"

Sara ignored him as she stared over at the dead souls.

"*Timothy?*" Sara asked, fighting off a sob.

19.

Sara squinted across the pit at what sure looked like her dead brother Timothy. He was wandering now among the dead souls. One side of his head was caved in, no doubt from the fall off the high balcony.

"Yes, it's your brother, Sara," Marek told her. "Timothy. Trapped here for all eternity. Help me free Cole of his burden and I'll see to it that Timothy is freed from this realm."

Sara was shaking badly, nearly passing out. She knew that back in the panic room her body was probably dying. Severe withdrawals could trigger cardiac arrest. As she lay on the stone floor of the chamber, she could no longer feel her heart beating.

She looked over at Timothy, desperate now. "Tim! Tell me what to do. You were always my rock. Remember when mom died? You were there for me. You told me what I needed to do. Tell me now. Can I *trust* Marek?"

Timothy nodded a "yes" back to her.

"Yeah, well, my mother is still *alive*," Sara said.

Using the last of her strength, she got back to her feet.

She glared at Marek. "And you, Marek, are a *liar*."

Marek looked sheepish. The image of Timothy flickered away.

Confused, Cole looked to Sara for answers.

"Cole, Marek was somehow projecting that image to trick me. If my brother's soul was truly here, I know what he'd say. He'd tell me to stop torturing myself over his death." She fought back a tear. "He'd be right."

She took Cole's hand and pressed it to her chest.

"No heartbeat, Cole. My body is dying back in the panic room."

"Then die, you junkie *bitch*," Marek growled. "But Cole's *tar'dor* will be mine, as it should have been all along."

Marek rushed toward them but was slowed by the dead souls blocking his path. In the other direction, Sara saw that the shimmering barrier was now failing and the creatures from the passageway were tearing through it, teeth gnashing, talons clawing the air.

Cole saw this too and tried to hurl himself into the pit, but Sara grabbed him and stopped him. He fought to get free of her.

"Sara, I *need* to do this. Let me *kill* it. Let me *end* this."

"Cole, don't you understand? Marek has been lying all along. The pit won't destroy it! It's the way back to our world. It *must* be. He wanted to take your *tar'dor* from you and escape with it by jumping into the pit."

"What if he's telling the truth?" Cole asked. "And the pit is deadly?"

"Then we die together," Sara told him. "My heart has stopped. I know it. So I have no time left anyway." She peered into Cole's eyes. "Dying is *never* an art, Cole. It's usually pointless. But sometimes it's the right sacrifice at the right time."

To one side of them, Marek had pushed past the dead souls and was now charging toward her and Cole. On the other side, the demons had broken past the barrier and clawed toward them through the entrance.

"I can't hold it anymore!" Cole bellowed.

The demon inside him surged within his chest.

Sara grabbed Cole and kissed him hard on the lips. Maybe it was just her imagination but from above a warm light seemed to penetrate the gloom of the chamber. It shone down on her and on Cole. She wondered again, as she so often did, whether there truly were angels. She hugged Cole—pressing her chest to his chest—and she hurled them both into the abyss.

20.

Cole jerked awake, gasping for air. He found himself on the floor of the panic room. Nearby were a couple of paramedics and cops.

Relieved to be alive, Cole felt his chest. "It's gone. Finally *gone*."

He turned to Sara to share the good news. She was pale and lifeless. A paramedic pulled her blouse apart and jammed paddles on her chest just beside her bra. Her body was rocked by a defibrillation shock. She gasped and spittle sprayed from her mouth.

The other paramedic checked her EKG.

"Her heart is beating again," the man said, relieved. He slapped her face gently a few times but she didn't wake up.

"Will she be okay?" Cole asked.

"What did she O.D. on?" the paramedic asked. "Speed? Smack?"

"Not an O.D. Severe withdrawal," Cole told them.

"Dose her or she might crash again," one paramedic told the other, and he injected a drug into her still unconscious body.

"You her boyfriend?" he asked Cole.

"No. Well, *maybe*. She kissed me," Cole said, smiling now.

"Great. Junkie love," one of the cops said. "Let's get them both out of here."

The paramedics fitted an oxygen mask on Sara and readied a stretcher for her. The deputies pulled Cole to his feet and locked him in handcuffs. Never before in his life had he been cuffed, but now it was twice in the same day. As Cole was led from the panic room, he could see where the police had used blowtorches to cut its door open. They led him to the elevator and, before long, he was back down on street level.

Cole was put in a squad car by one of the officers.

Before long, Sara, still unconscious, was rolled out of the building and put in the back of an ambulance by the paramedics. Her wrist was locked to a metal rail of the gurney. Cole watched as one of the medics climbed into the back of the ambulance with Sara along with a police officer. No doubt, the cop would read Sara her rights again once she woke up. And she *would* wake up, Cole knew. She was too strong a woman not to. The other medic hopped into the driver's seat and the ambulance pulled away.

As Cole watched the vehicle drive off, he grinned and whispered to himself. "She kissed me. She *kissed* me."

#

Sara's eyes fluttered open. She tugged the oxygen mask off with one hand. Her other hand, she realized, was handcuffed to a rail.

She looked around and saw she was in the back of an ambulance. There was a cop and a paramedic. Neither fact came as a surprise.

"You should leave that on," the medic told her, nodding to the mask. "We gave you clonidine. Know what that is?"

Sara shook her head no.

"It mitigates opioid withdrawal," the guy explained. "Temporarily. But you have serious dependency issues, young lady. You need to get into a program. Understand?"

Sara ignored the question as she felt herself regaining strength. She realized her blouse was open, her bra peeking out.

"Did you defib me?" she asked and the paramedic nodded.

Sara then noticed that the cop, the officer named Wilcox, seemed to be enjoying the view of her open blouse.

"Like what you see?" she asked. "Take a closer look."

"Watch your mouth, lady," Wilcox growled.

"No, seriously, take a real *close* look."

The cop looked to the paramedic. "Can you believe this girl?"

The paramedic's eyes then went wide as he stared down at her.

Sara grinned as the man gasped at the odd surging in her chest.

"Never see a *tar'dor* before?" Sara asked, coyly.

She unleashed it. As the beast leapt from her body, it snapped her handcuffs, then knocked the rear doors of the ambulance off their hinges. Before it could get away, she called out the leashing command Cole had taught her: "*Auwk mym doth be en thay.*" It obeyed, and she yanked it back inside her. The driver screeched the ambulance to a stop.

"What the hell is going on back there?" the man yelled.

The cop and the other paramedic were too stunned to answer.

Sara hopped from the back of the ambulance and strode off with a spring in her step. She felt good. She felt *strong*. She knew the paramedic was right, though. She needed to get into a program. And she would. Narc Anon. It would take time and much effort but she would defeat *those* demons, the opioid ones. And she'd find her friend Nia and visit her in the hospital and make sure she was okay. She'd find some way to make amends for burning down the sanitarium. She'd find a way to help Cole too, for the poor guy was surely in a panic now at being taken into custody.

All that could wait, for she had a new pet to get acquainted with.

She paused in the street to let a taste of the demon emerge from her mouth, all fangs and sharp teeth and raw snarling power.

Sara Sarque threw her head back and she roared.

255

AUTHOR'S NOTE

Dear Reader, Thanks for reading my collection of stories. Much appreciated! Since you have come this far, I hope you will go a just bit further and take a moment to post a review at whatever site you found the book. Written reviews are most welcome, of course, but just rating the book by selecting some number of stars is really helpful feedback. Anyway, happy reading!

CASSIA:

CASSIA was awarded the **Silver Medal** in the 2022 Readers' Favorite Contest in the Medical Thriller Category. CASSIA was also a **Finalist for the 2022 Eric Hoffer Award Grand Prize**.

"An electric storyline, impeccable character development, and thought-provoking implications make Mallery's work a **must-read for all audiences.**" - *The U.S. Review of Books*

"The storyline alters from drama to thriller in a flawless manner, the pacing of the action is well done. **An excellent read.**" - *The San Francisco Book Review.*

"All the components of a **truly stunning psychological thriller** are found within the pages of 'Cassia,' from the characters to the dark and haunted scenery, and the twists abound. ... You will not see this one coming, and it is so worth the read." - *Reader Views*

"Cassia is a **powerful thriller** by D. C. Mallery that permeates your psyche. ... At the heart of this story is a lurking moral dilemma that makes the novel more thought-provoking than most thrillers." - *Readers' Favorite.*

"Mallery's mastery of pacing will keep readers hooked right to the surprise ending. **An effective, thought-provoking medical thriller.**" - *Kirkus Reviews*

ARTEMESIA:

"With captivating suspense, the author takes the reader on a **hair-raising roller coaster ride** as they understand who the killer is and begin to guess who the next victim will be. ... This compelling story's persuasive dialogue and fast pace provide a **mystery that every reader will love.**" - *The U.S. Review of Books.*

"A searing, curious look at ritualistic homicides boosts this **striking thriller.** ... The story's latter half ... hints at supernatural elements, but the author coats them in ambiguity until the **sensational denouement.**" -- *Kirkus Reviews.*

"D.C. Mallery keeps pulling the rug from under your feet with **tantalizing reveals and unpredictable twists and turns that you never see coming.** The plot is dark and deliciously twisted, filled with riveting characters who have multiple layers to peel away." - *Readers' Favorite Reviews*

"D C Mallery is **a mastermind** and pulls together his characters, scenery, and plot in a way that **readers will not be able to put his books down.**" - *The San Francisco Book Review.*

"The storyline is innovative and unpredictable, **a fresh addition to the psychological thriller genre.** ... It's intense and twisty, with well-paced action and attention to detail. **Exquisitely crafted mind-bending intrigue, it's a distinct read you won't soon forget.**" 5 Stars -- *Reader Views Reviews*

DARKSIGHT:

"An **action-packed thriller** full of authentic human drama skillfully depicted. ... an intelligently conceived work, driven more than anything else by fully developed characters in the throes of real human emotions." - *Kirkus Reviews*

"An engaging female protagonist, a mind-bending plot, and some marvelously gruesome pseudoscience make DARKSIGHT **a true page-turning thriller** about the fine line between emotional blindness and physical sight. ...DARKSIGHT is **a scintillating read.**" - *IndieReader*

"Mallery's novel is a **fast-paced thriller** that is part X-Files mixed with a dash of CSI." - *The US Review of Books*

"'Darksight' by DC Mallery is an **insightful psychological suspense** that will take you on a thrilling ride! ... The heroine begins as a person with depth, but as she faces challenges, she really evolves into a woman of incredible strength." - *Reader Views.*

"DC Mallery has clearly done his research as *Darksight* **is brimming with science and technology that makes it feel like a Michael Crichton novel.** ... Ultimately it is a book that asks what you would do if you could have your one big wish come true: your sight restored...but there is always a caveat, and sometimes those caveats cost lives." - *San Francisco Book Review.*

D C Mallery is a writer of suspense/
thrillers and other novels. Short stories
and screenplays too. He can be
found at www.dcmallery.com and on
Twitter and Instagram @dcmallery.

www.ingramcontent.com/pod-product-compliance
Lightning Source LLC
Chambersburg PA
CBHW020550180626
46810CB00007B/2447